Watch Over My Child

By

Roberta Kagan

Gilde's story,
Book three in the Michal's Destiny Series

CONTACT ME

I love hearing from readers, so feel free to drop me an email telling me your thoughts about the book or series.

Email: roberta@robertakagan.com

Check out my website http://www.robertakagan.com.

Come and like my Facebook page! I love interacting with fans on the page:

https://www.facebook.com/roberta.kagan.9

Follow me on Bookbub to receive automatic emails whenever I am offering a special price, a freebie, a giveaway, or a new release. Just click the link below, then click follow button to the right of my name. Thank you so much for your interest in my work.

https://www.bookbub.com/authors/roberta-kagan.

Disclaimer

Table of Contents

Chapter 1

Gilde

December 1, 1938 The first Kindertransport

Gilde Margolis stood beside her sister, Alina, at the train station. Her arms were folded across her chest and her small black valise sat on the ground beside her. It was that eerie time of morning before the sunrise, when the shadow of night had not yet begun to lift and the world was still cloaked in darkness. A dusting of snow fell like ashes on her hair, appearing more pale gray than white in the limited light of the station. Even though she was bundled up with a heavy coat over an itchy wool dress, thick black stockings, and long underwear, the icy fingers of winter reached deep under her clothing and into her skin. At twelve years old, Gilde was still a child, but circumstances were forcing her to embark, alone, upon a journey that would lead her far away from everyone she knew and loved.

"Gilde, look at me and listen to me, please….," Alina her eighteen-year-old sister bent to look into Gilde's golden brown eyes which were glazed with tears. Alina was shaking, her trembling hands were raw from the cold as she brushed a strand of blonde hair out of Gilde's eyes. Alina forced a smile and trying to keep the fear out of her voice she continued to speak. "Gilde, I know you don't want to go to Britain and, believe me, I don't want to let go of you." Alina put her hands on both of Gilde's shoulders "Since the day you were born we have been inseparable and I already miss you terribly even though you haven't left yet. " Alina cleared her throat and mustered a half smile of encouragement. "But I know that getting out of Germany right now is the safest thing for you. And you have to realize, Gilde, that it's harder for me than you can imagine to let you go so far away without me. I want to protect you the way I always have. But, I've turned this over in my mind a thousand times and you see, sweety, I truly believe that you will be safer if you get out of Germany."

"Why can't you just come with me?"

"We've been over this, Gilde. I am too old. I can't go. The authorities won't allow it. This program is for children only. But you are lucky to have been chosen to be a part of it. Thank God you will be out of Germany and far away from Hitler."

"I don't feel at all thankful. I want to stay with you and Lotti and Lev and wait for Mommy and Papa to come back."

"Gilde, we don't know when they will return. For now, you will be in good hands in Britain. A family has agreed to care for you until everything settles down here in Germany and then you'll be able to come back home and it will be safe.. "

"I'm scared, Alina. I don't want to go all alone. I will be so far away from you, and I won't be here when our parents get back…."

"I know, Gilde. I wish I didn't have to send you." Alina said. Then she thought, if our parents ever come back. God help us.

"You don't have to send me," Gilde said, her voice was firm and angry.

"Yes, I do!" Alina took off the gold Star of David necklace

that's she'd received as a gift from her parents for her sixteenth birthday and slipped it over her little sister's head. "Wear this until we are together again."

"But Alina, Mama and Papa gave that to you. I know how much you love it. I couldn't take it."

"You're not taking it away from me, Gilde. You're just holding on to it for me until we are together again."

"Please … don't make me go." Gilde reached up to her neck and gripped the Star of David and held it in her small hand.

"You have to go, Gilde. I love you and that is why I am insisting on this. Please, trust me." Alina made her voice as firm as possible.

Lotti and Lev were waiting on the other side of the station they wanted to give Gilde and Alina a few minutes alone to say goodbye. Lotti walked over with Lev at her side. She hugged Gilde and then Lev hugged her as well. Tears stained Lotti's cheeks and her eyes were red and swollen. They had been friends of the family for many years. And after Gilde and Alina's parents had been arrested by the Gestapo Lotti and Lev had insisted that the two girls stay with them. It had all began on the most horrible night of Gilde's young life, when bands of wild ruffians had attacked the Jewish neighborhood where the Margolis family lived. They'd come through the streets looting and killing anyone that was outside. They shattered the windows of all of the Jewish owned shops. Alina had been on her way home with her fiancé Benny when Benny was attacked. Taavi Margolis, Gilde and Alina's father heard Alina screaming and ran out of their apartment to help Benny. He'd demanded that Alina get inside the apartment with her mother and sisters. The three females watched in horror as Taavi tried to stop the angry mob from kicking and hitting Benny with clubs. But the thugs were relentless. Then the police came and Taavi, not the attackers, was arrested. The police took him away in a black car that made a terrible alarming sound. All night the two girls and their mother sat up waiting and praying for Taavi's return. When he'd not returned by the following morning, Gilde's mother had gone to the police station to beg for her husband's release. That was over two weeks ago, on a night that would become known as Kristallnacht, the night of the broken glass. Neither of Gilde's parents had been seen since. For several years before Kristallnacht, Lotti and Alina had been working with a group that ran an Orphanage for Jewish children. After Kristallnacht the orphanage received an offer from the British Government. They had arranged for a transport of Jewish children from the Orphanage to be taken to Britain to live with British families who had volunteered to take them and keep them safe. As soon as Alina and Lotti heard about the program both of them pled with the authorities to take Gilde along with the group. After a lot of meetings and begging, Alina and Lotti were successful in securing a place on the transport for Gilde. Gilde was going to live with a family in London where she would be taken care of until the end of the war.

And now the time had come to leave Germany. Gilde was standing at the train station as a frozen breeze wept across her face. With her knees quaking and tears freezing on her cheeks she held desperately on to Alina's hand for the last few minutes before she boarded the train into the unknown.

Alina knew that if it weren't for that fact that Lotti had been volunteering at the Orphanage for many years and then gotten Alina a job there, it was doubtful that Gilde would have been able to join the rest of the children on this rescue mission. 'It is for the best, isn't it?' Alina had asked Lotti on the day that Gilde had received her acceptance letter. Lotti had assured her that it was, but the question still plagued Alina, even now, even after she'd made the decision to send her sister on the transport.

"Gilde!" a heavyset boy of fourteen came loping over to Gilde. As he ran towards Gilde he slipped on the ice and fell. His friend Elias, another orphan of the same age, who'd been walking with him, laughed loudly.

"You've always been so clumsy, come on, let me help you up," Elias said giving Shaul his hand.

Shaul's face was red with embarrassment.

"Good Morning," both Shaul and Elias said to Gilde

"Good Morning," Glide said without enthusiasm.

Elias pushed back his dark hair that was falling over his forehead. Even at fourteen, it was already obvious that he was destined to be a handsome man.

One of the teachers came over and handed Gilde and each of the boys a square of cardboard that had been made into a large necklace with two pieces of thick string. Written on the front of each of the cardboard tags were numbers. Gilde looked at the number.

"What is this for?" she asked.

"So that when you get to Britain your new family can find you and identify you. They have a card with your number. That's how you will know each other," the teacher said.

"I don't need a new family," Gilde said tossing the card back at the teacher.

"I'm sorry," Alina said picking up the identification number and putting it over Gilde's head. Shaul read it, "Your number is 24, Gilde. I'm 82, and Elias is 79."

"Now we are nothing but numbers," Gilde said sarcastically, shaking her head.

"Please, Gilde. Don't fight this. I know it's hard. But you have to go," Alina said. She had been trying so hard to stay strong, but now she was crying too.

"All right, children, form a single file line and say your goodbye's it's time to board the train." One of the nurses who Alina had become friends with during the years she'd worked at the Orphanage was organizing the children for boarding.

"Come on." Shaul took Gilde's hand, but she shook him off violently. Then she stood steadfast and would not move.

"Alina? Do I really have to go? Really?" Gilde's eyes were wide and pleading.

Alina nodded her head "Yes. But don't forget to write. Write often."

Gilde's shoulders began to shake as she cried silent tears.

Elias put his arm around Gilde. "Let's go, Gilde. You'll sit with me. This is going to be a great adventure. You'll see…" He carefully led Gilde into the line and after a few moments, it was their time to board. Elias took Gilde's suitcase and carried it up the stairs, and then he extended his hand to help her. Gilde turned to look back at her sister and Lotti with one more pleading glance.

"Don't make me go," Gilde said. Alina could hear the pain in her sister's voice.

"I love you," Alina said. "Write to me. Don't forget…."

Shaul boarded behind Gilde.

They slid into their seats. Gilde went in first so that she could look outside, then Elias sat beside her and Shaul next to him.

Now Gilde could see her sister, Lotti and Lev through the small window. Elias was trying to distract her. He was talking. But she couldn't hear him. Her ears were ringing too loud with fear. Then the whistle of the train sounded and Gilde jumped. The train rattled and sputtered as it sprung to life and began its journey to an unfamiliar land far away from everything Gilde loved. She craned her neck turning all the way around to look out the window until the familiar forms of those she'd grown up with grew smaller and finally disappeared.

Gilde knew it was cold but she hadn't felt the bitterness of it until now. It stung like an icicle had punctured her heart. When she looked down, her hands were red and trembling. Elias, who was usually so arrogant, cocky, and distant, was very kind today. He took her hands in his. "We'll be all right. You'll see. I've read a lot about Britain."

"Yeah, me too," Shaul said trying to somehow integrate himself into the conversation.

Gilde just shook her head. She was gently rocking with the rhythm of the train as it rattled along the track. Her life was shattering, and although she appeared calm, she was stifling the desire to scream and kick the seat in terror. It felt as if the train were taking her into a dark tunnel where she would never know what had happened to her family. Letters? This was the only communication she would have with Alina. And her parents? Just occasional pieces of paper? No smiles, no hugs, no kisses goodnight? Where were her parents? Were they alive? A shiver ran down her spine. What if they were dead? Her Mama and Papa dead? Shaul and Elias were orphans, she didn't know when or how they'd ended up at the orphanage, but they had been orphans for as long as she'd known them. So, how could they ever understand how she was feeling right now? In fact, she couldn't even talk to them about it. Gilde wrapped her arms around herself and shivered from the cold. Then she leaned her head against the window of the train car and tried to fall asleep so she didn't have to talk. As she sat quietly feeling sorry for herself, she felt something warm being laid on top of her. She opened her eyes to see Elias had taken off his coat and was covering her with it. He smiled at her. She smiled back, but she still felt very sad and alone.

Eventually, the warmth of the extra coat combined with the motion of the train coaxed Gilde into a deep intoxicated sleep. It had been several days since the last time she'd slept through an entire night until morning without waking at some point shuddering from a nightmare. She was sleeping so hard that she hardly noticed when Shaul had put his scarf between her face and the iced up window. There was a pulse to the railroad almost like music. Glide's body rocked along finding peace in the continuous pace, until the train jumped forward then back and came to an abrupt halt. She opened her eyes slowly but she was quickly forced back to the terrifying reality of her situation, when she saw two men in Nazi uniforms enter the train car.

"Open your suitcases. Now!" They were yelling "Shnell, Shnell."

Because she'd been awakened so frighteningly, Gilde felt lost, unable to move. She was disoriented, but she knew she must comply with their orders and quickly. Gilde looked in the overhead compartment where she'd stored her valise earlier, but she couldn't find her suitcase. The officers were tearing through everyone's things, throwing their belongings all over the train car.

"They're looking for valuables." Elias whispered to Gilde, "Get your suitcase and open it. If you have anything of value, give it to me now."

Immediately Gilde's hand went to Alina's necklace.

"Hurry, give it to me before they see it," Elias said

Gilde slipped the necklace off of her neck and handed it to Elias. He put it down his pants. She gave him a look of disgust.

"I'm sorry. I had nowhere else to hide it."

"Shnell. Where is your suitcase?" The Nazi inspector pushed Elias against the train window. Gilde saw Elias' hand form into a fist. Gilde knew Elias well enough to know he was angry and ready for a fight. She got up quickly and opened her suitcase and Elias's. Then she rubbed Elias's fist and shook her head mouthing the words "no."

Elias looked at Gilde took a deep breath then unclenched his fist. Gilde knew that Elias wanted to hit the Nazi, to fight back. But she also knew that he didn't stand a chance against the gun that she saw at the Nazi's side.

When the inspection was over everything that Gilde owned was scattered like bits and pieces of broken dead leaves on the seat and the floor of the train car. Shaul helped Gilde to gather up her belongings and his own. Then he found Elias's things and tossed them to him. Shaul and Gilde carefully refolded their clothes. Elias just threw his stuff back into his suitcase and slammed it shut.

Then for a few minutes everything was quiet. "What do you think they're going to do? Do you think they'll come back and arrest us?" Gilde asked Elias

He shrugged "Don't know."

When Gilde looked around the train car she saw that all of the other children's eyes were filled with fright and apprehension.

"I'm afraid they're going to come back." Gilde whispered to Elias

"Nahh." He smiled trying to look strong and confident, but Gilde could see the fear in his eyes. "If they were going to take us they would have done it already."

Shaul was sitting in his seat, his face pale, his eyes darting to and from the door.

Then the train rumbled, and sputtered, and they were in motion again. Gilde sighed with relief. Shaul wiped the sweat from his forehead with the forearm of his coat. And, Elias stood up and reached into his pants. He handed the necklace back to Gilde. "Put this somewhere that they won't find it, or they'll take it away from you if they stop us again," Elias said.

She nodded. Then Elias sat down by the window and looked out. He didn't speak for several hours. Gilde felt sorry for him, she knew that he felt ashamed for looking weak and unable to fight back against the Nazi. She tried to think of something to say to make him feel better, but she couldn't think of anything. So, she just sat there staring straight ahead, having to put her trust in God as to what the future held, with Alina's necklace gripped firmly in her palm.

As they inched their way towards Holland, Gilde held her breath. She was so tense, so worried that at any moment the Nazi's would board the train and take them that she bit through the side of her mouth and tasted blood.

"Only a few more miles." Elias said "And we'll be out safely."

Shaul wasn't speaking. His leg was twitching and he kept looking around the room.

When the train finally passed through the border into Holland, all of the children stood up and cheered. From the way that they were cheering, Gilde knew that they had all been tense until this very moment. Gilde smiled wryly. She wanted to be happy, but she was leaving everything she loved in Germany. Yes, she was thankful that the danger of being boarded and arrested had passed. But, Alina's face flashed before her, and then she thought of the little room that they shared in the apartment over her father's store. She visualized her old worn teddy bear with the pink bow around its neck, that was beginning to shred with age. Her father had given her that teddy when she was very young. She hadn't taken it with her because she had limited space. Now she wished she had packed it and left some of her other things behind. The train came to an abrupt halt, shaking the passengers back into their seats and then forth. At first it felt like there was some trick, some cruel trick. Gilde looked at Elias, who smiled at her reassuringly. "We're in Holland." He said.

She wasn't sure what that meant. Did that mean that they were safe? If so, then why were they stopping?

The train conductor came in to the car and the children were escorted into the station building. A pang of fear twitched in the back of Gilde's neck. But then they were greeted by Dutch women with friendly smiles who gave them hot chocolate and cakes.

"See, I told you we were going to be fine." Elias said smiling and biting into a small cake. Shaul had crumbs all over his coat. Shaul and Elias ate and drank until they were almost sick. But Gilde had no appetite even though she had not eaten for two days. Her insides were twisted in knots and as hard as she tried, she couldn't overcome the terror of uncertainty and the longing to return to the familiar.

The group of Jewish orphans spent a couple of hours with the Dutch women. But before too long, Gilde was on a bus to the ferry that would take her closer to her destination.

London. Gilde thought about London as she wrapped her arms around herself and closed her eyes. All she knew of London was the old song about the bridge falling down. London was a foreign place filled with people who did not speak the same language as she did. How would she ever communicate with them? Both of the boys had fallen asleep. She looked deeply into their faces. When he was awake Elias looked so strong and capable, like a man, but when he slept it was easier to see that he was only a fourteen-year-old boy without a family without anyone in the world but himself to lean on. And Shaul, dear Shaul, he sort of reminded her of her old teddy bear. Her heart ached. These two boys were all she had left of her previous life. They would be the only ones in her new life who would remember Alina, and Lotti, the only people who she could still laugh with her about Mrs. Shienberg the history teacher's sheitel that was never on straight or complain about how demanding Mr. Bulmanstein's was about homework . Of course she could write to Alina and Lotti, and she would, but it might be years before she could look into their eyes and hold their hands again. And what of Papa and Mama? If only she knew. That was the most difficult part of this already terrible adventure. She would be far away, too far to see anything with her own eyes. She would have to believe whatever Alina or Lotti told her. Again, for the one thousandth time, she asked herself the same terrifying questions. Were her parents still alive? Were they dead? Were they suffering? She asked herself these questions silently, because in truth she had no one to ask, no one had an answer.

Chapter 2

Gilde 1938

When they arrived in London, Gilde, Elias, and Shaul, stood at the train station shivering as the snow fell in sheets and wearing their large cardboard identifying number signs around their necks. Shaul was claimed first. An old woman with a hump in her back, bundled up in several wool scarves, wearing a heavy coat and hat and carrying a thick blanket came over. She claimed him by his number showing him her matching card.

"My name is Mrs. Barlow. Come on now." She wrapped the blanket around Shaul's shoulders. "I was right. You didn't have a coat warm enough for the English winters. Well, never mind. For now, this blanket will do."

Shaul looked at Gilde and Elias. "I don't know how we will find each other," he said.

Gilde shrugged her shoulders holding back the tears. Another familiar face gone from her life in a matter of seconds.

Shaul hugged Gilde, then he hugged Elias, who surprising Gilde, allowed Shaul to hug him.

"Goodbye. I hope we'll see each other again."

Gilde bit her lower lip as Shaul was led away. She glanced

over at Elias. He nodded reassuringly, but she saw the sadness in his eyes.

Gilde was next. Awkwardly she hugged Elias. He pinched her cheek. "It's gonna be fine," he said with a smile she didn't trust to be sincere.

"How will I ever find you again?" she said feeling as if she had said far too many goodbyes since that terrible night when her little neighborhood had been brutalized.

"I'll find you, Gilde. Don't you worry, we'll be back home in Germany in no time. Now you go ahead and be a good girl. All right?"

He sounded so much older so mature that it made her feel even more lost.

"I'm afraid, Elias. I don't want to go home with these people. I don't know them."

"You have to go home with them, Gilde. You have to try and make the best of it. Before you know it the three of us will be back together. Just like the three musketeers' right? You, me, and Shaul.'

"I hated that book." She looked away.

"Gilde, please?"

She hugged him again "Be careful, Elias. Take good care of yourself. And please, don't forget to find a way to come back and see me."

"Come on, Gilde, I could never forget you? I'll find you. You'll see." The mother who was taking Gilde in to live with her family, gently led her away. Quickly she glanced back and saw Elias quickly wipe a tear from his cheek with the back of his hand.

As she followed her new family, Gilde put her hand in her pocket and wrapped her fingers around the Star of David necklace that Alina had given her. She thought of her sister's face and felt a deep emptiness in the depths of her soul.

The family who offered Gilde shelter had the surname of Kendall, they had two daughters. Elizabeth, the older girl was married and lived in Scotland with her husband. The other, Jane, was fourteen years old, two years older than Gilde. George Kendall, the father, was a dentist in London, he'd come from a long line of dentists and had a full and busy practice. The Kendall's weren't rich, but they were comfortable. Mrs. Kendall, Rosemary, was active in her church and in charity groups and well known amongst her peers for kindness and generosity. She was always bringing a casserole to a new mother or helping to make the arrangements for a neighbor's funeral. So it had come as no surprise to George when his wife had come to him and suggested that they take in a Jewish child who was in danger in Germany. George Kendall adored his wife and so he indulged her. He was far too busy to tend to the business of the house that was up to Rosemary. His wife had wanted the little Jewish girl from Germany and he'd readily agreed. At first Gilde was not friendly with the family. She felt awkward and out of place. All she wanted was to be left alone. The family tried to make her feel welcome, but although she was polite, she found it hard to be warm. They spoke English and very little German which made communication difficult. Glide knew how hard they were trying and she understood the magnitude of kindness they were bestowing upon her. In fact she was constantly reminded of how her sister and all of the staff at the orphanage made it clear to her just how fortunate she was to escape Germany and to have been taken in by a family in Britain. The Kendalls had opened their home and their hearts to her, a stranger, and a Jew. She was grateful. But she didn't want to be in Britain. Gilde wanted to go home to be with her sister, to await her parents' return.

It was Jane who was finally able to reach Gilde. They were

close in age, and an understanding began to grow between them. Since they didn't have a common language Jane, who had always been an amateur artist, began to draw pictures to communicate with her new houseguest. Gilde began to draw crude illustrations to further the correspondence. From there they began to share words in their respective languages. Gilde was enrolled in school, but she was unable to understand the language in her classes and none of the teachers were able to communicate effectively with her. Her marks in school suffered and she was terribly melancholy. Jane was her only friend and although Jane tried to bring Gilde around her peers, Gilde was having a hard time fitting in.

In the morning, the girls ate porridge and tea with milk. Gilde missed the hot cocoa that they sometimes served at the Orphanage, but she tried to remember to be grateful to the Kendalls for their sacrifice of sharing their home with her. Jane's kindness and patience wore Gilde's resistance down. It was a frigid winter. Gilde and Jane watched the other children through the picture window in the living room. The children were outside skating and although Jane had given up skating several years earlier, she took Gilde outside. She brought two pairs of skates, an old pair of hers and one that had belonged to her sister. They joined a group of children who were outside enjoying the winter and spent the better part of the day slipping and sliding on the ice. They communicated through laughter and by that evening Gilde and Jane had become good friends. Although because of the two years difference in their ages, they went to separate schools they walked for several blocks together each morning before they separated. While Gilde and Jane were together, Gilde felt comfortable, but as soon as she saw Jane disappear around the corner, she felt alone and began to think about her family. School work was difficult for Gilde because she was just learning English and everyone spoke so fast. But, when she joined the drama club, Gilde found a home at school. Since she was a child she loved to be on the stage, singing and dancing. Now, that she had a reason to learn the language, it was coming more quickly to her. Drama club was fun, however, unlike in Germany, here in Britain, she was not the star player. In fact, she was more in the background with the techs. It was too hard to understand her broken English for the director to cast her in a role. Still, she was making friends, finding her way in her new home. On Saturdays when Jane babysat for the neighbor's children, she took Gilde with her and even shared her pay with Gilde. At first, living with a non-Jewish family was strange for Gilde. Growing up, the Margolises were not religious, but they'd always kept the Sabbath. They had not adhered to all of the Jewish laws, like complete rest to the point of not flipping a light switch on Saturday. But every Friday evening, Michal made a special dinner and the family lit the Sabbath candles. So, it took Gilde several weeks to get used to Friday nights not being a special time of family celebration. On Sundays Gilde went to church with the Kendalls. They didn't force her to go, but Jane went and the girls had become inseparable. It was fun to get dressed up for church, even if her clothes were Jane's hand-me-downs, and Gilde loved the organ music and the singing. She still missed her parents and her sister, but she was settling in and every day she was becoming more at ease in her new home. At first, she was angry with Alina for forcing her to go to England. And even though she missed her sister, it took her almost a month to send her first letter to Alina letting her know that she had finally begun to adjust to her surroundings. When she'd first met them, Jane's friends had teased Gilde because of her accent. But as time passed, and mostly because of Jane, Gilde was accepted into a group of girls who loved American movie stars and tried like mad to get their hands on pictures of them from American magazines. These were Jane's good friends and because of Jane they accepted Gilde.

Chapter 3

Elias

Elias lay naked on the rug beside his young female teacher, Mary Kent. Their affair had been going on for four months now. It began three weeks after Elias attended his first class with Mrs. Kent. She'd asked him to stay after school and help her mark papers. Elias, who had never been a good student, and wasn't much interested in academics anyway, just shrugged. "Sure," he'd said. Although, he had never had sex he an instinctive feeling that Mrs. Kent was attracted to him and the idea excited him. The girls his own age had a way of leading a fellow on, making him believe that he might score and then at the last minute, bam, they'd just pull the rug out and say "No, I can't do this. We can't go this far." It drove him crazy. At almost fifteen, his hormones had begun to go crazy. And the way he looked, turned the heads of all of his female classmates. Elias was tall, well built, and handsome with dark hair and strong features. From his appearance, one would think he was in his early twenties. He sat in the classroom with his arms folded across his chest, never opening his book, or participating in class discussions. Instead he just there with his long legs stretched out in front of him and watched Mary Kent. His eyes scanned her body and when their eyes met, her face turned red and she had to look away. But, he knew that she saw and felt his desire and he also knew that he had an invisible rope around her and he was pulling her towards him. Once she'd asked him a question during a class lecture, and he had the audacity to say right in front of the rest of the class "Sorry, I wasn't listening. I was looking at you."

She hadn't expected that answer from a student and her face turned scarlet with embarrassment. The teacher in her knew she should send him to the Headmaster. But, as a woman she couldn't. Mary had been taken with his cocky arrogance from the moment he walked into her classroom. And the way he looked at her sent shivers up her thighs. In the two years since she'd graduated from University and began teaching she had never been attracted to a student before. It was against every rule, but she couldn't control herself. Elias was something special. He was a mixture of anger and gratitude. He oozed sexuality, but at his age it was hard to believe that he could be the great lover that his body said he was. And that accent, that accent when he said her name sent shockwaves through her nerve endings. At first Mary fought her attraction to the boy. After all Elias was seven years her junior and really only a teenager. But more importantly, Mary had gotten married only a year before she met Elias. And until all of these strange feelings for Elias had risen in Mary, she thought her marriage was a good choice. Her husband Jack was a quiet intellectual. A kind and gentle man but unfortunately, unemotional and without much passion. But when she weighed the pros and cons about Jack, she decided to marry him because they shared the same love of teaching and he offered friendship and stability. He taught history. It had all began between them when they met in the teachers' lounge at school. Then a few months after they started dating, Jack was offered a job at another school where he got a better position with a pay raise. One night when they were having dinner at an Italian restaurant he told Mary about his job offer and that he planned to move. She wished him well and told him that she'd miss him. He'd looked down at the table cloth and said that he cared for her and it was then that he proposed. It wasn't a romantic proposal. In fact it was rather matter of fact. But, Mary had married him because she was afraid that the years were passing quickly and she might end up an old maid. Since she was a young girl, Mary's parents had made it clear to her that she was not beautiful. Of course, she did the best she could to be as attractive as possible. Her clothes were always clean and pressed. Her hair was neat and styled. Anyone who met her would have said she was pleasant to look at but not striking in any way. This knowledge of being less than pretty had weighed on Mary's mind her entire life.

Then Elias, who was just a boy, had come along and changed everything.

The whole thing had begun on an afternoon four months earlier. Mary's mind drifted back to that day. Elias had gotten into a fight during class. A well-known bully, George Seaword, who most of the boys in class followed out of fear, began calling Elias "The German." George made fun of Elias's accent and broken English. At first, Elias ignored the boy, but when Seaword stuck his foot out and tripped Elias as they were coming into class after lunch, Elias caught himself before he fell. Then without another word he turned around and punched Seaword in the face. Seaword was sitting in his desk, but the punch was so hard that the desk fell back into the student's desk behind him. Seaword got up. He put his hand to his nose and felt the blood. Looking at his hand and seeing red, Seaword reared back and took a shot at Elias who was too quick for him. Growing up in an orphanage, Elias was well seasoned in street fighting. Blocking Seaword's punch with his left forearm, Elias swung a hard right directly into George's stomach knocking him down. Seaword was having trouble catching his breath as he lay on the floor. The blood from his nose was running down his cheek. Then Elias got on top of the bully and held him down in a choke hold with his arm across his neck.

"The next time you bother me, I'm going to beat the hell out of you. If you think this was bad, you don't know what bad is, you are in for a real surprise, because next time I won't be so gentle. Now if you don't understand me because my accent is too thick, you better ask one of your friends to translate for you. Because if I were you, Seaword, I'd be real careful of me," Elias said.

After glaring at his enemy with a stare that could frighten the devil, Elias got up and sat down in his seat. He wiped Seaword's blood from his fist on to the hip of his black pants. Mary Kent had never seen any of the boys not back down to George before. She was impressed. Elias had so much going against him because he didn't speak perfect English, but he'd proven he was not afraid to stand up for himself. Seaword had been a problem for many of the teachers. So even before he'd set his sights on Elias as his next victim, Mary had expected trouble from him. What she had not counted on was Elias's courage.

Mary didn't mention the fight. She could have taken both boys to the Headmaster's office, and she probably should have. But she didn't. Instead, once everyone was seated, she said,

"George Seaword, would you like to go to the nurse?"

"No. I'm fine." He said. He'd wiped most of the blood from his nose on his shirt sleeve and it seemed to have stopped bleeding. It probably wasn't broken. Mary thought

"All right, take out your math books. And we'll begin." Mary said

The blood was drying on Seaword's face and on the floor.

Elias smiled at her and she felt the heat of his desire. This was not the first time a student had gotten a crush on her. In fact it had happened with so many other boys during her short teaching career and she'd ignored their stares. But, Elias was not like one of the boys, intellectually she knew he was only fifteen, but emotionally to her, he was more like a man than a lot of the older men she knew. He looked at her like a man, not like the other students in the past. Perhaps it was because Elias had been orphaned at birth and grown up in an Orphanage that he was mature beyond his years. He spoke very little, but what he said, he meant, and what he didn't say with his voice, he said with his eyes. Mary knew she was making a mistake even as she asked him to stay after class. What she was about to do was wrong, but she couldn't stop herself. In fact it was Mary who had started it. It began on a Thursday afternoon.

After the rest of the class left and Elias and Mary were alone, she felt uncomfortable. She couldn't look directly at him.

"Do you think you should telephone your foster family and let them know that you are going to be late?" Mary cleared her throat. Perhaps she would just ask him to mark papers. I mean this was sheer madness.

"It's all right, Mrs. Kent. They don't pay too much attention to my comings and goings. I sort of do whatever I want."

Mary Kent nodded. "Well, I have to lock up this classroom, so perhaps we can go into my office and you can help me with the papers there."

The sexual energy was pulsating like an electrical storm firing off inside of her. She could lose her job, lose her marriage. He was only fifteen. What was she thinking?

"Me?" He laughed. "I can hardly get through class … let alone judge somebody else's work."

His English was improving rapidly. She had two students in other classes that were part of the same Kindertransport program of Jewish children sent to safe homes in England from Nazi Germany. They had not progressed nearly as fast. There was no doubt in her mind that Elias was a bright boy even though he didn't take his schoolwork seriously.

"I think you're smarter than you realize." She smiled

"Do you?" He laughed. "I don't know. I need to find a job, something that pays me. School is a waste of my time. I mean the Blossoms have been very generous in taking me in, but I would rather work and be on my own."

And it was true, the Blossoms were a fairly well to do family. Mr. Blossom had a position working in the bank. Their children were grown, married and on their own. They'd taken Elias in when they had attended a retirement party at Mr. Blossom's office. All of the guests at the party were buzzing with the news of what had happened on that terrible night when the Jews were attacked in their homes and on the streets in Germany. There had been several frightening broadcasts over the BBC. The bank president, Michal Eppleshine was Jewish, and he'd announced that he had planned to take a child from the Kindertransport. Patricia and Sebastian Blossom glanced at each other. It would be a strategic career move to show their generosity by offering their home to a needy youngster. Eppleshine would appreciate the kindness. And besides, Patricia Blossom was appalled to hear how the Jewish children were being treated in Germany. It certainly wasn't easy for the Blossom's to open their home to a stranger. Since their children had grown up and were gone from the house they'd enjoyed a peaceful existence. But overall it was a wise choice, and so they'd put their name on the list of those willing to take a child. And that was how Elias came to live with the Blossoms.

Elias followed Mary Kent into her small office. She carried a pile of papers and put them down on her desk. Then she turned around to close the door. He saw the sway of her hips and his heart beat sped up. She walked back to sit behind her desk. Now, Elias felt bolder because they were alone.

Elias walked over to Mary and twisted a curl of Mary's hair around his finger and smiled at her. "You're so beautiful," He whispered in a husky hoarse voice.

No one in Mary's entire life had ever called her beautiful.

She shook her head and stared at him. "Don't do that," she said as strongly as she was able to, and she wished she meant it. Elias lifted her out of the chair and held her in his arms. Then he pushed her up against the wall and kissed her, and then kissed her again. His hand slid up her blouse, cupping her breast and she was lost.

That was the beginning. Every day when she got up in the morning and headed off to school, she promised herself that she was going to end it. But as soon as they were alone and he looked at her in that way that he had of looking at her that made her tingle, then when he took her into his arms, she forgot her promise. She was guilt ridden, sick to the very core with shame, but Elias was like drug and she was addicted.

And now so many months later, they lay on the rug in her office naked.

"What kind of job do you think you can get without an education?" Mary asked him gently touching his well muscled chest.

"I don't know. I just know that I want to get some kind work and make some money. I can't stay here and waste my time sitting in a classroom."

"It would be a real shame for you to drop out of school." She said.

"I love it when you act like my teacher. It makes you even sexier than you already are…"

No one had ever called her sexy. Mary was breathless. It would be best if he left school. But she didn't want to see him fail, and quite frankly, she couldn't bear to let him go. "If I can get you a job here on the campus perhaps as a caretaker, after classes will you stay in school? You'll be able to earn some money, but at least you'll still be getting an education. You're a bright boy, Elias. And you're going to need to have some education behind you if you want to find a decent job. You don't want to spend your life doing manual labor do you?"

"You think that you could find a job here at the school for me? I mean you'd do that for me?"

"I don't know, but I am certainly going to try." She meant it, she had so many reasons to try.

It wasn't difficult for Mary to secure a few hours of paid employment each day for Elias. There was always cleaning and repairing to be done around the building, and a student would work cheaper than an adult would. She talked to the Headmaster and explained that Elias was with the Kindertransport and he was an orphan. She explained that he was living with a family and that he felt funny asking them for financial help. So, it would really be good for him to earn some money of his own.

He was hired. It was that easy and that quick. Elias's schedule included a free hour between the end of his classes and the beginning of his job. During this hour, he was expected to eat his dinner and get ready to work, but instead he spent the time with Mary.

Every day they met in the classroom at the end of the school day and then went to her private office. Mary knew that he was falling in love with her. And as odd and impossible as it seemed she thought she might be falling in love with him as well. She told herself that he was just a boy, but her heart and her body told her a different story. If she got caught, Mary was certain that she would lose her job and most likely she would be blackballed and unable to find another job teaching anywhere. I must be insane, she thought, but she was unable to stop. For the first time in her life, Mary felt beautiful, reckless and excited about being a woman.

When they were in class, Mary diverted her eyes from Elias's gaze. She was afraid that one of the other students might detect the current that ran between them. But once they were alone, the passion she had for him was all-consuming.

It was rare that any of the other teachers stayed as late as Mary and Elias did. For the most part they wanted to be on their way as quickly as possible, most of them marking papers and completing lessons for the following day from their homes. But one afternoon after school a female colleague who was a friend of Mary's knocked on the door to her office. Mary was not expecting any visitors, and the knock sent her into a panic. She and Elias had been lying on the floor. Neither of them fully dressed. Alarmed Mary got up quickly and straightened her clothes but, there was no place to hide the boy.

"Mary…" It was Miranda, she recognized the voice. The two women had been friends since Mary started teaching. "Mary, are you alright in there?"

"Get dressed, and straighten up. Hurry." Mary whispered to Elias.

"Yes, yes, give me a minute."

Mary checked to be sure her blouse was buttoned properly. She glanced at Elias he had his clothes on, but he was still disheveled. With her hand she smoothed down Elias' hair trying to make him look presentable.

"Mary are you sure you're alright?"

She nodded at Elias "Are you ready?" she whispered.

"Yes" he nodded back. Then Mary tried to smooth his hair one more time and then her own. She took a deep breath and opened the door.

"Elias came in to see me about his science project." Mary said. Even as she told the lie, Mary cringed at how stupid she sounded.

Miranda gave Mary a look for disbelief. Then she shook her head and Mary knew immediately that Miranda was aware of what was going on between her and Elias in that office. Perhaps it was seeing the look on her Miranda's face that sobered Mary. What she had been able to hide from herself before was now very clear to her. The truth was that she had been engaging in sexual activity with an underage student. Shame and embarrassment caused her face to flush. This had to end. It had to.

"We can talk later." Miranda said. Then she turned and walked away.

Mary couldn't speak. She knew Miranda well enough to know that her secret was safe. But what if one of the other teachers or the Headmaster had been at the door? All of this time she had been making excuses, trying to ignore the dangers of her behavior, but now it was slapping her right in the face. . She would miss the boy, she would miss their wonderful sexual trysts, but this incident with Miranda felt like a warning and it made her realize that she was walking a serious tightrope. Today could have been disastrous. If it had been anyone else at the door and she and Elias were caught it would end her career and her marriage. She would have nothing.

"I think you should go, Elias. Go to work." She was shaking.

"Mary?"

"Please, leave me now. We can talk tomorrow. I need to go and see what Miranda wanted."

"But, you seem so upset. I don't want to leave you yet. Let's talk about this…"

"Leave me alone now, please, Elias?" her eyes begged him and he knew that it was no use to pressure her.

He nodded and then he took his books and went to work. The following morning when he came to school a teacher's aide, a stocky red haired boy with a face covered in freckles, was standing outside of Mrs. Kent's classroom.

"Hold on a minute there, Elias. You've been transferred to another class. It's right down the hall." The boy pointed, "It's that way."

"What? Why?" Elias asked

"Don't know. I just know I was told to stand here and tell you to go to the room down the hall when you came to class." It was clear that the red haired boy was afraid of Elias. But Elias had no heart to fight with him. He wanted to talk to Mary. He tried to look inside Mary's class, but the door was closed and the aide stood in front of the small window built into the door.

"I'm real sorry, but you can't go in there." The aide said, his voice cracking with fear. Elias knew he could easily have taken the boy, one punch in the stomach would have disabled him long enough for Elias to go right into Mary's classroom. However, he didn't want to cause trouble for Mary. His head was spinning. He needed time to think. As he walked down the hall to his new class, Elias began turning possible scenarios over in his mind. Had they been discovered? Elias wasn't really concerned about his own welfare. If they kicked him out of school, so what? But Mary, he cared what happened to Mary. She might be losing her job. The uncertainty of what was happening was making him frantic and he was far too young to control his emotions. Had he caused all of these problems for her? The only way to find out the truth was to go to Mary's classroom and ask her. To hell with the other students, to hell with the administration. He was too distraught to wait until after school. That was far too long to sit and contemplate what might be happening. Elias had to know right now.

After the aide walked away, leaving Elias at the door to his new classroom. Elias turned around and went back to Mary Kent's classroom. By the time he arrived class was just getting into session. Mary looked haggard. She wore a severe matronly dress and her hair was pulled back away from her face into a ratty looking bun. He could see the deep lines and dark circles around her eyes and assumed she'd not slept well. She stood in front of the class holding a book in her hand when she looked up and saw him through the window in the door.

Their eyes met. Elias opened the door and walked in. Mary's eyes grew wide. The expression on her face was begging him to leave.

"Mary?" he said. The rest of the students turned around. "I mean, Mrs. Kent. I need to talk to you."

"We can talk later, Elias." Her voice was trembling with fear and warning. But that didn't stop him. He couldn't wait until later, the anxiety was too much for him.

"I need to talk to you now."

"I am in class now." She tried to sound like a teacher instead of an emotional lover.

"Why have I been transferred?"

"Elias, please … go to your classroom"

One of the girls who was sitting in the front row giggled

nervously, otherwise the rest of the students were silent.

"Why are you doing this to me?" he said holding his hands out to her.

"Elias, go, please leave, we can talk later…."

He walked out of the room, but he didn't go to his classroom. He was far too upset. Instead, he waited outside her office. He sat on the floor next to her office door until school ended. When she arrived, he stood up and glared at her. Then cocked his head to a side as if to demand an explanation. Elias was struggling against a flood of emotions that felt as if they might drown him. Yet he was trying like hell to appear strong.

"What happened?" he asked.

"I can't do this anymore. I am afraid of losing my job, my marriage?"

"You should have thought of that before we started."

"I know. I don't know what I was thinking."

"Well, so now what?" He said trying to take her hand, but she pulled them away "Listen, Mary, we can be more discreet. We can meet outside of the school. It doesn't have to end like this," he said trying to steady his trembling lower lip. Don't cry. He told himself. Men don't cry.

"Elias, I think it's best if we stop this now. I am sorry. I am so sorry. It was selfish of me. You looked at me with such admiration. I was taken in by all of it, but it's wrong. You're young and I'm married, and even worse, I'm your teacher. I am so ashamed of myself," she said looking away from him. Passion cannot be turned off like a switch and she didn't want him to see how she felt about him by the look in her eyes. Her heart ached, but she knew she must force this break up before things got really bad.

"Mary, I love you." He almost choked on the words.

She shook her head. "Please don't say that."

"What can I say? What the hell have we been doing all these months?"

She felt sick. What had she been doing? This was just an amazingly sexy and attractive boy. But the fact of the matter was that he was in truth, just a boy, and her student and she was just a woman who needed attention. "I'm so sorry, Elias. But it's over."

He threw his hands in the air and shook his head. She walked into her office and closed the door. She leaned against the wall and began to cry, heart wrenching sobs. Feelings didn't just disappear. What had she done to herself? What had she done to Elias?

Elias couldn't move. The door to the office was closed to him and so was Mary's heart. His legs were weak and he felt glued to the floor. Somehow hoping against hope that she would change her mind. He stared at the door willing it to open. But it didn't. Elias felt tears welling up in his eyes, but he refused to cry. He wouldn't do that. His throat was raw with suppressing his feelings. For a moment, Elias thought of banging on the door with his fists and yelling until she opened it. But what was the point? She didn't love him, and so nothing else mattered. *Pull yourself together.* He thought. *She's done with you.* He'd shed a single tear. With the back of his hand he wiped his eye harder than necessary. Then he left and went downstairs to work in the caretaker office. At least his boss wasn't there. He didn't want to face anyone right now. His shift was only three hours that night and somehow he got through it.

After work, he couldn't go right home, he walked for an hour watching his shoes as they hit the pavement. The family who'd taken him in was kind enough. He hadn't expected more. But he felt restless living under their roof, learning, and following their rules. In his mind at fourteen the relationship with Mary and the pain of his broken heart, had made him a man. A man should be on his own, supporting himself and carving out his own future.

The next day, Elias didn't go to school at all. Instead, he went into the west end of London to look for work. Real work, work that paid him real money, not the few pounds he earned as a part time school caretaker. It didn't take long for him to find a bookie willing to hire him to run numbers. Elias never returned to school or to the family that sponsored him. He moved in to a flat in Soho with two other boys who were working for the same bookie. And so began a year of illegal activity, gambling, loan sharking, selling drugs, and dabbling in pimping prostitutes.

On a bright day in mid-February of 1939, Elias stopped into the local pub to pick up payment from a client who owed his boss. Elias had been instructed to do whatever was necessary even use violence to get the money. This was not an unusual situation. Elias had proven to his boss that he could be effective at strong-arming a customer who was holding out on making his payments.

He walked into the pub and ordered a beer. It was there that he saw Glenda. She was only a few years older than he, but she was glamorous and worldly, not used up and hard like the rest of the hookers he'd met since he had become a part of the underworld. He watched her sitting at the bar. When she noticed him watching her, she smiled. Elias returned the smile. Glenda walked over and introduced herself to him.

"Would you like to buy me a drink?" she asked.

"Sure," he said.

Damn, she was sexy, not pretty, but crazy sexy. She had a thick layer of fire red lipstick on her full sensuous mouth that made him think of all the things he could do with those amazing lips. He wanted to grab her and take her to bed.

"I'm expensive. Can you afford five pounds?"

"Yeah, why not?" he said his heart was racing with desire. He'd had sex with some of the other prostitutes that worked for his boss. He'd never paid for it before, but it had been a long time since he met a girl who excited him the way Glenda did. It was worth five pounds just to have the experience.

"Good, then" She smiled and those lips drove him nuts "Get ready, little boy, because you're in for the ride of your life."

Chapter 4

Shaul

Shaul was living in London in a poverty-stricken area with an old woman, it was hard to say how far past 80 years she was, but what Shaul did know for sure about her was that she had a big heart. He had a small room of his own, which had once been a pantry right off of the kitchen. The old woman's name was Martha Barlow and age had caused her memory as well as her eyesight to fade. Sometimes she would look blindly at Shaul, disoriented, and ask him who he was and why he was in her flat. He would have to calmly explain and answer her questions. Sometimes she would lash out in anger and throw something at him. He'd leave the house, but when he returned she would be back to normal and have completely forgotten the incident.

As Martha Barlow got used to Shaul she began to tell him bits and pieces of her life. She had never married or had children of her own, but when she was younger she had been a teacher. That was when she'd studied German. Shaul was glad that she spoke enough German to communicate with him. There was very little heat in the flat and Shaul was always cold. Martha put a hot water bottle in his bed before he got in to warm it up for him at night. It was all she had to give. However the bottle only heated a small section of the bed and although he wore his coat and socks to sleep he shivered all night. Within two weeks of his arrival he'd developed red patches and blisters that itched mercilessly covering his hands and feet. Martha called the condition Chilblains. She tried to explain that he must refrain from scratching due to the threat of infection, but the urge to scratch was overwhelming and sometimes he broke the skin until it bleed. Shaul was also rapidly losing weight due to the lack of food, and he was always hungry. Still he tried not to complain even during Miss Barlow's fits of anger. He could always tell when a bought of insanity was coming on. Her eyes slanted until they were merely slits, and her face contorted until she no longer looked like the same person. When this strange condition came over her, she would begin calling him Charles and screaming accusations at him. He wasn't sure what exactly she was saying because she was speaking in English. Ranting far too fast for him to comprehend very much of what was being said. But what he did know was that she pointed directly at his face referring to him as Charles. During one of these episodes, she attacked him with a wooden spoon. She began chasing him and hurling herself at him but she was slow and he escaped into his room. Several hours later, she'd forgotten the incident entirely. He could endure the lack of food and warmth, but these bouts of madness frightened Shaul. It was not that he didn't appreciate her kindness, he did, but he was unnerved by the unpredictability of her behavior. What if she attacked him with a knife in his sleep? He might never see it coming. During a period of sanity, Martha Barlow insisted that Shaul register for school, but when he attended on the first day he was bullied. The other students teased him about his broken English, his accent, and his rash. By the end of the week he'd been subjected to so many cruel jokes and ridicule that he stopped attending. Miss Barlow tried to encourage him to return but he refused. When she was feeling up to it she tried to teach him herself. But most of the time Shaul hid in his small room, and read some of the dusty old books that Miss Barlow kept on the shelf in her living room. He assumed the books were remnants of her teaching days. Occasionally the old woman, feeling nostalgic, told him grandiose stories of her youth. They were stories of love, and of the many suitors that had once adored her. However, he was never sure if she was telling the truth or if she was delusional. But unless one of her fits came on, when she told the tales, she never mentioned Charles.

Shaul was convinced that something life altering must have happened to the old woman with a man named Charles, but he had no idea what it might have been. He only knew that whatever it was it had been something that caused her to go through some kind of a personality change and he dreaded the times when her eyes turned to slits and her lips drew thin and she began to curse and call him Charles.

Chapter 5

Shaul 1939

Don't you really think you ought to be in school, son?" Martha Barlow wore a heavy cotton robe. It had once been white, but was now stained and yellowed with age. Her bones cracked as she sat down at the kitchen table beside Shaul and poured herself a cup of hot water. Most of the time Martha drank hot water because she hardly had any tea and she tried to save what she had for special occasions.

"I hate school."

"Do you then?" She said handing him a thick cracker spread with a dark thick foul smelling substance. "Eat now, you have to eat."

"I hate this too." He said "I don't mean to be an ingrate but it's terrible What is it?"

She laughed. "It's called marmite. It's good for you."

"Do you like the taste? He asked, his eyebrows raised and his head cocked to side.

"I'm used to it, Shaul. I've been eating all my life. To me it tastes just fine. Now, eat. You have to eat and it's all we have. "

"I supposed if you're used to it, it's probably not that bad...

"You seem to be rather unhappy here. I suppose it must be hard." She muttered shaking her head. "Well, it's true our food is different than what you grew up on. Here give me that bread with the marmite and I'll give you a plain slice of bread."

"Thank you. It's not that I'm not grateful. I'm just having some trouble getting adjusted."

"It's understandable."

Shaul looked at the old woman. It was clear to him that she had two sides, sort of like the man in the book "The strange case of Dr. Jekyll and Mr. Hyde" that he'd read. When she was kind, she was the sweetest old lady he'd ever met. But that other side frightened the hell out of him.

The plain bread was much better. "I wanted to tell you some good news. I got a job. I hope it's all right with you that I am going to go to work instead of back to school. I've also decided that I am going to pay you some money for rent and food and for everything you do for me." Shaul said

"Now you surely don't have to do that, Shaul. You would be best off getting yourself an education, so you could land a good job in the future."

"I wanted to help with expenses. I know it must be difficult for you. You certainly didn't have to take someone in to live with you. The least I can do is lend a hand. And besides, I am not going back to school."

"That's a shame. You should. You really should finish your education while you have a chance. But if this is what you've decided there is nothing I can to change your mind. What kind of a job did you get?"

"Helping the milk man make his deliveries. I will take the bottles to the customers and collect the payments. It sounds fairly easy. The milkman said he could pay me a few pounds a week and give me some milk to bring home. I thought the extra would be helpful to both of us."

She nodded. "I am a teacher. I could teach you at home if that's what you prefer…"

"I do…." He said "That would be much better for me. I don't' fit in here and the other students are constantly giving me a hard time"

"I understand how challenging it must be to be in a new country trying to learn a new language at the same time as you're attending classes and trying to make new friends."

"Mrs. Barlow?"

"Yes, Shaul."

"Can I ask you a question?"

"Sure I suppose you can."

"Why did you take me in?"

"Oh, now that's a long story."

"I would like to know. I mean, if you don't mind telling me."

"Would you now?"

He nodded. She watched him, her old eyes studying him.

"I don't normally tell anyone this story…" She said.

"You can trust me. I don't know anybody here and I wouldn't tell anyone even if I did…. I promise to keep your secret." He said

"Yes, I suppose you would now."

He nodded.

"All right then. It just might be good for me to get this off my chest. You see I haven't ever talked about any of this before. But let me put on a pot of tea, and since this is a special occasion, I'll use a little of the tea and the sugar. You just sit back Shaul and I am going to tell you a tale from my past."

She reached up and took down the well-worn tea kettle that hung from a hook on the low ceiling. After filling it with water, she added a spoonful of the precious tea leaves she kept in a glass container. Then she turned on the flame on the stovetop and sat back down in a chair at the table across from Shaul.

"Well…this story is certainly one sad memory that I have buried very deep in my heart. But I am an old lady and probably don't have many more years on this earth, so give a listen. Old Maid Barlow, as the ladies all call me in town, was not always an ugly old woman. No, Shaul, I was not always this way."

Chapter 6

Martha Barlow

Martha Barlow sipped the tea "I love a good cup of tea." She said. "I put a drop of sugar in. It's good isn't it?"

"Yes, very good. " Shaul nodded.

The old woman smiled at him "So, back to my story. I'll bet you think I was always old and ugly. That's what the young always think of the old. But I wasn't. No, Shaul, I wasn't. In fact, I was once very beautiful. Here…" She got up and opened the drawer to her china hutch. "Look at this picture."

He took the old yellowing wrinkled photograph that she handed him and gazed at the image of a young laughing blond. Her eyes twinkled as she held up a toddler.

"This was you?"

"Yes."

"That's your child?"

"Oh no. That's Charles' son."

"Who was Charles?"

"My employer, my savior, my lover, but most of all my downfall."

Shaul bit his lower lip.

"I was a young governess, a teacher. I worked for Charles and his wife. My job was to teach their children academics as well as manners. Charles and his wife came from old money. They hired me mostly to alleviate them of any responsibilities for their children. Charles' wife was busy with her friends and parties. Charles was not as busy. He was home a lot of the time and always trying to talk to me. At first I didn't pay him much attention. After all, the missus was the one who hired me. I was instructed to talk to her if I needed anything. But as time went by, I found that because she was a busy socialite and he was at home most of the time reading or working on something in the office he had set up in the back of the house. Because he was readily available it was easier to go to him with questions or requests for the children. The strange thing was that he loved to play with the children. That's rather rare for a man. First we became friends. He would come outside when I had taken the children out for exercise, and he played with them. It was attractive to me to see how much he loved them, and how willing he was to act like a child himself. Before I knew it, things between Charles and I escalated, then one night, we became lovers. Of course, it wasn't long before I became pregnant and although I tried to hide my condition, his wife spotted it and confronted me. Both Charles and I tried to lie, but she had a sharp eye and knew the truth. I was fired and sent on my own. Fortunately, I'd saved a little money. So, I moved to the east end of London and rented a flat. I heard nothing from Charles. I was quite sure he was done with me. And, the pain I felt from his abandonment was greater than anything I'd ever experienced. But, I had to stay strong, my child was coming. James was born in the early spring. The neighbor lady, Meg, who lived in a small flat in the same building I did helped me with the birth. You see, I had no money for a doctor or a midwife. But we managed. I was alright at first. But on the third day after James's birth I began feel terrible pain in my belly, my head ached so bad I couldn't lift it from the pillow. Then I began to burn up with fever. And to be quite honest with you, I wasn't sure I'd survive. I sent my lady friend to see Charles to tell him of my predicament. I asked her to beg him for money to take care of his son. She went to see him and took little James with her, because I was too ill to care for him. I was in a bad way. The worst part of all of it was that my milk was not coming in. Not that I would have been confident in feeding it to him after all, my fever was high. If he caught the illness from me, he would surly die. Meg returned looking many years older than when she'd left. Her face was drawn and I knew that her meeting with Charles had not gone well. She told me that he denied Jamey was his. I knew that my son was his spawn; I'd never lain with any other man. It was hard to believe that Charles had turned his back on me so easily. However, now anger had replaced hurt in my heart and I was determined to live. Over several perilous weeks, I struggled with bouts of sweating followed by bouts of shivering cold. Meg, bless her soul, she's dead now, found a wet nurse for James. For me it was touch and go for a while. That was until Meg went to the home of the local doctor and begged him to see me. She offered to clean his house for six months in exchange for one visit. He agreed. When he came he shook his head. "She has the child bed fever." He said "there is nothing I can do. Either she'll live or die. But the odds are she won't make it. I'm sorry."

All of that effort and then he left. It was a long recovery period. I probably should have died. But, I didn't. God had other plans for me I suppose. In fact, I believe, that you, Shaul, are part of those plans. You see God saved my life, so that I could be alive to do something good. When I heard about the Jewish children who needed homes to escape from Hitler, I knew that I was meant to take one of them in." She smiled at him

"Where is James?" Shaul asked.

"Oh, well, the story doesn't end there. You see Charles

had a fire in his home a year later. He and his wife were at a gala of some sort when it happened. Both of his children and their present nanny were killed. A few months after the fire, Charles came to see me. I was surprised that he still had the address Meg had given him. But he came. When I saw him standing in my humble room my heart skipped a beat. I couldn't believe that he was here. For so many months, I had dreamed of this moment. You see, I thought he'd come for me. I had prayed that one day he would realize that he loved me and come back to me. I could hardly speak to ask him if he wanted a cup of tea. Fool that I was, I wanted to fall into his arms and forget any hurt or pain he'd caused me. I was ready to forgive him, no matter what he did. I loved him that much. But he didn't say he loved me. Instead, he asked me to give James to him. I had not been aware of it, but he told me that his wife was no longer able to bear children. The pain of having my hope thwarted was like a thunderbolt right through my heart. I sunk down into the sofa and worked hard not cry. He didn't seem to notice. Instead he told me that James was the only blood line he had left. I couldn't look at him. He had taken so much from me already, but now…now I could give James a life he would never have with me. With me, he would spend long hours working in a factory or worse a coalmine, and probably die young. I was a certified teacher, but I couldn't work in a school because I had no one to watch James. I would educate him to the best of my ability but then he would be on his own to find work. Believe me; I gave it a lot of thought. This was my son, my heart, my only child. I had raised him since his birth on my own, given him all I had, all I could give. Many nights I went to bed without eating so that I could be sure, he had enough food. But now, even though it would take everything away from me, I was being given the opportunity to give him a better life. He would be an heir to a fortune. I steadied my voice so that James could not hear the emotion in it and I asked him what his wife felt about taking James to live with them. She wanted him Charles told me. She would love him as if he were her own. I shuddered. James was sitting on the floor on an old worn blanket that had holes in it. When the winter came again, there would be the struggle to assure that there was enough heat. Living with me, James had much slimmer chances of surviving to adulthood. Can I have the night to think it over? I asked, although I already knew I was going to send James with him, I just wanted one more night with my son before I said goodbye forever. Charles nodded and left.

When he returned the next day, I had James ready to go. Everything he owned was packed in a small cloth bag. You're making the right decision. Charles said to me. He took my son in his arms and I put the handle of the bag in his hand. Then quietly they left. I never felt so alone or lost in all of my life. I wept. I don't know for how long. But the following day, I got up and went to look for work. The small bit of money I had saved was running low, and now I had time to go to a job. As I passed the trash can outside the building I happened to see the bag I'd packed with James's things in it. Charles had tossed James's past into the garbage, along with me."

"Have you ever seen your son again?"

"I never saw him again. I tried, but I when I went to the house, the housekeeper would not allow me to come in. Then one day I read in the paper that James and his father were killed in a boating accident."

"You're son is dead?"

"Yes. And I blame Charles for everything. Everything."

"I'm sorry."

"So am I."

Chapter 7

1939 Gilde London

Because of her language difficulties Gilde was behind in school. But with Jane's help, she was advancing.

Thomas walked Jane and Gilde home from school. He stood outside the Kendall home talking to them for several minutes. He was tall and well built, with eyes and a smile that could melt a girl's heart. Gilde tried hard not to be taken in by Thomas's charm and good looks. But she was only fourteen and it was difficult not to be swept up like all of the other girls were by Thomas. She watched them together and was envious, Jane who at sixteen was already a classic beauty, and Thomas, who in her mind was a handsome hero. In Gilde's mind the two of them looked like something out of one of her romance novels. How could she not secretly want to be Jane? Wouldn't every girl want that? It was nothing but a fantasy, this longing to be in the arms of a good-looking man like Thomas. Nothing but a dream. Still, Gilde knew that she should not even be thinking about Thomas in that way because Jane had told her that she was falling in love with him.

As time passed and Gilde got to know Thomas better she began to observe things she'd not seen before. Like when Thomas talked to Gilde and Jane, it looked like his feelings for Jane were not nearly as strong as hers were for him. But what Gilde began to notice was that unless she was imagining it Thomas was attracted to her. As much as that had been a fantasy of hers, the reality of it frightened her. Because no matter how much she liked him, Gilde would never betray Jane.

They had walked home from school one afternoon as they did every day spending the last few minutes talking outside before Thomas left. Jane and Gilde then went into the house. Jane was exceptionally giddy. She was making jokes and the sweet chime of her laughter was contagious. They shared the camaraderie of best friends who were akin to sisters. Gilde knew how fortunate she was to have Jane as a friend. After all when Gilde first arrived it was Jane who pulled Gilde out of her depression and helped her to make friends in her new home. Because of Gilde's constant social interactions with Jane and her friends, she was quickly learning English. And again, because of her friendship with Jane she spoke English with her accent, the boys called it cute instead of being critical of her. If it had not been for Jane, Gilde would surely have been ostracized for her German background. But, Jane made it clear to everyone that Gilde was no friend to Hitler. Some of the other children in school made Anti-Semitic remarks to Gilde, and when they did, Jane was the first to defend her friend. And so, as time ticked by, Gilde began to feel at home in her new country.

Many nights the two girls stayed up late talking in bed even though they had to be up early for school. They whispered so as not to wake the family. Gilde talked about her parents and her sister. But Jane couldn't think of anything except Thomas. She talked about him incessantly and told Gilde how he had kissed her once. It was the quick peck of an inexperienced boy, but to Jane it was reassurance that she and Thomas were destined to be together forever.

A few days later when the girls got home from school and before dinner, the girls went into the room they shared and laid their books down on the desk. Then they both changed from their school uniforms into more relaxed clothing.

"I think he's going to ask me to the winter wonderland dance." Jane giggled. The entire school was buzzing with excitement about the upcoming event. Jane already had several invitations. She was popular, because she had all the qualities that the girls admired. She was pretty, perky, friendly, and smart. It seemed to Gilde that everyone liked Jane. But, Jane would smile sweetly as she refused the invitations from the other boys because she was waiting for Thomas. And although Gilde was two years younger, the older boys were just as interested in her as they were in Jane, but in a different way. Where Jane was the sweet innocent girl next door, Gilde was foreign exciting and exotic. The boys were intrigued, but they weren't sure she would make good wife material. Their mothers wouldn't be so eager for them to marry a Jewish girl from of all places, Germany. Something about Gilde was blatantly sexy. Her long golden hair and curvy body put thoughts into their heads that kept them up at night acting in ways that they were ashamed of in the morning. However, for Gilde, Britain was becoming a lovely place to live. It was not that she didn't miss her family, she did, but she was still young and because of Jane she was adapting. Gilde was quickly becoming a part of a group of friends that made her life fun and exciting.

Standing together Jane and Gilde were physical polar opposites. One dark, one light, one tall, one short, but anyone could see they were the best of friends.

The lunch table where Gilde and Jane gathered every day with their friends was starting to clear out. The bell had rung and everyone had five minutes to get to class. Gilde gathered her books and began to clean up the small area where she'd sat.

"Wait, I need to talk to you," Jane told Gilde.

"I don't want to be late," Gilde said.

"It's important. Please?"

"All right." Gilde put her books back on the table and sat down. She was never late, so if Jane needed her, she would stay and if it meant that the teacher would yell at her and embarrass her in front of the class for being late, then so be it.

"Thomas asked me…" Jane was shaking. Gilde could see that she was excited but nervous too.

"To the dance?"

"Yes!"

"When did he ask?"

"I was sitting here at the lunch table. You know I always get out of science class early. No one was here in the lunchroom yet. Thomas must have known that I get here early every day, because he came walking into the cafeteria and didn't seem at all surprised to see me. Then he just walked over as casual as anything and asked me."

"And you waited all through lunch to tell me? You must have been going crazy keeping quiet?" Gilde asked. She was smiling broadly. She knew how much this invitation meant to Jane.

"I had to. There were too many people around to talk about it during lunch." Jane giggled. "I am so excited."

"You really like him."

"You know I do."

Gilde smiled. "Yes, I do know and I'm so happy for you." She was glad to see Jane so happy. It would be nice to feel that way about someone.

"Who are you going to go with?" Jane asked

"I don't know. There is no one I am especially interested in." Gilde shrugged her shoulders.

"You look sad, what's wrong?" Jane looked at Gilde concerned. "I know a few of the fellows asked you to the dance."

"Yes, they did, but I don't really like any of them."

"So what is it?"

"I don't know."

"Yes, you do ... come on … let's have it." Jane looked into Gilde's eyes with concern.

" Even if I did have someone to go with, I don't have a dress that is fancy enough for a dance."

"You silly goose. Did you think I wasn't going to let you wear one of my dresses? Of course. I planned on it. Listen, how about this … you get first pick from all of my dresses. Even before I choose."

"I couldn't do that. You pick first, then, if you're sure it's okay, I'll choose from what's left."

"Yes, it's okay. I want you to go to the dance. And I want you to look beautiful, so after school we'll raid the closet and find the perfect dress for you."
"Oh, Jane, you are so good to me. You are such a good friend." Gilde smiled. Jane rubbed Gilde's shoulder and got up. But for now we'd better hurry up. The second bell already rang, and we are both really late." Jane got up. Gilde followed her. Then they began to walk down the hall together towards their classes.

"If you're sure you don't have anyone special you want to go with, do you want me to see if Thomas has a friend? Then we could go double date."

"Sure. That would be fun."

"It would, wouldn't it?" Jane said smiling. Then she turned the corner to her class and Gilde kept going straight ahead to hers.

Chapter 8

The Dance

Thomas did have a friend Brian Kent. But unlike Thomas who was popular and athletic, he was a quiet studious boy with thick glasses. The two boys arrived at Jane's house each of them carrying a corsage with a single white carnation for their dates. Gilde was surprised that Thomas had chosen Brian as her date. He had so many other friends and Brian seemed so dull.

Both girls had spent hours getting ready. They had set their hair on pin curls the night before, then took them out and carefully styled their hair in waves. Now that they were dressed in their party attire they were excited. The two couples walked towards the school. Jane, usually so vivacious was quiet. Her infatuation with Thomas made her self-conscious and shy. Since Gilde was not invested emotionally in either boy, she felt free to be herself and so she did most of the talking. She had a wonderful gift of making people laugh by finding the smallest idiosyncrasies in her teachers and friends and then mimicking their voices. However, her jokes were all in good fun and never malicious. She was even able to imitate Thomas so well that when she did he roared with laughter.

They arrived at the school. The gymnasium was decorated for the dance.

"Would you girls like us to go and get you some punch?" Thomas asked.

"Yes, thank you," Jane answered

"Gilde? Would you like some punch?" Thomas cleared his throat and looked over at Brian

"Yes, Gilde. Would you like some punch?" Brian asked

Gilde laughed. "Sure, two glasses are better than one."

"NO, I meant can I…?" Brian stammered.

"I was only joking. Of course, Brian, I would love a glass of punch." Gilde said and she noticed Thomas smiling.

Thomas asked Jane to dance. As Thomas took Jane's hand and led her to the dance floor, Gilde looked at Brian.

"I'm not much of a dancer, I'm afraid." He said. So, Gilde and Brian sat on the chairs that had been set up in a row around the circumference of the dance floor. There was very little to talk about. Brian stared at his shoes and Gilde hummed along with the music. Jane and Thomas danced two dances then headed back over to Gilde and Brian.

"I'm going to ask Gilde to dance, it it's all right with you," Thomas said to Jane "It's not fair to her that Brian doesn't dance."

"No, it's fine. I quite agree. In fact it's very kind of you." Jane looked up into Thomas's crystal blue eyes and smiled. *It's no wonder all the girls want to go out with him, he is handsome and such a gentleman. I can't believe I am so lucky to be his date tonight*, she thought.

Thomas led Gilde to the dance floor. He put his arm about her waist and they began whirl around the room. "You look quite lovely tonight," he said.

Gilde giggled. "Thanks," she said.

"The gold in that gown accents your topaz eyes. You know you're eyes are the same color as a topaz stone, but they have tiny bits of glittering gold."

"Oh…" Gilde was embarrassed and at a loss for words.

"It's true."

She looked down. He put his hand under her chin and raised her face so that their eyes met "It is true…"

"Jane picked it out. It's her dress." Gilde said. Gilde had never thought of herself as pretty. She always thought of herself as funny, but never as a beauty.

"Well, Jane is a sweetheart isn't she?"

"Yes, she is, She is my best friend. When I arrived here in England I had no one. Her family took me in and they treat me like one of their own children. And well, Jane, she has been like a sister…and like an angel."

"But … she is not nearly as beautiful as you. You know, I asked Jane to the dance because I was sure that she would find a way to bring you with her. I didn't know if you would have a date or not, but I knew that if I was with Jane, I would see you. And then when Jane asked me to bring another fellow. Well, I thought ... that's perfect. I'll bring the least attractive fellow I know and then Gilde will have to notice me."

Gilde wanted to run away, her head was spinning with so many conflicting emotions. While she was surprised and flattered and his words made her heart beat quicken, Gilde adored Jane and Jane loved Thomas. She had made her feeling clear to Gilde so even the slightest attraction to Thomas on Gilde's part was a betrayal. Her body was responding to his handsome smile and tender words, but even though she was young, her brain told her to resist. And because of this Gilde didn't want to hear anything else he had to say.

"I think I'd like to go back to my seat now." She said tossing her head back and walking quickly.

"You're not angry, I hope?" he said a little too loudly. But she didn't answer, she had already begun to walk away.

Chapter 9

Thomas

After the night at the dance, Thomas began coming to see Jane at least two evenings a week. Jane was always giddy, ecstatic. She hummed or whistled as she made the bed in the morning. She giggled at the slightest thing. But most of all she talked about Thomas insistently. Gilde listened biting her lower lip, wanting to be a good friend, but in fact. She was worried about Jane. Gilde didn't have the heart to tell Jane what Thomas had said at the dance. More than anything, Gilde wanted Jane to be happy. And because she knew the truth she knew it was only a matter of time before he broke Jane's heart. All day while she was in class, Gilde would try to decide what to do. Would it be her fault if Jane got hurt for not telling Jane the truth? But how could she tell her? What could she say? Anything she said would hurt Jane.

One night as the girls were getting ready for bed, Jane sat down and took Gilde's hands "I've made a decision, Gilde."

Gilde sat on the bed beside her "About what?"

"I want to marry Thomas, Gilde. He's the one for me. I am sure of it." Jane said

Gilde didn't answer. Outside the sky opened up and a flood of rain fell upon the roof. The pounding of the rain overhead was in sync with the pounding of Gilde's heart. A loud crash of thunder followed by lightening unnerved Gilde. She felt like God was telling her that lying to Jane was a sin.

"I think he feels the same way about me, don't you think so?"

"I don't know. I hope so." Gilde lied. She knew how he felt, but she couldn't get the words out.

Gilde was distraught. But Thomas was not giving up and every time Thomas came around, he made Gilde even more uncomfortable. He stole glances at Gilde when Jane turned her back. Smiled at Gilde and whispered "You're so pretty." When Jane left the room. Thomas was hard to resist. And all this attention towards Gilde from the most attractive and desirable boy in school was wearing down her resistance. The only thing she could do was try to stay away from him. But when she left the room, he would find a way to include her in whatever he and Jane were doing. If they were playing cards, he'd insist that Jane invite Gilde. When they went out for a soda, he'd tell Jane to insist that Gilde join them.

"You don't want to leave her at home. It's rather rude, don't you think?" He'd say, and Jane would nod and then she'd plead with Gilde to join them.

Jane awoke early one morning sneezing and very congested.

"I'm going to stay in bed today, Gilde." Jane said "I feel terrible."

"Let me make you some tea before I leave for school."

"Would you mind?"

"Not at all"

When school was out, Gilde tried going an alternate route to avoid Thomas, but he found her. Just as she was going up the walkway to the house Thomas came up the street and rushed up to walk beside her.

"Want some company?"

"I don't think it's a good idea," Gilde said. "Besides, I am home already. So, I'm going to go inside. Jane isn't feeling well. I want to see how she's doing."

"Gilde, what can I do to make you see that I really like you?"

"Nothing … nothing at all. There is nothing you can do so stop, please stop."

"Why don't you like me?"

"Because Jane likes you and I love Jane."

"Jane and I are just friends."

"Is that what you really believe?" Gilde stopped dead in her tracks and turned around to look right in his eyes "Don't you see how she looks at you?"

"I've never given her any reason to believe that I feel any differently."

"You've kissed her."

"Just a quick peck goodnight," he said and his voice became hoarse. "Not the way I want to kiss you…"

"Don't…" Gilde said. But Thomas didn't listen. He took her into his arms and pulled her close to him. Trembling she dropped her books. Then he kissed her with such passion that she felt her knees buckle. Her heart was racing. Thomas smelled like good cologne. She wondered if the fragrance had rubbed off on her coat. Would Jane smell it?

"I have to go," Gilde said, but her hands were trembling so badly that she could not pick up her books. She tried to put them together but dropped them again. Gilde was almost in tears.

"Here, let me help you." Thomas bent down and began to

gather her books. The papers in her notebook had scattered on the ground and the wind was carrying them away.

"I need those papers." Gilde said weakly, unable to chase them. She felt as if she was frozen to the spot where she stood. Gilde wanted to run away. Instead she watched as Thomas collected her notes and brought them back in a pile. He handed them to her.

"Thank you. I have to go," she said.

"Gilde, I felt something when I kissed you. Something special, magical, one of those once in a lifetime things. I know you felt it too."

She whirled around at him holding her school work and books in trembling hands "It doesn't matter what you feel or what you think I feel. Nothing will ever happen between us, Thomas. I told you that and I meant it."

"Gilde? Let's talk to Jane. Let's tell her how we feel."

"I feel nothing for you. And don't ever try to kiss me again." She ran up to the door of the house and fumbled with the key. Then she closed the door behind her. It was hard to catch her breath. But at least she'd gotten away, away from those all-encompassing feelings that Thomas brought on, that confused the hell out of her and, away from his melting blue eyes to the safety of her surrogate family and the love of her best friend.

Chapter 10

Damn him. Gilde thought about Thomas. He had spoken words that planted a seed in her mind and that seed had begun to grow. She thought about him more often than she wanted to. In fact, the harder she tried to push thoughts of Thomas out of her mind, the more vivid the thoughts became.

Thomas began to come by the house even more often than he had before. When he looked at Gilde she saw the longing in his eyes and hoped that Jane would not see it. When Thomas spoke to Gilde she heard his voice grow softer, the change was subtle, but distinctive enough for her to hear it and for it stir something inside of her. These feelings she felt growing from a tiny reed into a massive oak tree for Thomas were emotions that must be squashed! He must never know that she thought about him at night, or that she felt warm all over when he said her name.

Chapter 11

1939

Shaul was having a terrible time adjusting to life in Britain. He wasn't in school, he worked with an old man and had no contact with anyone his own age. The red rash that he'd had the previous winter had returned. Still, even as miserable as he was he tried to continue working with the milkman. In the morning, Shaul drove the truck out to the farm and picked up the crates of bottles then he picked up his boss who did the driving and they began to make their deliveries. In February the milkman who Shaul worked for was given a new route in another part of town.. Here the homes were larger with more lawn space. It was by far a more affluent neighborhood than the inner city where they had been working, but because the homes were further apart the delivery work was more difficult. Since his boss was only the driver, Shaul had to go to the door, take the order, return to the truck, fill the order, and then return to the house with the delivery. The walkways from the house to the street were longer and because of this servicing the same amount of customers took more hours than it had in the past.

A light snow was falling and dusting the street like a sprinkling of powder one afternoon as Shaul and his boss were completing their daily rounds. They had just finished loading several crates of empty bottles when Shaul looked up and saw a girl walking with a bunch of other girls. She had long dark hair that hung down her back in a single braid. The girls wore plaid skirts, thick dark tights and heavy jackets. Shaul gazed at the brunette and thought she was the prettiest girl he'd ever seen. Then as he stood in the shadows still watching he recognized a familiar face amongst the group. It was Gilde. She was a year older, her clothing was different, but he was positive that it was Gilde. He'd missed her, he'd missed Elias too. But Shaul felt too clumsy and awkward to go over and say hello while Gilde was with her friends, especially while she was with the brunette who he thought was so striking. So, he waited and watched to see where the girls went. From behind the milk truck he saw Gilde and the beautiful girl with dark braid wave goodbye to the rest and head up the walkway to the door of a two story house.

Shaul didn't want the girls to see him. If Gilde had been alone he would have gone up and said hello. But as it was, she was with the girl who looked like a Goddess and Shaul was far too intimidated.

Then from across the street, Shaul heard a male voice. "Gilde, Jane, wait up…"

Jane…Shaul heard her name. Now he knew that her name was Jane.

"Thomas." The girl called Jane said.

A handsome dark haired boy ran across the street. Shaul could not hear what they were saying, but he could see both girls smiling at the boy they called Thomas. He wondered what it would feel like to be that handsome boy. What would it be like to have two pretty girls giving him all of their attention? It was cold outside, but none of them seemed to notice. They were giggling and Shaul suddenly wished he had friends his own age. It had been a long time since he'd seen Elias or Gilde and he missed being a part of a group of friends. Well, at least now he knew where Gilde lived. When she was alone without Jane, Shaul would talk to her. He wondered if she had been in contact with Elias. Was it possible to miss life in an orphanage? It was just that when he'd lived in the orphanage, he'd had friends, people who accepted him as he was, regardless of his clumsy body and awkward social skills.

He kept watching Gilde with her friends. She was smiling, and she was even prettier than he remembered. Somehow she'd adjusted. He had not. In fact, he'd decided that he hated everything about England until his eyes lit upon the girl called Jane with the long dark braid.

Chapter 12

Shaul Spring of 1939 London

Winter which was always difficult for Shaul, had finally passed. And although spring brought with her a great deal of rain, for Shaul it was more tolerable. The angry red rash called chilblains had begun to disappear, and he finally had some relief from the terrible itching.

Thoughts of Gilde's friend, the girl called Jane, kept Shaul from sheer madness. It was his guilty pleasure to create a fantasy world in his mind a world in which he was a part of the group of young people who he had seen with Gilde. He was Jane's boyfriend, and he was handsome.

Every day when he was on his route delivering milk in the area where he saw Gilde and Jane he would search for them. Sometimes he saw them together, but he never went up to speak to Gilde. He kept promising himself that the next time he saw them he would approach, but he never did. He just couldn't bring himself to talk to Jane, so he kept hoping to find Gilde alone. Shaul knew Gilde well enough to speak to her, but so far every time he'd seen her she was with the girl of his dreams.

In his mind, Shaul began to expand on his fantasy life. It was a complete story that began with his first meeting with Jane. He daydreamed that she was taken with him, that she found him irresistible. In fact, in his vision, she pursued him.

She asked him to her house for dinner and introduced him to her family as her boyfriend. They took long walks and talked about everything. He imagined the two of them taking a train out to Brighton to spend a day on the beach. Instead of the flabby, pale boy that he was, in his fantasy, Shaul was more like Elias. He smiled as in his minds eye he saw his complexion cleared of rashes and breakouts, tan from the sun, his body lean and muscular. He lay on a towel on the sand beside Jane the goddess of his heart. This life inside of Shaul's head was not reserved for any special time. He began to imagine Jane's presence with him all day as he made his deliveries. At night after he made sure that the old woman had eaten something and was safe in her bed, Shaul would go off to his own small area in the house to dream of Jane. No woman had ever touched him intimately nor had he ever touched a woman. However, his imagination was powerful, creating love making so real that he became immersed in it. When he passed Jane's house on his route, he watched for her. If he she happened to be outside, his heart raced wildly. But, he still could not find the courage to speak to her.

Chapter 13

Gilde Fall of 1939 London

Each night the women in the Kendall family including Gilde prepared the evening meal together. Mrs. Kendall insisted that dinner be a special family time. Once the food was prepared, they each carried serving plates to the table.

George took his place at the head of the table and then he reached over to the stand behind him and turned on the radio to the BBC.

"George, not at dinner, please," Mrs. Kendell complained

"Just for a few moments," George Kendell said. "I heard something today and I want to see if it's true."

"George." Rosemary shook her head. "All right, but only until all of the food is out and we all sit down, then I want you to say grace and we will dine like a proper family."

"Very well." George nodded. He knew that his wife felt that mealtime should be a period of pleasant conversation of each member sharing their daily activities. Most days he complied, but not tonight. Tonight was different. George was concerned about the state of the world. There had been suspicion that Hitler was going to invade Poland. That day while he was at work George had heard rumors that the Nazi invasion of Poland had begun and he had to know if the gossip was true. Although his wife was oblivious to the threat to Britain, George was not. He paid attention to the news and world affairs and he could see how ruthless Hitler was and he felt it was only a matter of time before his beloved country was in danger. Rosemary had always been sheltered, that, George decided, was his own fault. He had always made light of things so that she wouldn't worry. And even when they'd adopted Gilde and Rosemary was so horrified by the things that were happening in Germany, George had assured his wife that her home in Britain was perfectly safe. Rosemary had accepted George's comforting words without question. But, although he reassured his wife, George was not so sure that Britain was safe at all. Hitler, the lunatic in Germany was on a quest to conquer the world and he was quite positive that it was only a matter of time before Britain was part of that sinister plan.

George and Gilde were in the dining room when the announcer on the radio said that Germany was bombing Poland.

They looked at each other, eyes wide, both of them silent.

It was true then. George needn't listen anymore. He'd heard the news.

Jane and her mother were busy talking in the kitchen. Gilde knew she should go back in and help them bring out the rest of the plates, but she felt a shiver go up the back of her neck. When she'd first left Germany, Gilde had been convinced that the Nazi problem would be over quickly and she would be free to go home within a few months. But of course, when she'd left Germany, she was just a child and she'd been easily convinced. Now even though she was still just a child she could see things more clearly. It had been a year since she'd been in Britain and things looked bleaker than they did before she left. Instead of being forced out of power by some miracle, Hitler was growing stronger. The mail between Germany and Britain was slow, and it had been several weeks since she'd heard anything from Alina. The last letter she'd received said that Alina had not heard from their parents. It also said that Alina was planning to move, but it did not say where, just that she was leaving Berlin. The letter also told Gilde, that Lotti and Lev were alright. But arrests of Jews without reason continued and were growing in number. Then Alina said that she might not be able to send any more letters for a while. She gave no explanation. Gilde read that part over twice to be sure she'd read it correctly. The very idea of not hearing from her sister sent shock waves through Gilde. She longed to talk to anyone from her family, even Lev or Lotti, but this silence was maddening. She'd sent a letter to Lotti but had received no answer. Now, she wondered if the letter had ever found its way into Lotti's hands. It seemed as if the world had turned upside down and fell into a whirlpool of chaos. And now with Germany invading Poland, Gilde was even more distressed. Did this have something to do with why Alina would not be writing anymore? Was Alina in danger? Gilde was pretty sure she remembered hearing Lev and Lotti talking when she was still at home. They'd said that Hitler had promised never to invade Poland. Was her memory correct? Did it matter? Hitler was a madman, no one could know what he might do next. Intellectually Gilde knew that she should be glad to be out of Germany. After all she was safe, one of the lucky ones. She was living in a lovely home with a wonderful family, and she was grateful for all the Kendalls did for her every day, but her heart still missed her parents, her sister, and her friends. Gilde missed her life, the life she'd known before Adolf Hitler came into power and shattered everything. It was true, Jane had become her best friend and she loved Jane. With Jane's help she'd adjusted and made so many friends, but sometimes she still felt so alone and lost. She felt like a derailed train car going off a cliff. If only she had some way of finding out happened to her loved ones, if only she could be sure they were safe. Then maybe she could find some inner peace.

Jane and her mother were still in the kitchen. Gilde heard water running. Then a spoon clanging against a pan. The house smelled of baking. It was a delicious smell of safety and home and usually it soothed Gilde. Not tonight. The terrible news she'd just heard was ringing in her head. . But neither Jane nor her Mother had heard the news on the BBC. They were too busy in the kitchen to pay attention. As Jane and her mother carried the sparkling glasses and pitcher of water to the table, George Kendall, trying to act as if everything was quite normal, reached back and quietly turned off the radio. A look of knowing passed between him and Glide. Then everyone took their places at the dinner table. Rosemary smiled at her husband, he returned the smile and patted her hand. She was such a good wife, a kind and generous woman and he was glad she was ignorant of what he'd just heard. At least for now she would be spared the anxiety he felt.

"Shall we begin, George?" Rosemary asked.

"George nodded "Yes, dear. Dinner looks scrumptious." he said and then reached out to join hands with the family. They all joined hands around the table and George began to say grace. When he finished the family ate. Usually George enjoyed hefty portions, but tonight he could hardly eat.

"Are you feeling alright, George?" Rosemary asked

"Yes, I had a big lunch at work today."

Gilde didn't mention what she'd heard on the radio and Mr. Kendell didn't say a word about it either. They both seemed to know that it was best that Jane and her mother be kept in the dark about this new development in the trail of Nazi devastation. Jane was too busy getting ready for the school year to begin to pay any attention to the news. She was trying on clothes to see what still fit and what didn't. Rosemary was helping Jane and Gilde sort through their things, so she too did not leave the house or see the news. There were clothes to be taken in, and hems to be let down.

So much to do. And that was why the news came as quite a shock to Rosemary and Jane when George turned on the radio two days later to learn that France and Britain had declared war on Germany. Although George loved to shelter the women in his life, to protect them from the harsh realities outside their home, this was one terrible truth that he could not keep from them. The world as they knew it was in flames exploding around them. Britain was at war.

Chapter 14

Thomas came to the house to see the girls the same night that war was declared. They sat outside on lawn chairs in the Kendalls' well-manicured yard. It was September and the weeping willow tree had begun to shed her leaves. The faint sound of a child's laughter came from one of the other yards on the block. And the smell of something savory cooking wafted through the air. Thomas's face was flushed. It was easy to see that he was excited by the prospect of war and heroism. Gilde was angry with herself because although she fought the attraction, his passion made him even more appealing to her.

"I am going to enlist. I am going to defend my country against the Nazis."

"Fool," Gilde said crossing her arms around her chest. She wanted to sound curt, but in fact, she was terrified for him. His fervor made him look brave and exciting, but war was not a game. Although she'd never experienced it, Gilde knew this instinctively. She'd seen the Nazis in action when they'd attacked her small neighborhood. What would they do to the British in an all-out war? What would they do to Thomas?

"I'd be a coward to sit back and let the country fight without me." He said

Jane gasped. All the color left her face.

"Don't worry about me. I can take care of myself" Thomas said, sitting up proudly.

"You're too young. You're only sixteen. They won't take you." Gilde said turning on him with a glare of distain for upsetting Jane.

"I'll lie. I'll tell them I'm eighteen. They need volunteers. They'll take me."

"Don't go…" Jane said. "Please, Thomas." She grabbed the sleeve of his shirt. And it broke Gilde's heart to see how much Jane cared for Thomas.

"I have to Jane."

"I know your parents must have talked about the Great War. Mine did. Oh God, Thomas. You could be killed, easily." Jane said there were tears in her eyes. Gilde took Jane's hand in both of hers. She'd been young when she left Germany but even she could remember Taavi and Michal talking about the horrors of the Great War and she dreaded what the future might hold for all of them. Gilde was not only worried about her new family, about Jane and Thomas, but although she didn't speak of it, her nerves were on fire when she thought about her parents and Alina. Lotti and Lev as well.

Jane took her hand from Gilde's and began to rub Thomas' shoulder. "I couldn't stand it if something happened to you, Tom." She said

Gilde tried to sit still, but her body was trembling, and although it was cool with a light breeze, but not cold outside, she was freezing. It all seemed more than she could bear. She'd been ripped from her home and her loved ones only to be thrust into a war that was sure to bring even more tragedy.

Then Thomas turned to Gilde. "You're shaking."

"I'm all right," she said clearing her throat.

"Are you sure, Gilde?" Jane asked.

"Yes, yes, I'm fine…" she lied.

Then Thomas took Gilde's hand and ignored the fact that Jane was sitting right beside them. "Marry me, Gilde. Marry me before I leave," Thomas said.

Jane looked from Gilde to Thomas and then back to Gilde again. The shock on her face was alarming to Gilde.

"What? Thomas, are you out of your mind?" Gilde glared at him and pulled her hand away. "First of all, I have no romantic interest in you and you have a lot of nerve even asking me something so outlandish."

"It's not outlandish, Gilde. You know how I feel."

Gilde felt like she might puke "This is all too much for me. Please don't do this, Thomas." She stood up and walked away from Thomas. She wanted to put physical distance between them. Chronologically Gilde was a child, but she had the face of an angel with long golden hair and the curvaceous body of a woman.

"You know I am in love with you. And I see the way that you look at me. I am not blind. I know what you're feeling. I can see it in your eyes." Thomas got up and walked over to Gilde. Then he put his hand on Gilde's arm and tried to pull her towards him.

"You're insane," Gilde said shaking his hand off.

"Have the two of you been seeing each other…behind my back?" Jane stammered cocking her head to one side as if suddenly realizing she'd missed something that was going on right under her nose. "Behind my back?" she repeated, her voice told Gilde she felt betrayed.

"No, we have not," Gilde said with strong conviction

"But, I have told you how I feel," Thomas said "And although you won't admit it, I know you feel the same way about me, Gilde."

"You are wrong, Thomas. I told you I have no interest in

you and I mean it. How dare you do this to me and Jane? How dare you!" Gilde said she was almost crying when she turned to look at Jane whose face was drained of blood and had turned a pale gray. "Jane, please you must believe me, I have no feelings for him, none at all. And... Nothing has ever happened between us." Gilde said. Where she had been cold before, now she was sweating. Her face was red with anger.

"You say you have no feelings for me. But I don't believe you. The only reason you deny you care for me is because you love Jane and you know how she feels about me. War is upon us, Gilde. Who knows if any of us will survive? Think about it, Gilde. Don't' give up this chance to be with someone you love. I know you love me. I can see it in your eyes, even now."

"You are one arrogant bastard," Gilde said.

"Gilde, tell me the truth. How do you feel about Thomas?" Jane said. "Because if you care for him and him for you then I want the two of you to be together."

"I don't care for him. Not at all," Gilde lied, she did care for him, but she cared for Jane much more.

"I don't believe you," Thomas said.

"Well, it's true, In fact if I have any feelings for you at all right now, I would have to say that I hate you. I hate you for doing this to me and Jane." Gilde said then she fixed her eyes fiercely on him. She was shaking and her hands were clenched in fists. There was nothing more to say, Gilde turned and walked back into the house leaving Thomas and Jane outside to talk alone.

Later that night when Jane entered the bedroom she shared with Gilde the light was off, but Gilde was still awake. Jane quietly undressed then got into bed. For a long time they were both silent. Then Jane whispered "Is it true, Gilde? Do you love him?"

"It's not true."

"I want you to know that if you do, I understand. I know you would never want to hurt me. I know you would lie and give up your own happiness in exchange for mine."

"I don't care about him at all. He can go straight to Hell for all I care."

"He told me that he had feelings for you for a long time. He told me he told you. Why didn't you tell me?"

"Because I couldn't. I didn't know what to do, I didn't want to hurt you. I don't want this to come between us, Jane. You are my best friend."

"But if it is you he wants not me. And if you feel the same way about him then who am I to stand in your way…"

"I said I am not interested in him."

"Gilde, I know you well enough to know when you're lying," Jane said.

"Why do you want me to tell you that I am attracted to Thomas? Why, Jane? Why do you want me to say that? Of course I am attracted to him. So is every girl in school. But, that doesn't mean that I would ever act upon it. I find him handsome, but I love you. You are like my sister. And you have loved him and from the day I met him I knew that. So, I would never let my own feelings towards Thomas go beyond friendship. And I swear I never will."

Jane was silent.

"Janey?"

"It's alright, Gilde…."

"No, it's not. How can I make it right?"

"You can't. It's not your fault. The facts are the facts. Thomas is leaving to go to war. He may or may not return.

God help us. But regardless of anything, he doesn't care for me the way I care for him. So, there is nothing more to say," Jane said.

"Jane…"

"Go to sleep, Gilde…" Jane said turning over. Tears ran down her cheeks and wet her pillow.

Chapter 15

After Thomas left, something crucial had changed between Gilde and Jane. On the surface things were the same, but Gilde could feel that Jane had pulled away. The easy laughter between them became more stilted. Before the girls had giggled well into the night sharing secrets, but now Gilde could feel that Jane was guarded around her. She couldn't tell if it was because she hadn't told Jane about Thomas' feelings or if it was because Jane knew that she had been attracted to Thomas all along. And the worst part was that the invisible wall Jane had built between them kept Gilde from asking. Still all of their outside activities remained unchanged. Every Sunday after church, Gilde and Jane met with their friends. But, now most of the boys had gone off to war and the group was almost all girls. And, although no one dared speak the words aloud, each of the girls feared it was only a matter of time before the death notices would begin to arrive.

Chapter 16

Gilde 1940

Food was needed for the troops and therefore food rationing began. The Kendall's were given a ration book for Gilde as well as for their own family, but the rations were low and everyone had to make to do with much less.

Things were moving quickly in the world.

In May of that same year, Winston Churchill became Prime Minister.

Hitler's lust for power was insatiable and on May 10th he invaded France, Holland and Belgium.

By late May the German's had reached the British Chanel.

Then on June 22, 1940 in a railroad car in the Compiegne Forest, France surrendered. But Churchill makes it clear to the world that Britain would never surrender. Even if it turned out that Britain must fight the Hitler alone.

Less than a week later Norway dropped into the hands of the Nazi's.

Although it had been a year since Thomas left, things were never the same. Thomas's interest in Gilde had put a rift between Gilde and Jane, where they were once best friends they were now more like polite roommates. Gilde assumed by the hours that Jane was keeping and the way that she was primping, that she was seeing someone. But, Gilde couldn't be sure because Jane never introduced her boyfriend to Gilde. Instead she drifted farther away with each passing day. Most nights Jane did not come home for dinner. She got home late and went straight to bed. The late night sharing of their deepest secrets and giggling until the sun began to peek through the darkness no longer happened. Jane had become secretive and distant. And Gilde was saddened by the loss of her dearest friend. Many times Gilde tried to re-establish the old deep friendship, but something was lost and could never be regained.

Thomas had made this mess of her life, and Gilde couldn't forgive him even though she knew he didn't realize how important her relationship with Jane was to her. How could he? Thomas had never been separated from his family and friends the way she had. Jane had been her lifeline in Britain and now without her, Gilde was lost.

The nights Jane joined the family for dinner had become few and far between. But one night Jane stayed home because she said she had an announcement to make to the family. After they'd finished eating the small meal that the rations allowed, Jane told her parents that she was planning to begin nurses training in order to go to the front and help the wounded soldiers. Gilde was not surprised that Jane hadn't told her. In the past, before Thomas, Jane would have discussed this with Gilde long before she'd brought it to her parents' attention. But, the Jane who was once her best friend, was gone and in her place was a quiet somber girl who kept secrets from Gilde The Kendall's tried to discourage their daughter. They were frightened for her. However, Jane was determined. She told them that she planned to go to the battlefront where she could be of use and care for the wounded soldiers. Gilde, too, tried to talk to Jane. She was worried. "Jane, you're putting herself in real danger, you could easily be killed," Gilde said, but Jane just smiled a sad distant smile. The next day she signed up for training.

Because she no longer had Jane's friendship to depend upon, Gilde joined a local drama group. She'd always wanted to be an actress. If she didn't have her German accent, there was no doubt she would have been cast in a lead. Gilde could sing, dance, and act. Her beauty mesmerized the audience, but her German accent repelled the British. They were at war with Germany and even though Gilde was as much an enemy of the Nazis as the British, because she was born in Germany, they saw her as a German. So, she worked with the tech's to design costumes out of old fabric and build a set with almost no materials. Since the war began, and without Jane's friendship to buffer, the other girls in the crowd she and Jane had been a part of began to grow standoffish towards Gilde. Gilde was lonely and more homesick than she'd been in a very long time. She wasn't a practicing Jew, so she always attended the rehearsals at the drama club on Saturday afternoons. On such a day in early September, the rehearsal ran late into the afternoon. It had been a long tedious rehearsal and the director refused to dismiss the cast or crew until his was satisfied. It was getting dark and Gilde felt bad because she doubted she'd be home in time to help Mrs. Kendall prepare dinner. She began walking quickly towards the corner where she could catch a tram when she heard a loud blast. The ground moved beneath her. It was as if the world had exploded. The German's had bombed London before but this was more intense. People came dashing out of the shops and into the street, many of them screaming. Others just stood where they were paralyzed in shock. A small child was sitting on the pavement where she had fallen, her thumb in her mouth, weeping in fear. The sound of the bombs, the roar of the planes and the cries of the people combined to a deafening scream that pierced Gilde's soul. Although at least a hundred people had come out of their apartments and stores into the street to see what was happening and Gilde was in the middle of the crowd, she had never felt so alone. German planes hovered overhead surrounded by smoke that was billowing up from the blaze below. The sky had become a cloud in shades of gray. So thick was the smoke, that Gilde's eyes were tearing and she coughed unable to breath. Orange flames burst into the air like fireworks from nearby buildings. Gilde was unable to move. Her feet seemed to be glued to the ground. Her body was suddenly chilled and trembled in terror. The stack of school books she'd been carrying fell from her hands, but she did not bend down to pick them up. Instead, she watched the panic all around her frozen in the moment. An explosion erupted in front of her. Her eyes grew large as body parts flew through the air like broken tinker toys. She fell backwards into a pile of broken glass from a store window and hit her head on the pavement. Then she heard screaming and got up as quickly as she could. Her head ached, and she was dizzy. Everything around her seemed unreal and spinning. When a splash of blood slapped her in the face, it woke her and now she could move her feet. Her legs were unsteady, but she began to run. Then just to her left she heard another blast, and saw another burst of fire, so she turned right and began running again. Gilde had no idea where she was going, all she knew was that she had joined the herd of people who had become frightened animals. Running, just running without any idea of where to go. Blood dripped down her cheek and from her forearm, but she wasn't sure how badly she was hurt. She could feel no pain. So much glass and debris were flying through the air. Then a man came out of one of the stores and grabbed her arm. He pulled her into the shop, then through a hallway and down a flight of stairs to a dark cement basement. Her heart pounded. She didn't know this man, but she was too frightened to resist. The bombs continued falling outside and she felt as if this might be the end of the world.

Chapter 17

1940 London Shaul

It was late on a Saturday afternoon. Shaul had never been religious so he had never taken off work for the Sabbath. It was a long day and Shaul was exhausted. He had not seen Jane, the beautiful girl today. But, he'd created an entire scenario in his mind. It eased his loneliness to pretend that she was his girl and that they were engaged. The fantasy kept him from thoughts of suicide. Without his dreams, all he had to look forward to was his work with the milk man and the home life with the old woman. He saw Gilde two more times but that was many months ago before the war began, and would have approached her, but she was with Jane and he was so afraid that once he met Jane he would have to accept reality when she rejected him. So, he'd stopped looking for Gilde and Jane and decided that he would rather keep the dream alive than die in the reality. Shaul knew that so many of the men his age had enlisted and were on their way to fight Hitler, but he was a coward. He knew it and he hated himself for it. He'd always been clumsy and was afraid that he would not be able to stay alive in a battle. So far there was no draft and as a long as the enlistment remained voluntary, Shaul could make believe that he was staying behind because the old lady needed him. It was true, she did. He brought in money and milk every week, and he was glad to be able to help. But, deep in his heart Shaul was ashamed because he knew he was afraid to go to war and that was what kept him from enlisting.

It was late afternoon in early fall, the trees had begun to shed their leaves. It was the time of day when the sun was just at that point in the sky when she was about to surrender her reign to the moon goddess of the night. In the glow of the late afternoon sun the leaves were a blanket of vivid color. Fall was a beautiful time of year, but for Shaul it was also a reminder of what was to come. The miserable English winter. He had still not gotten used to the cold and the terrible rash that came with it. The hot water bottles in the bed did little to soothe him and he dreaded the months ahead.

Mr. Brighton, the milk man, and Shaul's boss, was rattling off orders but Shaul was hardly listening. "I'm tired, I haven't been feeling well lately. Clean the wagon. Bring the empty bottles in and wash them." Brighton said

Shaul nodded his head. The routine was the same every day. He didn't need the instructions, but Brighton seemed to feel that he had to repeat them every afternoon. Brighton went inside. Shaul was glad that his boss was gone. Now he could let his mind wander and think about the lovely Jane. He began to unload the empty bottles and to line them up.

In his mind he and Jane were dancing, a waltz. She was floating in his arms. He could smell her perfume and feel the warmth of the small of her back under his right hand. Shaul looked into her eyes. He wasn't sure of the color, he'd never been close enough to Jane to see the color of her eyes. So, he fantasized that her eyes were aqua blue. She smiled at him. He leaned down and felt her lips brush against his.

"I love you, Shaul" She said in his fantasy. He felt his body respond, as his penis grew hard.

He was suddenly ashamed. What if old man Brighton came outside? What would he think if he saw Shaul lining up the milk bottles with a bulge in his pants? Think of something else, Shaul said to himself as he tried to shake the feeling. It was difficult, he wanted this dream to be true so badly that he couldn't get the girl out of his mind. He filled the sink with just enough water to wash the glass bottles and began carefully loading them in.

A loud deafening boom broke into Shaul's dream life, then the ground beneath him began to rumble. Shaul was thrown back and fell upon the ground. In the distance he saw a fire spring up with angry red arms reaching to the sky. Black smoke began to emerge from the flames. Then there was another explosion louder and closer than the first. A roar came from above him, Shaul raised his head and through the openings in the wood panels of the barn he saw a formation of planes rumbling by all of them bearing the Swastika the Nazi insignia. He trembled laying on the ground unable to move. Get up, he thought, Get up and get into the truck and get out of here. This wasn't the first time London had been bombed, but this was the first time it had happened so close to Shaul. He forced himself to run towards the truck, but just as he was opening the door another bomb hit the ground and the truck rolled like a tinker toy on top of him. He felt the enormous weight crush his insides. As he took his final breath, Shaul realized that this was an all-out attack. London was under siege.

Chapter 18

1940 London Gilde

Gilde could feel the earth trembling even deep underground in the basement where the man had taken her. She looked around her and saw a family. A woman, possibly, the mother of the rest of the brood. She was heavyset with frizzy light brown hair in a single knot on top of her head. An attractive boy with honest eyes in his late teens and a sporty but attractive girl a few years older than Gilde. The man who'd rescued her looked older than the mother, like he might be in his mid to late fifties. Gilde assumed he was the father, or perhaps the father was at war and he was the grandfather. She couldn't be sure.

"Don't you recognize me, Gilde?" The young girl said. "I'm Sharon Lawrence. I was in Jane's history class. We've met before"

Gilde shook her head.

"I met you with Jane at the library once. It was a long time ago. But when the bombing started, my father pulled us all down here. But just as we were going into the shop to come downstairs I saw you outside and I recognized you. I told my father that I knew you and that he had to bring you down here with us so you would be safe. So he went back out and got you. These are my parents, that's my brother," the girl named Sharon said.

Gilde looked at the girl in disbelief. It was hard to understand why her father would take such a risk. "Thank you," Gilde stammered.

Sharon's father smiled. "I'm glad I could help." He said

"Don't be afraid," the mother said to Gilde "You're safe here with us. It looks to me like you've been hurt pretty badly. Let me get you a towel. Your head is bleeding, your arms and knees too. Let's clean you up so we can see how deep those cuts are. My son William has medical training, so if you need stitches, he can probably help."

Sharon's mother pulled up a chair and got a towel from a shelf. While she was cleaning the back of Gilde's head, Gilde noticed that the men both wore Yarmulke's. This family were Jews. When the father had pulled her in to the shop she had been too stunned by everything happening around her to notice what kind of business it was that they were in. The store was upstairs. Most of the shops on this street were two story buildings with basements. The shop owners and their families lived upstairs.

"My name is Gilde Margolis." Gilde said to the rest of the family "Thank you, Sharon, for remembering me and asking your father to help me, and it's nice to meet all of you."

Sharon smiled.

Mrs. Lawrence blotted the blood from Gilde's head, her arm and her face. The hair on the back of Gilde's head was crusted with dried blood. Gently the older woman parted Gilde's golden locks. "Well, you were lucky. None of these wounds are very deep."

William walked over. "Let me have a quick look, Mother." First he looked at the back of Gilde's head "I'm sure it hurts like the devil but it doesn't need stitches." He said. Then he took her arm in his and looked for glass inside the cuts. "It's dark in here, but I don't think that you have any glass in these."

Next William knelt and they were eye to eye. He smiled at her. Tenderly he touched the cut on her cheek. Gilde winced "I'm sorry. I know it hurts."

"Will I have a scar on my face?" She asked

"No, I don't think so .You can rest assured that your pretty face will be just as lovely as always in a couple of days when that heals."

"I really can't thank you enough for helping me." Gilde said. Her head hurt.

"You have an accent. Where are you from?" The mother's eyes turned to slits as she looked at Gilde skeptically. "It sounds like a German accent? Are you a German?"

"I'm from Germany, but I am not a German. I mean I was born in Germany. But Hitler has decided that because I'm a Jew I am not a German."

"Judaism is a religion not a nationality," Sharon said "If you're from Germany, you're a German. I hope you aren't a spy, are you?"

"A spy? No. I am certainly not a spy. I am lucky to have escaped from Germany with my life. Judaism is not just a religion it's also a nationality, at least it is in Germany since Hitler took over. In Germany, if you are Jewish you have no rights as a German citizen. You are a Jew not a German. You have no country. My parents were arrested one night when all of the Jewish businesses were vandalized by the Nazis for no reason at all. First, my father was arrested for trying to defend my sister's fiancé who was murdered on the street. Then my mother went to the police station to try and help my father and she never came back. Being a Jew is a crime under Hitler," Gilde said.

"How is that possible?" Sharon's father asked. "I mean don't get me wrong, they don't like Jews much here either.

But it's not as bad as that."

"I don't know, how it is possible that they are arresting innocent people, but it's very bad for Jews in Germany, very bad," Gilde said.

"We have plenty of anti-Semitism, Sam," the mother said to the father. "Don't be such an idealist. We're Jews. You know that no matter where we live because of our religion we are never really safe."

"I know I am young and have not seen a lot of the world. But from what my parents told me, there has always been anti-Semitism. But I am telling you, what is going on in Germany is beyond anything I could ever have imagined. Even now as I am sitting here in Britain, I don't know if my parents are alive or dead. The last letter I received from my sister said that the mail was being censored. She said she wasn't going to be able to write to me anymore. Still I tried to stay in contact. I wrote to her again, but she never answered. I can't say whether she ever got my letter. You see, I was sent here with a group of Jewish orphans by a charitable organization that made arrangements with families who were willing take us in. The program was called the Kindertransport. It was only because my sister and a close friend of our family worked at the orphanage that I was accepted in the program. But only young people were allowed to go, my sister would have gone with me but she was too old. If I had not been brought here to your country, who knows what might have happened to me."

The woman had kind eyes, the color of a light grey dove. "We are the Lawrence's. I am Lenore, this is my husband Sam, my daughter Sharon you already know, and my son William. You're in the basement of our jewelry store. We live in an apartment right upstairs. My husband fixes watches and cuts stones and diamonds."

Gilde smiled. "It's nice to meet you. Thank you so much,

Mr. Lawrence, for bringing me here. I guess I just froze from fear."

The eruption of a bomb outside shattered the conversation and everyone in the basement jumped.

"It's hard to believe that we are at war. William wants to join the Navy, but I am hoping that he will reconsider. He's a brilliant boy. He would be of better use to the world as doctor than a soldier," Mrs. Lawrence said.

Gilde could see that Lenore Lawrence was terrified for her son to enlist and she couldn't blame her.

"I understand how you must feel," Gilde said. "Hitler has ruined so many lives. I cannot understand how all of these terrible things can happen. I feel as if my world in Germany was turned upside down and now Hitler has followed me here to Britain."

"I don't even know why we have put ourselves into this war. If Hitler attacks Poland why do France and Britain have to be a part of all of it?" Mr. Lawrence said.

"Because if we allow the Nazis to take Poland, next it will be France and before long it will be us." William said. "That's why I have to fight. Do you understand that at all, Father?"

Mr. Lawrence sighed and shrugged his shoulders.

Gilde watched the family and felt her heart break for them. It was strange to speak to Jews who spoke English with an English accent the way the non-Jews spoke. She wondered if they spoke Yiddish too. But somehow, she didn't feel that this was the time to ask them. Every time a bomb fell outside the building, Mr. Lawrence whispered a Hebrew prayer of thanks that they had been spared. Gilde's father had not been one to say prayers, but she'd heard Lev say them especially on the Jewish holidays and the memory brought tears to her eyes. Lev and Lotti. They were such good friends of the family. Lotti was not Jewish, but she respected Lev's religion and he in turn respected hers. How she longed to be in the warm safe blanket of her home, of her family and friends. She had to keep believing that they were all still alive, because the thought that they might be gone forever was too painful to accept.

A young couple came rushing down the stairs into the Lawrence's basement. The man was tall and thin, the woman tall and thin as well but shorter than the man.

"Lenore, its sheer madness outside. People are looting the stores. Is all of your inventory upstairs in the store?"

"No, not the diamonds, the watches or the gold. Only the gem stones and a few silver chains."Mrs. Lawrence said.

"Maybe I should go up and try to salvage what I can." Sam Lawrence said

"Don't be a fool. It's too dangerous. If the gem stones and the silver get stolen, at least we still have the diamonds, gold and watches.

"Our building was hit. We can't get into the basement. I am afraid to try. Can we stay here with you?" The neighbor lady asked

"Of course," Lenore said, "I wouldn't have it any other way." Then she turned to Gilde. "Gilde, these are our neighbors. They own the butcher shop next door. Jeffrey and Marge Weiss."

"A pleasure to meet you," Gilde said noticing that the man had the black hat, long black coat, white shirt and black trousers, that she'd seen Orthodox Jews wear in Germany.

The woman smiled and touched Gilde's arm. Her head was covered and she wore a long skirt and a blouse with long sleeves and a high neck. The man did not meet Gilde's eyes nor did he get close to her.

"They're orthodox Jews," William said.

"Son, that's very rude." Mr. Lawrence stared at William.

"Well, it's true. I just wanted Gilde to understand why Mr. Weiss was acting so strangely towards her."

"William, please," Lenore said as she shook her head. "The way my son behaves you'd think he was still a child instead of a man."

Gilde smiled at William. He returned her smile. She thought he was incredibly attractive. His eyes were the color of the ocean like his father's and his hair was the color of a copper medallion she'd once seen in the window of a jewelry store.

At ten minutes after six, an all-clear signal was sounded.

"I don't think we should go out there yet." Sam said

This was not the first time London had been bombed, but it was the first time London had been bombed so relentlessly.

And Sam was right. They could hear the chaos outside. Then at eight o'clock the bombing began again.

The bombs rained over London through the night. Gilde knew she should somehow try to get home. The Kendalls would be worried. But she dared not venture out into the darkness with all that was transpiring that night. Everyone sat listening to the thunder of the outside world and each of them feared that the next explosion would fall upon their heads and the building above them would collapse leaving them to die of suffocation.

Chapter 19

The bombs had stopped during the night and the following morning it seemed to be quiet enough for Gilde to go outside and try to make her way back to the Kendalls. The Weiss's had left an hour earlier.

"I should get home." Gilde said "The family I am staying with will be worried about me."

"Before you go, let me go upstairs and get some water so I can help you clean up those cuts properly." Mrs. Lawrence said.

William followed Gilde and his mother upstairs. "I might as well clean them off for you and take a better look in the light of day, just to make sure that there isn't a glass in your skin." He said

"Very well, Wil. You can take care of it for her if you'd like." Mrs. Lawrence said "Would you like some tea or something to eat before you go?"

Gilde was hungry, very hungry, but she didn't feel comfortable taking the Lawrence's rations so she declined the offer and thanked the family. As she made her way out to the street Gilde saw that all of the glass display cases in the shop were shattered. Gilde felt so bad for the kind family who had helped her through the night. They'd lost so much in the bombing. There had been no time for Mr. Lawrence to empty the cases. Gilde assumed that looters had taken most of what was in the shop because only a few pieces of jewelry were scattered throughout the broken glass. The door to the building had been blown off its hinges and lay in the street. Gilde's heart broke for the Lawrence's. Her father had been a business owner. She remembered how much pride and work he put in to keeping his shop before the Nazi's stole it from him and gave it to an Aryan carpenter. Gilde wished she could stay and help clean up, but she had to get back. So, she walked through the opening and began to make her way home. London was almost unrecognizable in its destruction. Buildings that had once stood tall and strong now lay in piles of debris. Dead and dying were everywhere. The smell of fire and the dust from the ruined buildings sent Gilde into a choking fit of coughing, her eyes burning as she kept walking towards home. A couple of children wobbled aimlessly through the streets in search of their parents. A little girl stared at Gilde, looking lost and dumbfounded.

"Where are your parents?" Gilde asked. The child could not be more than five years old. She didn't answer. Gilde bent down to where she was the same height as the little girl so as not to be intimidating. "Are you all alone?"

The child stared at Gilde blankly, but her eyes were as wide as a full moon. Still, she did not speak.

"Let me help you…" Gilde said and began to walk over to the girl. As she got closer, the child panicked and began to run through piles of rubble. Gilde thought about chasing her, but she had to get home. She was worried about Jane and the family. The child disappeared into the remains of a broken building, then Gilde caught a glimpse of the little girl's blue coat as she ran all the way through the building and into another.

Gilde said a silent prayer for the little girl, then she began running towards home. At any time the planes could come back dashing over her head and another bomb could land anywhere even right on top of her. Twice she slipped on the rocks and crumbled stone that had once been buildings, scraping her knees and elbows, but she got up and continued running. Her adrenaline was too pumped up for her to feel any pain. Sometime during the nights bombing, a big red bus had fallen straight into a hole in the street. The crevice was so deep that Gilde felt a chill as she looked at it. From where she stood she could see a pile of bodies on top of each other inside the train car. She ran faster.

Finally she arrived at the street where she lived with the Kendalls. It too was in shambles. She'd been worried about the Kendalls. But somehow in the back of her mind, she'd expected their house to be spared. How could she have been so foolish? She thought she would return and the house where she lived would be just as she'd left it. But it wasn't. In fact, it was leveled to the ground. Her heart raced. She bit her lower lip so hard that she tasted the salty taste of blood. Gilde was afraid to look through the piles of wood and brick, she was afraid of what she might find. Her head was spinning and she was dizzy, she gagged but didn't vomit. It had been too long since the last time she'd eaten and her stomach was empty. Still she felt the bitter bile rise burning her throat. Bending over at the waist, she forced herself to breathe deeply several times between fits of coughing. The dust from the rubble made it hard to breathe. Even if she cried out for help, there was no one around to hear her. So, alone and horrified, Gilde began to search for the remains of the surrogate family who had taken her in.

She found them, but not all of them.

The bodies of Mr. and Mrs. Kendall were brutally deformed, bloody, missing limbs, their faces distorted in pain. But, strangely, she could not find Jane. Jane had already begun her nurse training, but she was still returning home at night. So, Gilde had expected to find her. But, unbeknownst to Gilde, Jane was not at home when the bomb's fell. Gilde looked at the destruction all around her then she sat down on a pile of bricks that had once been a part of the neighbor's home and began to cry. Her hands were filthy from the search, but she didn't notice. She covered her face with her hands and wept.

"Jane … Where was Jane? Was she alive or dead?" She whispered, Jane's name over and over. Gilde said nothing else, although her heart longed to say so many things. She wanted to tell Jane how much she meant to her. She wished she had some way to convince Jane that she would never have betrayed her with Thomas or anyone else. But most of all, she wanted to express her deep gratitude to Jane for making her welcome, for making her feel at home when she was so far from her family. If she had the chance she would thank the Kendall's for al l they'd done for her. Had she ever thanked them? She couldn't remember now. Gilde felt the bile rise in her throat. Thank you, Mr. and Mrs. Kendall, thank you for all the sacrifices you made for me, a stranger. I know how hard it must have been for you to take a child in to your home. If I didn't tell you, it was because I wasn't thinking. I was so young when I came here, all I could think about was what I was leaving behind. I never took a moment to think of how all of it affected your family. I appreciate everything you did, all of you. I do. If only she had one more chance to say these words … but, now it was too late.

Chapter 20

Gilde 1940

After discovering that her adopted parents had been killed in the bombing, Gilde didn't know where to go. She thought about going back to the Lawrence's flat but she'd just met them and it felt like such an imposition to show up on their doorstep. Gilde wandered the streets shaken to the core and afraid until she saw the home of a friend Laura Paulson a girl she knew from school was still standing. It was not really her friend, it was Jane's friend, but Gilde knew Laura well enough to explain the situation and ask if she could stay at least until she could figure out what to do next. The family lived a few blocks away, and they were lucky the building that they lived in did not take a direct hit. Gilde knocked on the door.

Mrs. Paulson, Laura's mother answered. Her eyes were wide with shock when she told Gilde to come in. However Laura's mother gently made it clear that Gilde was to keep her visit temporary.

"You see, Gilde, Mr. Paulson has been out of work. Things have not been easy around here for us. He just recently got a job and because we barely have enough to take care of ourselves, we can't take on the responsibility of another child. So, please, try to find another place to stay as quickly as possible."

Gilde stayed the night and the next day she and Laura walked to school together. All day during class, Gilde was worried about what the future would hold for her. After school she walked back with Laura to the Paulson's home.

Gilde and Laura went to Laura's room "My mom is serious. We had it real bad for a long time. It was awful." Laura said as they laid their school books on the dresser.

Until now Gilde hadn't thought about the Paulson's financial problems. But as Laura was talking to her Gilde remembered that Mrs. Kendall had brought food to the Paulson home several times. She even remembered overhearing bits and pieces of a conversation between Mr. and Mrs. Kendall about the Paulson's situation. She overheard Mr. Kendall say that he felt terrible because he had seen the Paulson family standing in soup lines.

Gilde didn't know what she was going to do, but she did know that staying with Laura was temporary. She had recently turned fourteen and if need be she would drop out of school and find work. But who would hire her? She had no skills. And now she had no family, no address.

The Paulson's tried to be tolerant, but Gilde could feel the undercurrent and she knew that she was imposing upon them. Laura's older brother made comments about Gilde's German accent several times and that made Gilde feel even more unwelcome.

Every morning for a week, Gilde went to school with Laura. The student's because their parents had told them, and teachers, because many of them still remembered, constantly talked about how the Germans used poisonous gas in the Great War. The teachers warned the students of the horrible effects they would suffer if Germany gassed them. Everyone was required to have their gas masks with them at all times. Gilde, listened to the others talking about the effects of the gas and she was terrified. It quickly became commonplace to see everyone she came in contact with carrying a cardboard box around their neck with their gas mask inside.

London had become like a chamber of horrors to Gilde. When nightfall came the Germans rained a sea of bombs on the city leaving fires in their wake, then in the morning the dead and injured were found under the rubble of churches, schools, and apartment buildings. Each night Mrs. Paulson blocked out the windows of her home with black paper to make sure that the house would appear dark and that way it would not attract the bombers. A law was passed that once the sun set no lights in any building could be lit, the city must appear dark to any overhead planes. Gilde couldn't get used to the deafening roar of the warning sirens. They unnerved her.

As each day passed, the atmosphere with the Paulson's was becoming more tense, like a rubber band pulled to the breaking point. . There was not much food and Gilde was always hungry, but she restrained herself from eating. She knew she had to leave. The idea of leaving was scary but it was time to look for another place to say, because the Paulson's were making it clear that they wanted her to go. An organization had come to the Paulson house offering to evacuate the children to the country during the bombing, and the family was seriously considering sending Laura and her brother.

One afternoon Gilde was helping Mrs. Paulson clean the apartment. She tried to make herself useful so that she wasn't such an imposition. She was on her knees washing the kitchen floor when Mrs. Paulson said in a soft voice "Gilde, have you thought about somewhere else you might want to go? I don't want to hurt your feelings but times are tough. Perhaps you could contact the Central British Fund for German Jewry, and see if they have another family who would be more financially suited to take a child from the Kindertransport. Or you could go to the country. They are evacuating all of the children from their homes. We are thinking about sending Laura and Dave. But if they go we'll have to send their ration cards with them and that might make things harder on us. Besides that Dave just got a job and we sure could use that money. It's just that we aren't as well off as the Kendalls were. I hope you understand."

"Yes of course. I'll contact the Committee. " Gilde stammered. What could she say? It was terrible to be living in a place where she knew she was not wanted.

Gilde didn't have a lot of choices. It had been difficult enough asking the Paulson's to take her in their home. Now she would have to ask another family to make the sacrifice. Gilde hated to be such a burden, but she had no idea of where she might find employment or how she could ever live on her own. She thought of all of Jane's friends. They had been much friendlier with her before she had the falling out with Jane. It was highly unlikely that they would want to help her. Then she thought of the Lawrence's. They'd been so kind, and they were Jewish. She was embarrassed to go back and ask them for help. So she'd contacted the Central British Fund for German Jewry and they told her that all of the children from the Kindertransport were going to be relocated to the country. The country? She'd just gotten used to London. She'd just begun to feel comfortable at the little theater group she'd joined. Although most of the young people from the theater group would probably be leaving the city with the evacuation too. Without Jane she was lost, and now they wanted to move her again. The woman from the committee had implied that the Kindertransport children would be used as farm workers. It was an option. But before she took it, Gilde decided that she was going to swallow any pride she had left and go and talk to the Lawrence family and see if they would take her in. They might say no, but she had to try.

The following morning, Gilde walked to school with Laura, who seemed to be getting tired of having her around as much as her parents were. As they trudged down the familiar streets Laura didn't speak. At first Gilde tried to make conversation but Laura's short one-word answers discouraged her. In the beginning, when Gilde had first arrived, Laura seemed happy to have the company. Mrs. Paulson had decided that Gilde would sleep in Laura's room. As the weeks passed, Laura became more standoffish and easily annoyed. When they arrived at school, Laura went to class. Gilde didn't want to tell Laura about her plans in case the Lawrence's said no to her. So, she watched Laura disappear down the hallway. Then she turned around, left the school and walked to the Lawrence's Jewelry store.

The door had been put back into place even though it was badly damaged, and the mess of broken glass and rubble from broken concrete right outside the shop had been cleaned up.

I can't believe I am about to beg these strangers to take me in. Gilde thought. Then she opened the door to the store and went inside. The shards of glass had been swept from floor but only two display cases remained standing. They were empty. Gilde wondered if there was any Jewelry left or if it had all been stolen during the looting. Mr. Lawrence must have heard the door open because he came out of the back room. His thin white hair was disheveled and he had as slight limp, but he recognized Gilde right away and a big smile came over his face.

"NU, Gilde? How are you?'

He did speak Yiddish. She almost cried when she heard the old familiar greeting "Nu"

Gilde said "I am alright. But I have to talk to you and Mrs. Lawrence."

"What is it? You need help? Money? What?"

"Yes." Gilde said. "I am afraid I need help."

"All right, come on. Let's go sit down in the back and we'll talk."

He took her to a room with a table that was covered with equipment, papers, magnifying glasses, and various old broken watches and small chips of gem stones. There was a large box lined in black velvet. Mr. Lawrence saw her look at the box

"That's what I have left in inventory. No use in putting it back. The bombs keep coming. If and when I have a customer, I bring out the box. So? It works for now." Sam Lawrence said. He kept the diamonds and gold in a safe, he used that stuff to trade with the black market, but there was no need to tell Gilde about that.

"Yes, I think it's a smart idea." Gilde said.

"Sit, sit…"

She sat down. There were two chairs. He was sitting in one the other chair was dusty.

"When the bombs fell, the family I was living with were all killed." Gilde said taking a heavy breath. "I have nowhere to go."

"My God, Gilde. You're just a child. That's terrible."

"Yes. I know. I am distraught. But I am also desperate for a place to live."

Mr. Lawrence nodded his head. "We don't have much. Everything is so hard to come by now with the rations and all. But I have a few friends, and so we're not starving on these rations. I am even able to get some kosher food sometimes. Before the war Lenore tried to keep a Kosher house, but now, it's not easy. We do the best we can. We trade our ham and bacon rations with our neighbors for other things. It all works out. Anyway, I'm rambling." He smiled "Of course, you're welcome in our home. A nice Jewish girl like you. And we don't have much, but, what we have we'll share with you."

"I also have a ration book. I'll give it to you for my food." Gilde said "Do you mean I can stay with you?"

"Of course. If my Sharon or my William were in a strange city without anywhere to stay, I would hope that a Jewish family would take them in. So how can I turn my back on someone else's child?"

"Oh Mr. Lawrence. You don't know what this means to me." Gilde started crying.

"Shaa. It's alright. We even have a room just for you. I am sorry to say that against our will, William enlisted. You can use his room"

"Should we talk to Mrs. Lawrence before you say yes?"

"Sure, but I know what she'll say. She'll be happy to have you. A nice Jewish girl. Why not? Maybe when William comes home, you and William might decide you like each other. And who knows it could be a shidduch. Well...who knows, anything can happen, right? But for now, you'll move in. Sharon will be so happy. You know she has a hard time keeping friends. She says she's always the outsider when she's with Gentiles. But she has some Jewish friends from our Synagogue. She'll introduce you. Jews always have a rough time keeping non-Jewish friends. I guess that's why we're the chosen people." He looked at Gilde and saw the questioning look in her eyes. Then he laughed. "Don't worry. It's been going on like this for centuries. Our people are strong; we have always survived anti-Semitism, we always will. Maybe someday we'll even have a country of our own. Eh? A dream, huh? Why not, everyone should have a dream."

"Do you think my parents will survive in Germany?"

"I believe that they will."

"And the Nazi's?"

"They'll end up defeated, with their heads buried in the sand. That's where they belong isn't it?" He laughed "Don't be so serious. Everything always has a way of working itself out. You'll see. We try to laugh in this family. We laugh even when maybe we should cry." Sam winked at her and he even though he looked nothing like Taavi, he reminded Gilde so much of her father at that moment.

Gilde smiled at him

"Come on, let's go upstairs and tell Mrs. Lawrence to roll out the red carpet because we have a house guest."

Sam Lawrence was right. The family opened their arms and took Gilde in with a warm embrace. For the first time in a long time, Gilde felt wanted and safe. She knew they were strangers, and they owed her nothing. At any time they something could happen and they could say go, like the Paulson's did and she'd be back out on the street. But for now at least, she had a home, and even if it was only temporary, she could make believe that she was surrounded by people who cared about her. To make things even more like a fairy tale, she had her own room. It had been William's room. His things were everywhere, but that was just fine. She saw his wooden jewelry box on the dresser with his gold mezuzah inside. In a drawer next to the desk was a medical journal, probably one of his books from school. A few items of clothing hung in the closet, and a pair of shoes he'd worn were on the floor beneath them. . She couldn't remember a time in her life when she had so much privacy.

Later that night, when everyone had retired to their rooms. Sam and Lenore were alone in bed. Most nights they just turned off the light and fell into a deep slumber. But tonight, Lenore turned over to look at Sam before she extinguished the light. A look of worry was on her face and a deep furrow had formed between her brows. "Why did you agree to this, to take this stranger in to our house, Sam?" She asked

"I had to take her in, Lenore. She was alone with no one to turn to. She's so young, almost still a child. Can you imagine her alone on the street? What would become of her? She's a Jewish girl, Lenore. If we don't' help other Jews nobody will"

"But we have so little, Sam. You've already sold most of my mother's diamonds, God rest her soul. All that we had from before the war is dwindling fast. The business has gone straight to hell. Who needs jewelry when they don't have anything to eat? We are in trouble Sam. I don't know how we are going to manage"

"Like we always do, Lenore. We might have a little less for a while until this is all over but we share what we have it's a mitzvah. And, she seems to be such a good girl." He said

"Yes, I suppose she does. But what if we lose the war? Then we will have nothing."

"If we lose the war, no one will have anything. And whether this poor child is with us or not, won't make any difference as to whether we survive or not. Have a rachmones."

"I do have a rachmones, it is a pity. I am just worried. You know that if we had plenty I wouldn't hesitate for minute. But Sammy, we have gornisht, nothing."

"We have each other. And we have plenty of love. Let's at least share our love with this poor little girl."

"Sam, what am I going to do with you? You're such an old fool." Lenore shook her head.

"You're angry that I told her it was alright for her to move in?"

"How can I be angry, Sam. Your heart is so big. I have to be thankful. I am a lucky woman to have such a good husband. Kenahora. Pooh, pooh, pooh" She spit a little over the side of the bed and said kenahora, so that the evil eye would not notice her good fortune.

"So you understand?"

"Of course I do. It will be hard for us, no doubt, but you're right. We couldn't turn her away. It would be a sin. She'll stay here with us. We'll do what we can."

Chapter 21

1940

Mr. Lawrence was right. The entire family opened their arms and took Gilde in with a warm embrace. Sharon offered Gilde instant friendship and after school Gilde began to help in the Jewelry store. It was her choice, Mr. Lawrence never asked. But she wanted to learn and she learned quickly.

"You know my own children don't have any interest in the business. I've tried to teach them, but no. They want nothing to do with it. You are going to be quite a stone cutter someday."

Gilde watched as Sam Lawrence cut diamonds and she learned. Within a few months, she could fix a broken watch and he began to allow her to cut less valuable gemstones. At night Gilde and Sharon helped Mrs. Lawrence black out the windows as the bombings continued.

The theater group that Gilde had joined was too far away from the Lawrence's apartment and Mrs. Lawrence didn't want Gilde to go out at night.

"It's dangerous anyway, that a girl should be out alone? Especially now with the bombing too? I think you should quit, Gilde." Mrs. Lawrence said.

So, Gilde quit. But she enjoyed the Friday night Sabbath dinners, and the occasional Yiddish words that the family spoke. She felt warm and wanted and she hadn't felt that way since the Kendall's died. The family walked to temple on Saturday morning and Gilde went with them. She watched Sharon and learned to wear modest clothing. Not as modest as the extremely orthodox neighbors , the Weiss' that Gilde had met during the bombing, but conservative clothing that was not too tight or exposing.. The family tried to keep a kosher home, and for the first time, Gilde was beginning to understand Judaism as a religion and not only as a nationality.

There was a mezuzah that had been attached to the corner of the building by the entrance door and because Sharon kissed her hand and then touched the Mezuzah every time she went in and out of the apartment, Gilde learned to do the same.

"So, tell us about your family." Mrs. Lawrence asked one night at dinner. "What do you hear from them?"

"Nothing. I sent another letter to my sister last week and I haven't gotten an answer. I don't know what to do." Gilde said

"So, you won't worry. You won't think about it. I'm sorry I brought it up. The war will end soon and then you're going to invite all of us to your parents' house for a nice dinner. We'll bring a roasted chicken" Mr. Lawrence said smiling and winking at Gilde

Gilde knew he was trying to comfort her. But the chances of her ever finding her family again were growing bleaker every day.

One Friday afternoon Gilde and Sharon were braiding dough to make Challah for the Sabbath when an idea came to Gilde. "Sharon will you help me learn to speak English the way you do? I want to lose my accent. If I can get rid of this German accent, I think my life will be a lot better here in Britain"

"Of course I'll help you. We're friends."

It was fun to learn to speak without her accent. Sharon would enunciate words and Gilde would say them over and over until she was able to sound just like Sharon. They put so much energy into the project that it helped distract them from everything going on in the world.

A committee came to the Lawrence home and offered to take Sharon and Gilde to the country.

"You two want to go?" Mr. Lawrence asked. "It would be safer."

"I don't want to go, papa." Sharon said

"Gilde?"

"If you want me to go, I will, but I don't want to. I feel at home here."

"So you'll both stay with us. I would prefer that anyway." He smiled.

Still, even though Gilde felt loved and wanted by the Lawrence's, every few weeks she tried to send a letter to Lotti or Alina, but she never received an answer.

Chapter 22

Elias

Elias was never one to pay much attention to gossip. When he heard rumors about himself, he brushed them off like dust on a dark coat. He'd grown up in an orphanage, had very little recollection of his family, and few ties to anything. So when he moved in with Glenda he wasn't concerned about his reputation. He had none. But Glenda was a hard girl, with a mind of her own. She knew that Elias adored her, but she had a special relationship with her pimp, Bart, and she wasn't about to give him up. Elias couldn't understand it, Glenda earned the money, but Bart controlled her like a puppeteer. There was no doubt that Bart was a handsome devil of a man, with Clarke Gable good looks, dark hair, brooding eyes. The hold that Bart had over Glenda drove Elias crazy. He hated to see Glenda with other men, but she ignored him when he begged her to leave what she called "the life." Elias was smart, very smart, and perhaps sometimes too smart. Many times when cash was not flowing, he'd devised illegal plans that had helped the bookies grow their business and in turn, he earned more money. His mind was quick and he learned fast. Since he was a child, he had been able to repair anything. In fact, he'd even built a radio with used parts he'd found and stolen from scrap yards. When he heard about a job opening at the local newspaper office, working the printing press, he applied. Although he'd never worked a printing press before, he lied and said he had experience. Elias was so convincing that the boss believed him when he said he could handle the job and would be an asset to the department. On his first day, the other men watched him and analyzed his ability to work the press. One of them reported him for lying. The boss listened to the complaint but decided to give Elias a chance to prove himself.

It was true, Elias knew nothing about printing Newspapers. But, Elias was learning. He would learn every aspect of how the machine worked and from then on, he would be the master. It was in this way that his brilliant but troubled mind operated.

There was no doubt that Elias knew how to be charming when he wanted to be. And because he was handsome by the end of the day the women typists were helping him to learn what he needed to know in order to run the press. They weren't experts, but they'd been at the job long enough to help Elias figure things out. By the end of the week, he ran the printing press like a pro. He'd gotten this job to prove to Glenda that he could earn a legitimate living. Perhaps this would convince Glenda to quit selling her body.

"I can support you. We can get married and have a normal life. I'm tired of working with bookies, and seeing you with John's. Wouldn't it be nice if we could just have a few children, maybe buy a house somewhere far away from here? Elias told her. But Glenda just smiled at him as he if were nothing but a boy.

It made him angry. He left the apartment walked for miles smoking cigarettes he'd stolen from the jacket pocket of one of Glenda's rich Johns. What the hell is wrong with me? Why do I need a woman's love so much?" He kicked a stone on the ground. Both of the women he'd fallen head over heels for were older than Elias. Neither of them treated him like an equal. Elias knew he was handsome. He worked hard to be a wonderful lover. And he'd heard girls his own age refer to him as a sexy young man with a rebellious streak.

All of these qualities made him appealing to older women, but they never seemed to take his feelings seriously. So, regardless of how much he tried to do for Glenda financially she refused to consider leaving her pimp.

Damn, maybe I am the way I am because I never had a mother. Elias thought. But he would never share that weakness with anyone.

Bart came to the apartment often. And every time he did, Elias would sit on the sofa glaring at him, not daring to verbally challenge him. Not out of fear of the fight, but out of fear of losing Glenda. He would leave the room as she took a wad of pounds out of the garter holding up her stocking and hand it to Bart as if he had done something to earn it. This ignited a fire in Elias' belly. One day after Bart had picked up the money from Glenda and left, Elias went into Glenda's bedroom to find her sitting on the bed and counting the few pounds that Bart had left her.

"Why do you do this? Sleep with strange men, let them do terrible things to you and then give all of your money to that bastard?"

"Because he loves me. He understands me."

"I love you," Elias said his heart pounding in his neck.

"You're a boy, Elias. He knows me. He knows things about me that you will never understand."

"Like what?"

"Like that I need someone to take charge. When he tells me what to do I feel safe."

"I could tell you what to do. Leave him. That's what you should do."

"Elias, you don't understand."

"And when you come home with a black eye and I know he is the bastard who gave it to you? What about that?"

"He only hits me because he loves me. He gets jealous when he thinks he's losing me. In fact, you and I are the only thing that I have ever stood up against Bart about."

"What do you mean?"

"He wants me to get rid of you. Bart says you are messing up what we have. I refused."

"And?"

"And, so far, he says that as long as I don't let you get in the way of him and I and what we have, you can stay."

"Well, that's generous of him. What exactly does he do for you, Glenda?" Elias asked his voice bitter with sarcasm.

"He protects me and let's me know that I am beautiful, desirable, loved."

"And the son of a bitch does all of this through pounding you with his fists when you don't behave."

"Please, Elias. I can't lie to Bart and if you don't stop challenging my relationship with him, I will have to send you away."

"How the hell can I convince you that the guy is using you for money? How many other girls does he have that he put out on the street just like you?"

"I don't know, maybe five."

"Five others, but he loves you, Right? Isn't that what you're telling me?"

"Listen, when I met Bart I was just a kid, not even thirteen. My mother died when I was born. I ran away from home really, it was my step father that I was running away from. I'd already miscarried my second child by my stepfather. He'd started raping me when I was eight and I couldn't take it anymore. I stole money out of his pants pocket one morning while he was still asleep. Then I paid for bus fare into London. But I had no idea what I was going to do when I got here. I hadn't thought that far ahead. All I knew was that I wanted to get as far away from my step father as possible. I wandered the streets for a few days, hungry and alone, and need I say, terrified? Then I met Bart. He was so kind and understanding. The first thing he did was feed me. "She smiled a nostalgic smile. "Then he put me up and for a while it was just him and me. There were no Johns in the beginning. That was the first time anyone had ever made love to me. It's a lot different than being raped."

"Yeah? Is it? Because in my book he was raping you. He was setting you up for this pitiful life where you sell your body to give him money and make him happy. Is that really all right with you Glenda?"

"You can't begin to understand my relationship with Bart. He is my oak tree, Elias. When I needed someone he was there. He has always been there for me."

"So what am I?"

"Bart says you're my companion as long as you don't cause problems."

"Damn, I wish you could think for yourself."

"I am thinking for myself, Elias. I love Bart. If you want to stay here with me, you won't try to change that. If not you can go now."

He knew she meant it. And Elias thought about leaving, but he was comfortable and happy with Glenda. So, he tried to make believe that in time he would be able to find a way to change her way of thinking.

Elias had an untamed sex appeal that made the girls he saw on the street shoot him smiles and sometimes even wink.

He would return their gestures. Occasionally he spent an afternoon in bed with a pretty girl, but for some reason his heart brought him back to Glenda. Sometimes he would take long walks and dive deep into thought about the women he had cared for. Mary and Glenda had not been as different as people may have thought. Although Mary had a respectable job and Glenda was a prostitute, both women had another man in their lives. For Mary it was her husband, for Glenda it was Bart. Neither of them thought of him as someone they would ever marry. He wondered if that might not be part of his attraction to them. He knew that neither of them would ever try to tie him down. He was confused in his own mind. What did he really want? Sometimes he thought he wanted marriage and a family but then when he met a sweet young girl who he might be able to marry start a family with, he would find that he was not romantically interested.

Glenda had made it clear that if Elias wanted to stay he was to make himself scarce when Bart was around. Even worse, Glenda also told him that if he forced her to choose between himself and Bart, she would choose her pimp. When Elias was angry with Glenda, he considered moving back into the small apartment he's shared with his friends. He could always go back to running numbers. He hated punching a clock and working a full day at the printing press. At least when he was living with the other fellows and running numbers, he had some form of self-respect. Here with Glenda, he felt like a chachka (he still remembered the Yiddish word for toy), something to be put back on the shelf and ignored when Bart came around.

Elias continued working at the press, but he didn't make nearly as much money as he'd made with the bookies, and he felt like a failure. Glenda earned more than he did and gave most of it to Bart each week. One evening after Glenda's John slithered out of the flat, she came into the living room where Elias was smoking a cigarette. He couldn't stand to look at her clients, because he knew what was going on in the bedroom and it made him sick. How could he ignore the moaning he heard through the walls? He knew Bart didn't give a damn about Glenda. If Bart cared at all, he would feel the same way about Glenda selling her body as Elias did. One of the hardest things about Glenda's johns was that even after they left, their smell would linger in the apartment and haunt Elias for the rest of the day or night.

"I'm tired. Have you eaten anything?" Glenda asked Elias. She was stretching her back. She wore a silk Japanese style robe. It must have been a gift from one of her clients. It was slit up the front and her long shapely legs were exposed as she walked.

"No," he said. When he thought about his life and his relationship with Glenda, he lost his appetite.

"Come on, come with me, let's go to the pub down the street, I want to go and get something to eat. There's nothing here."

Elias's shoulders slumped in defeat. "Why do you do this? I'll never understand it."

"I told you before, he loves me." Then she turned to him and glared "I'm tired, Elias. I don't want to go over this again."

"How can you be so stupid?" He shook his head. "If I were a different kind of a fellow I'd knock some sense into you."

"Oh Elias, you're too young to understand. I am his favorite. I am the only one that he really loves. Now please can we go and eat?"

"You can't believe that? I know you can't believe that he loves you. If he did he wouldn't use you like this."

"He isn't using me. I offered to do this for him, for us..."

"So, where the hell do I fit in to all of this?" Elias asked.

"Oh My God, you ask the same questions over and over. I told you I'm tired, exhausted. So, where do you want to fit in, Elias?" She put a cigarette to her lips and turned to him leaning down to the chair where he sat so that he could light it. Instead her grabbed her wrist and stood up. Elias was over a foot taller and far stronger than Glenda.

"Stop playing games with me!" he said, his voice was raised.

"You're hurting me." She looked at him and he saw the fear in her eyes.

He released her arm, he hadn't realized how hard he was squeezing her wrist. "I'm sorry." He cleared his throat. "I just want you to know that I care about you. I care a lot. I am working at this lousy job right now, but I promise, I'll do something great. I'll make money, plenty of money. Just quit this way of life, leave Bart. I love you, Glenda."

"Love doesn't pay the bills, honey." She said taking a deep drag on her cigarette

"Bart gives you just enough of the money you earn, to stay alive. Do you realize that?"

"He takes care of me. He manages everything. He finds the johns, makes sure they're not dangerous…."

"And have you had any that were dangerous? I would bet you have."

"Yeah, once or twice, I have had a problem or two." She shrugged. "It happens."

"See? Do you see? He's not doing anything to help you. If he loved you, he couldn't put you in danger. I know I couldn't."

"Oh, Elias, you are such a sweet boy." She went to hug him "Come on let's go get something to eat."

"I'm not a boy." He shrugged her off. "I am a man and you don't respect me."

"Of course I do…"

"No, you don't."

"So? If that's how you feel then what? You want to leave?" She asked

"You know what, Glenda? I think I do," he said. His pride was hurt. His ego was bruised, and he was furious. He went into the bedroom and packed the small cardboard suitcase that he'd brought with him when he was on the train to London from Germany. Then he went back into the living room. She was sitting on the sofa, a deep wrinkle had set between her eyes.

"You sure you want to do this? You sure you want to go?"

"No, I don't want to do this," he said, his hands were trembling with anger. "I want things to be different."

"I'm sorry, Elias. But, this is the way things are and the way they are going to be…"

He felt the blood rush to his face. He wanted to hit her to push her to knock some sense into her beautiful little head. But instead, he turned and walked out the door.

For several days, Elias did not return. He spent the nights sleeping on the street with a bottle of whiskey. In the mornings, he was too hung over to go to work. In a drunken stupor, to prove to himself that he was attractive and desirable, he tried to seduce a young girl who was having lunch alone on a bench in the park, but she ran from him. He saw the terror in her eyes and realized that he must look like a derelict.

Elias went into a public bathroom in the train station and tried to clean himself up. When he looked into the mirror his bloodshot eyes, and greasy hair alarmed him. He looked older than his years, and even worse, his decrepit life had made him look like he was ill. Elias washed his face, combed his hair, and straightened his wrinkled shirt. He rinsed his mouth with water, hoping to kill some of the stink of liquor on his breath and walked to the newspaper office where he worked. When he arrived, he was greeted with looks of disgust and a reprimand from his boss for not showing up for work for several days. Then he was given his final pay envelope and a swift dismissal. Now, not only was Elias miserable in his love life, but he had just been fired.

Dejected and disgusted with himself, he crawled back to Glenda's apartment. Since he had a key, he had no reason to knock. As Elias had expected, Glenda was asleep. Elias hated to accept it, but he doubted that she was alone. Many of her johns spent the night. The thought made him ill. He felt powerless as he threw the cardboard suitcase on the floor. His head was pounding. It felt like his temples were being hammered. After kicking his shoes off, he lay on the sofa and tried to fall asleep only to awaken and rush to the bathroom to vomit. Apparently, the noise of his retching awakened Glenda and by the time he came out of the bathroom room she was sitting on the sofa waiting for him.

"I don't know whether to ask you where you've been or if you are ill. But I can see and smell that you've been drinking," she said shaking her head.

"What happened to you?" he asked, her eye was surrounded by a deep purple bruise.

"Nothing ... I fell."

"You're lying to me."

"What difference does it make?"

"Did one of your johns do this to you? Or worse … was it Bart?"

"Elias, I don't want to talk about it."

"But I do," he said

"Well, that's too bad. You walk out of here and do what you please then you come back and start asking questions," she said and she got up and slowly went to the kitchen to put on a pot of water for tea. He followed her.

"You can't dismiss me this easily, Glenda. I want to know what the hell happened here."

"And I want to know where the hell you've been. I've been worried about you," she said.

"You have?" He softened.

"Yes."

"I was hurt," he said. "I drank until I couldn't drink anymore. I don't want this life for you, Glenda. I want you to leave Bart and all of this behind. I can try to get another job. We could get married."

She laughed a harsh laugh. "Now wouldn't that be nice? But, I can't and you know that."

"Who did this to you?" Gently he ran his fingers across the tender skin surrounding her eye. "It was Bart, wasn't it?"

She nodded, "Yeah, it was Bart. He was mad because I was worried about you and instead of working; I went out to look for you. He had sent a John over here and I wasn't home. I was out trying to find you. It made him real mad"

"When?"

"The day you left. I knew you were angry. I wanted to talk to you. I walked the streets all night. Then when I couldn't find you I gave up and came back here. When Bart came by to pick up his money in the morning, I didn't have anything to give him. He asked me what happened with the john he sent. I said I wasn't here and I never saw any customer."

"So, he hit you?"

"Yes."

"And then?"

"And then I went back to work. That night he sent some guy, and then he sent another one last night. He said if you came back that he wanted you out of here. So, I guess you'd better go because I am expecting him soon and he won't be happy to see you."

"And you, Glenda? What do you want?" Elias asked.

"I told you before, Bart comes first, Elias. I care about you, but I love Bart."

"So it's over with us?"

"It has to be," she said.

"You want me to go?"

She nodded.

Looking at her in disbelief, Elias picked up his suitcase and walked out the door. For several hours, he wandered the streets. He had lost his job, his ego was bruised and he was heartbroken. It was then that he made a decision. Britain was at war with Germany. He would enlist, join the army, leave everything behind him, and go to battle against the Nazi bastards who sent him to England in the first place. But first, he decided that he had a mission to complete, a mission that would make the world a better place.

Chapter 23

Elias knew where the pub was where Bart conducted his business. Elias waited outside, patiently until the bar closed. Bart was one of the last to leave. Elias watched from an alleyway between two buildings as a young girl with wavy red hair handed Bart a wad of bills. He counted the money and then patted her behind and kissed her. The girl went in one direction, and Bart headed the other way. Quietly, staying several paces behind and slipping into doorways, Elias followed Bart. Once they'd left the main street, Elias could see that there was no one around as he gained on Bart. Then from behind, Elias grabbed Bart by the neck in a chokehold and threw him to the ground.

"What the hell?" Bart said. "What's going on here?" Bart turned just enough to see Elias's face. "It's you, you little punk!"

But Elias wasn't listening or answering. He kicked Bart in the face several times, until the man's once attractive features were nothing but a bloody mess. Blood poured from his lips and nose, but Elias couldn't stop kicking him. All of the years of frustration and displacement boiled to the surface in this moment and he took all of it out on Bart. Elias could not hear the man's cries for pity, all he could see was the trail of johns smirking as they left Glenda's bedroom. A vision of Mary flitted across his mind, and then another of Glenda. The women he wanted always belonged to other men, men who didn't appreciate them the way Elias did. When his rage finally subsided, Bart was dead. Elias hadn't planned to kill him, he was only planning to beat the hell out of him, to show him that he was not just a nobody who could be pushed around. But, it had gotten out of hand and now Elias had committed murder. First Elias wiped the blood from his shoe on Bart's freshly pressed white shirt. Then Elias ran away, he ran as fast as he could for two blocks. Once he felt as if he couldn't catch his breath, he ducked into an alleyway and leaned against the building. He was hyperventilating. He'd just killed a man, a devil of a man, but a man nonetheless. Elias was a murderer. The realization was daunting. He sunk to the ground and sat there staring forward into the darkness in disbelief. His head ached, his shoulders were tight, and he felt a sudden wave of nausea come over him. Elias wretched and dropped to a sitting position on the ground. Until the sun began to rise, he sat in that alleyway with his head in his hands. Before he enlisted, he had to talk to Glenda, to explain why he did what he did. He knew she would be devastated and he had to explain that he'd not meant to kill Bart, but he had attacked him out of love for her and then things just got out of hand.

Elias went back to Glenda's apartment. But he was too late. The police were already there waiting for him. Glenda was crying. She wouldn't look at him. She just folded her arms around her chest and went in to the other room.

Anger bubbled up inside of Elias as he was riding in the back of the police car. He'd rid the world of a cockroach of a man. They shouldn't be arresting him, they should be praising him.

When they got to the police station, Elias was taken into an interrogation room. Two British police officers sat at the table across from him.

"Elias Green?"

"Yes, that's me."

"You killed a man last night?"

Elias shrugged "What makes you think that?"

"You're girl told us that it was you."

"What do you mean?" Elias asked in disbelief

"She knew it was you."

"Glenda?"

"Yeah, you got another girl?"

"No." Elias said shaking his head

Elias was more hurt by Glenda's betrayal than he was by the fact that he was in trouble with the law.

"You could face execution for this, you know that?"

"Yeah…" Elias didn't care. Right now he would have gladly taken his own life to end the terrible pain that was stabbing him in the heart.

"You're from Germany aren't you?"

"You ask a lot of questions."

"That's a German accent."

"I was on the kindertransport. Yeah, I came from Germany, but I don't support the Nazi bastards. I hate them worse than you do"

"Well, we have a proposition for you. You can either face jail or worse, a possible execution." The cop said

Elias shrugged.

"But, because your girl tells us you speak fluent German and because you were born there and you sound just like every other Kraut, we're going to off you the opportunity to go to Belgium and work as a spy for Britain. What do you think?"

Elias bit his lower lip. "Can I smoke?"

"Yeah go ahead." The cop said

Elias lit a cigarette. He liked the idea. He liked it a lot "Tell me more. Tell me what you would want me to do."

"It would work like this you'd have papers that said that you are a citizen of Belgium, German speaking. We'd have a job set up for you tending bar in a nightclub where we know that a lot of German officers meet and have a few drinks. When men are drinking, they like to talk and brag. Your job would be to keep your eyes and ears open and get us plenty of valuable information."

Elias' eyes lit up. It would be a real pleasure to be a spy against Germany. He'd like nothing better than to help defeat that son of a bitch, Hitler.

"Don't fool yourself, this is no easy job, and we'd always be watching you. So, you couldn't pull any shit, like turning on us and joining the Nazi's."

"You wouldn't have to worry about that." Elias said

"I have to say, I believe you." The cop said "So, what do you say?"

"I'll take it." Elias said. Then he put out the rest of his cigarette in the ash tray on the table.

"Just thought I should let you know before you start. There's a damn good chance you won't survive. If they catch you, they'll kill you."

Elias was leaned back in the chair. He looked the policeman square in the eye. "When do I start?"

"Right away."

Chapter 24

1941 June

On June 22, 1941 Adolf Hitler, made a catastrophic error for Germany. Believing he was unstoppable, he invaded Russia going to war against Stalin an enemy as formidable as himself.

Chapter 25

1941 London Late November

Winter was on her way, and the chill that she brought seized the city of London. The building where the Lawrence's lived and worked was cold and many times the family wore their coats inside the apartment and the store. Early, before dawn on a frigid winter morning there was a knock at the front door. Lenore Lawrence grumbled as she pulled back the blankets and forced herself out of bed to see who was there. She put on her heavy wool robe, then her coat and house slippers and shuffled downstairs. A cold wind rushed in as she opened the door but she hardly noticed. "OY!!!! Thanks be to God. Come in, come in. Hurry up its cold outside." Lenore said pulling her son into her arms. Then she turned and yelled up the stairs "Everyone come quick, Willie is home…"

The family, including Gilde came dashing down stairs to the shop. In the excitement, Gilde hadn't had a chance to get dressed. She still wore the thick flannel nightgown with the heavy wool sweater and cotton socks that she slept in every night.

"Willie, you're so skinny." Mrs. Lawrence said hugging him, "I'm so glad you're here. Let me make you something to eat."

"Wil, how did you get home?" Mr. Lawrence asked.

"I'm on leave Papa."

"How long can you stay?"

"I have four days, then I am being re-stationed."

"Re-stationed where?"

"I don't know yet. I do know that I'll be aboard a destroyer."

"Oy, William" His father said shaking his head.

"It's war Papa."

The family gathered around William, but Gilde stood back. She hardly knew him. But he looked over their heads and his eyes caught hers as she stood on the bottom stair. Her feet were with only her thin cotton socks.

"Gilde? " He said smiling. "I remember you."

"Yes. How are you?"

"Gilde is staying with us. The family she was living with was killed in the bombing." Mrs. Lawrence said. "She's staying in your room, so you'll have to sleep on the sofa."

"No. No please. I'll sleep on the sofa. Let William have his room."

"Don't be silly. Why don't you stay in my room with me and that way Wil can have his room back for the time he's here?" Sharon said

"Are you sure?" Gilde asked

"I'd love it. It will be fun we can practice your English…"

"Your English sounds pretty good to me William said. What happened to your heavy accent?"

"I'm trying to lose my accent."

"You must be freezing." William said to Gilde. Then he took off his coat and put it over her shoulders. A glance of approval passed between Mr. and Mrs. Lawrence.

"We raised such a gentleman." Mrs. Lawrence said

"Oh thank you. You didn't have to do that." Gilde said, but she was glad for the warmth. And she couldn't help but think that William looked very handsome in his uniform.

"Let me make you something to eat. You look so hungry."

"Ma, it's four thirty in the morning. I'm not hungry"

"So? So you can't eat because it's early in the morning? Why not? You say you're not hungry. You look hungry to me. OY Vey, you're so skinny. Well, I'm your mother, mothers can always tell what their children need."

"You want me to eat? I'll eat." William said to his mother, but he winked at Gilde. She smiled back at him and giggled a little.

"I want you should eat." Mrs. Lawrence said "It will make me feel good."

"All right then."

"Come, I'll put something together for you."

Chapter 26

For somebody who said he wasn't hungry William ate as if he hadn't eaten in a long time. The whole family sat at the table with him.

"So, how are you?" Sharon asked, "We worry about you every day."

"I am fine. I am in training."

"Is it hard?"

"Sometimes, yes. Because I am not a fighter by nature. I spent my childhood dreaming I'd be a doctor. My heart tells me that I am a healer. And I am working on the ship as a medic. The truth is that I can't even stand to kill an ant, but even so, I have to learn to fight in case I need to. And I have to stand up against the Nazi's. It wouldn't be right for me to stay at home with my family and go to school while Hitler is destroying our country. Besides if we don't fight the Nazi's they'll come on our shores and then we'll have to fight them here. That would put everyone I care about in danger."

"Not only are they destroying Britain but they hate the Jews." Gilde said "It was bad in Germany for Jews when I left. God only knows how it is now."

"We don't know. We don't hear or see anything. I assume it's pretty much the same for Jews as it always is. I wish I could promise you that your family is fine. But I can't. I won't lie. The German's are brutal. I haven't had any personal encounters with them yet, but what the other fellows say, is that they are cruel, heartless. I know this upsets you. So, let's try not to talk about it. There's nothing we can do right at this very minute. I am doing my part by serving in the Navy. I feel it's the right thing to do. "

"I am just praying that you'll come home to us safe. Willie, you haven't seen battle yet. I know you son, and you're not made for this." Sam Lawrence said

"Yes, but sometimes a fellow has to do what's right, even if he's scared beyond measure. It would be easy for me to stay here and be safe and comfortable with my family. But it wouldn't be right. And, I would always know, that no matter what happened in the end, especially if Germany wins, that I didn't do my part. I can't live with that."

"Don't let your Papa fool you, William. He's doing his part as well. Aren't you Sam?"

"Oh, Lenore. I am not doing nearly as much as William. "

"Yes, but you are making an effort."

"Your mother is making a lot out of nothing." Sam shook his head

"You're father has become a volunteer fire watcher. He watches a factory all night two nights a week. Even at his age he is trying to help."

"I didn't know this." William said. "But I am proud of you Papa."

"Everyone has to do their part. I wish I could do more."

"You're only human Papa. Don't be so hard on yourself. You should be proud. What you are doing can save people's lives and that's something important." William patted his father's shoulder

Chapter 27

1941

The following morning William slept late. Gilde and Sharon went to school. But Gilde couldn't wait to get home and see William again. When she'd first met him she'd thought he was attractive, but because they were in the middle of the bombing she hadn't really paid much attention to him. But now that he was at home and she was getting to know him better, she was beginning to like his open and honest way of communicating. He had admitted to being afraid. She was impressed that he had been man enough to show both weakness, and courage. The combination won her admiration. She liked him.

William was reading a medical journal when Sharon and Gilde got home from school that afternoon.

"So, how are my two favorite girls?" he asked smiling and looking directly at Gilde.

"Fine." They both said at the same time, then looked at each other and giggled a little.

"It's Friday night, you'll be here for Shabbat dinner. That will be so nice, Wil." Sharon said. "Gilde and I baked Challah. I hate that brown Hovis bread. It's so grainy and tasteless."

"How did you get the flour and sugar?"

"We used our rations, and you know Papa. He always finds a way to get what we need."

"Black market?" Wil asked

"Probably. Papa has so many friends and connections."

"You know how to bake?" Wil asked Gilde

"Your mother and sister taught me."

"Well, my mom and sister bake quite delicious bread. So, you're learning from the best."

"Since your home, I'll bet Papa tried to get some butter off the black market this morning. We've been using margarine, but Papa would want the best for you, Willie."

"The margarine has a strange aftertaste, but I don't mind it. We have it in the canteen all the time" Willie said

"At first I thought it was terrible, but I'm getting used to it too." Sharon said

"I've been getting used to a lot of strange food in the Navy. I can't keep kosher. It's impossible. But, I think God will forgive me." He said "However, right about now, real butter sounds like heaven."

Gilde smiled. "I know it's none of my business, but how does your father do it? He hardly earns much money in the shop anymore."

"He has a lot of inventory that's been handed down through his family. You know, jewelry and things of value. He trades it for food, sometimes to pay the rent, and for other things we need." Sharon said. Because of this we're probably doing better than most people."

"Gilde, would you like to take a walk with me?"

"It's cold outside, Wil." Sharon said

"I'll keep her warm."

"I'd love to." Gilde said

When they were leaving the house and William reached up to kiss the mezuzah something stirred inside of Gilde. William had a link, an artery that connected to the blood of her ancestors. He, like her, was a Jew. And that connection made her want to bond with him.

They walked for a few minutes then William put his arm around Gilde. She turned to give him a harsh look. "I only did that to keep you from being cold."

"Is that the reason?" She said trying to sound stern, but she couldn't help but laugh

"I can't lie. I did it because I like you. By the way, I never took you for being Jewish when we first met. You had a German accent and your blond hair is so light that I didn't think you were a Jew. In fact I heard your German accent and I was afraid you were a Nazi. Forgive me?"

"I already have forgiven you. I understand that my accent confuses people. They don't know what to make of me. I hate the Nazi's. That's why I am working with Sharon every day to get rid of this German accent. "

"So, tell me a little about you. Things I don't know, like what do you enjoy doing? What do you like to eat? Anything at all, as long as it's not sad. As long as it's not about the past and your home and family. Because when you talk about them, it burns me up inside. I want to make it right for you and I can't. It's not in my power."

"I know." She smiled then she looked at him and said "Well, I love apple and raisin Strudel."

"Kraut food." He said. Then they both laughed.

"I also love Sheppard's pie."

"Better. English, of course."

"Yes, and I love Cholent, and Mondel bread, and Challah,

and chopped Liver, and anything Jewish. I love Yiddish. I can't speak it anymore. My parents used to speak it mixed with German. But I've been away from them for such a long time that it seems I've forgotten so much. I understand a few words and when I hear them, they make me feel warm inside. I love to hear the prayers at Hanukkah."

"It's true, Yiddish is a lot like German. Can you still speak German?"

"Yes, but not fluently, a lot of it is fading away. Do you know the prayers?"

"Of course, what good Jewish boy who was Bar-Mitzva'd at the tender age of thirteen doesn't know the prayers?"

"Will you say them for me?"

"I'll do one better. I'll sing them, like a cantor."

Gilde held her breath while William sang in a beautiful baritone voice.

When he was finished Gilde wiped a tear from her cheek. "That was beautiful."

He shrugged. She could tell that the compliment embarrassed him. "You have a wonderful voice."

"You think so, huh? Do you sing?"

"Not the prayers. I don't know them."

"But you sing?"

"Yes, I do."

"Sing something for me."

She sang an old Yiddish song that her mother had sung to her when she was a child

"Oh Gilde, you're the one with the lovely voice not me. And, by the way, I didn't understand the words at all, but I liked the sound of the Yiddish too."

Chapter 28

In the morning Gilde heard the clang of the milk man's truck. She opened the door and took the container of milk and a small container of orange juice inside. Then she left the ration cards for the next day under the empty container. Mr. Lawrence had prepaid the milk man for the month.

She put the milk up on the windowsill where it would stay cold. As soon as William awakened, Mrs. Lawrence began preparing a quick breakfast of toast with just a drop of real butter. She gave William two pieces of the Challah while the rest of the family would eat the black bread. Next she skimmed the cream off the top of the milk for William.

"I feel like King David." William said to his mother smiling. "You should give some of this to Papa, and to the girls and to yourself."

"No, Willie, it's for you" Sam Lawrence said. "We want you to have the best. Don't we girls?"

"Yes, of course" Mrs. Lawrence said. "Yes," both Sharon and Gilde said in unison.

Sharon took the margarine down from the windowsill and with her back to William so he wouldn't see, she made up the regular rationed black bread toast for herself, Gilde and her parents. She knew that her parents and Gilde would agree with her that they wanted to save the precious butter for William. After all, he was only going to be there for a few days then he would be serving their country.

The next day the family walked to the Synagogue. The men and women were seated on opposite sides of the aisle. As the rabbi and cantor were saying the prayers Gilde glanced over and saw William watching her. She blushed and he smiled. Sharon noticed and she nudged Gilde with her elbow then whispered "I think my brother likes you."

The Rabbi gave a sermon on Abraham and how God told him to kill his son Isaac to prove that he loved God above all else. Then as Abraham was about to kill his beloved child, God spoke to him and told him to stop before he took Isaac's life. Gilde had heard this story before and it always frightened her. Even now as the Rabbi told it again to the congregation she found it unsettling. After the service was over a small spread of refreshments was served at the temple. Gilde met the other congregants who were friends of the Lawrence family. Sharon introduced Gilde to her girlfriends who all made a big fuss of William, and then the family left to walk back to the house where they would rest until sundown, when the Sabbath ended. William walked slowly beside Gilde. "So what did you think of the sermon."

"That bible story has always frightened me." She said

"Why?'

"Because I have never heard God speak and I've always thought that if a person was crazy they might think they heard God tell them to murder their son. And then they might do it."

"No, Gilde, Abraham was not crazy. He was the father of our people."

"But what if a mad man thought he heard God."

"I don't know. I think the story is more symbolic. I think it means that we should love God even more than we love our families." William said. "And if you remember, God didn't allow Abraham to kill Isaac. The whole thing was a test."

"I don't like tests like that." Gilde said

"I understand."

Gilde shrugged. "Do you really believe it ever happened? I mean do you think God ever talks to us?"

"Who knows? I can't say. But I will I tell you that I believe that there is a God because I have seen miracles in my lifetime. I don't want to brag, but I graduated from school early. I've been attending classes at the University where I've been training to go to Medical School, and I've seen people who should have died but didn't and were healed completely by prayer. It made me a man of God and a man of science at the same time."

She nodded.

"I have a surprise for you. Would you like to come with me after dinner, later tonight?"

"Where?"

"It's a surprise."

"Yes, I'd love to."

"But we can't tell my parents. They wouldn't like us to be alone together. They would think it was wrong."

"So, how will we get out?"

"When Sharon falls asleep you'll sneak out and meet me in the back yard."

"Oh, I don't know William." Gilde said "I don't want to get in to trouble."

"Do you trust me?"

She glanced up at him and nodded Yes.

"Good, then I'll wait for you."

"I don't know how long it will take for Sharon to fall

asleep and it's freezing outside."

"I don't care. I'll wait all night in the cold if I have to. Besides, I have to go and set up the surprise before I take you there."

"What? William what do you have up your sleeve."

"Shhh, I don't want the parents to hear." He said "You'll see. I think you'll like it."

Chapter 29

When Sharon fell asleep Gilde got dressed quietly and slipped her coat on. Then she went out the door and into the yard. As he promised, William was waiting.

"Come on, it's not very far." He said leading her.

Gilde was a little nervous. She'd never done anything so bold and she knew that if they found out, the Lawrence's would forbid it.

"It's alright." William said. He was carrying a cloth bag in his hand.

They walked for several blocks. Gilde began to regret agreeing to this. She was cold and her nose and eyelashes felt like they were frozen.

William led her up the walk of an old brick house.

"Who lives here?" Gilde asked "The house looks haunted."

He laughed "It does look haunted. But I think you'll like it once we're inside." He said "I used to come here with my friends when we were kids."

"Are you sure nobody is here?"

"Yes, I'm sure. The house is closed down in the winter, but I've seen people living here in the summer. I think it's a summer home."

"It's pretty big and set so far back from the street that it's like something out of an Edgar Allen Poe novel. Kind of scary. Are you sure that nobody is here?"

"Yes, I checked earlier. That's why I told you I had to set things up before we came.

They went inside and William put the bag down. There was a small pile of firewood in the fire place. Carefully he lit a fire "I set up the fire place with wood. I guess you could say I did a little shopping on the black market before I put this together."

Once the fire blazed and the warmth filled the room, the house wasn't frightening anymore. In fact it gave Gilde a homey feeling and a sense of well-being. It calmed her nerves and made her feel lazy and for the time being, safe.

"Now" William said taking a thin wool blanket out of the brown bag and spreading it on the floor next to the fire, "We are going to have a picnic."

"A what? It's the middle of winter."

"Yes, we are going to have a picnic right here by the fire. I got some special delicacies I hope you will enjoy." He began taking things out of the bag. I even got some chocolate. Now how long has it been since you've tasted a piece of luscious chocolate?" He laughed

She laughed "This is really sweet of you. You went to a lot of trouble. And it probably cost you a fortune."

"I have friends." He smiled and winked.

"Well, I can see that this took an effort."

"Of course it did. But you're worth it." His eyes were glistening in the fire light.

They ate, they laughed and they talked. The hours passed like minutes. William fed the fire two more logs, and then there were no more. And it was just before sunrise that the fire began to burn out.

"As much as I hate to leave, I know we should get back. My sister will get up and see you're gone and then we'll be in trouble." William said as he put out the rest of the fire making sure not to leave even a single burning ember.

He took Gilde's hand and helped her up. "Thanks so much for spending this evening with me. When I am out on the ocean it will be this memory that I'll carry with me."

As they walked back William reached over and took Gilde's hand. She didn't pull away.

"I had fun tonight." She said "I'm glad I went with you."

"Me too." He said.

When they got back to the house he watched her as she went up to her room.

Chapter 30

On Sunday Mrs. Lawrence made fried matzo for breakfast.

"I don't mean to be rude." Gilde said. "But I've never had this before. What is it?"

"We usually only have it for Passover. But it's William's favorite and so we wanted to make it for him. Sam, God bless him got some flour and I made the matzo yesterday with a little water"

"Well I certainly appreciate you're going to all this trouble, Ma. It's delicious. We sure don't get anything like this in the service. You probably had to use all of your egg rations to prepare it."

"You never mind about that. You just enjoy it, Willie" His mother said. Then she walked over and hugged him tightly. Her eyes were glassy with tears.

Sharon, Gilde and Mrs. Lawrence took very small portions leaving most of what was left of the rare treat for Sam.

"This is delicious. How is it prepared" Gilde asked

"Well, first I made the matzo yesterday. That was easy, just a little flour and water, roll it out into a cracker and bake. Then today I soaked the Matzo in water, added egg and a bit of onion. I'm glad you like it."

"I do. It's wonderful" Gilde said

Gilde was tired because she had hardly slept. But no one seemed to suspect anything about her and William being out all night. All day, no matter what Gilde was doing, she would glance up and catch William stealing glimpses of her.

"I called Lewis and Jake and told them that you were home. They are both coming by to see you today." Mrs. Lawrence said

"Good." William said but behind his mother's back he made a funny frowning face at Gilde and she had to look away to stifle a laugh.

As soon as they had a moment alone Gilde whispered to William "Why did you make that face when your mother said your friends were going to drop by? Your face was so funny I almost burst out laughing."

He laughed "You want to know the truth?"

"Of course I wouldn't want you to ever lie to me…" Gilde said with a teasing expression on her face.

"I didn't want to share my girl with them. I didn't want them to steal you away from me." William said, then sheepishly he said "I mean, I know you're not my girl…but…What the heck am I saying. I sure am making a damn fool of myself."

"No you're not. I think you're very sweet."

William's friends arrived and both of them were flirtatious with Gilde and with Sharon, but in a very respectful manner. Gilde was having fun. This had been a wonderful weekend with William and she was really starting to like him. She remembered what he said before and decided that if he asked her to be his girl she would say yes. His family had already won her heart and she could easily see herself as a part of all of this, maybe even as William's wife.

That night when Gilde and Sharon went to bed, Gilde fell

into a deep sleep. She'd hardly slept the night before and she was very tired. Most nights she had dreams of her family or nightmares of the bombings and the finding the bodies of the Kendalls. But that night she was too tired to dream. She slept so deeply that when she felt a hand on her arm she awoke startled. At first, she was disoriented in the dark. But then she made out the face and the form of the man who was standing over her.

"William what are you doing here?"

"I want to show you something."

"Seriously. It's the middle of the night."

"I know. Be quiet. We don't want to wake Sharon. Come with me."

Gilde got up and put on her robe. They walked down stairs. The house was quiet, everyone was asleep.

Before he'd awakened her, William had laid Gilde's shoes and coat by the door. He gave her the shoes "Put them on."

She shook her head and smiled but she did as he asked. Then William helped Gilde with her coat.

He put on his own coat and opened the door for her. She followed him outside to the back yard.

"I wanted to show you the North Star. Do you see how bright it is tonight?"

She nodded.

"It's beautiful like you. When I am gone and you are feeling sad or alone come out here and look at the North Star. When you see it, you'll know that where ever I am I can see it too. And, I am thinking of you."

He gently touched her face. "I don't ever want you to feel alone and lonely again."

He kissed her and she felt safe in his arms. And even though it was terribly cold, the warmth of his heart melted her entire body into his. "You remember what I said this afternoon when I was acting like a complete idiot?"

"No? When were you acting like an idiot? I must have missed it."

'You know…." He hesitated and then his voice got soft and gravely. "When I called you my girl."

"Oh yes, I do remember something like that."

"Gilde?" He cleared his throat. "Would you? I mean, be my girl?"

"Yes, William. Yes."

"Oh, I'm so happy I can't even feel the cold." He said

She giggled. "Me too."

"I have an idea. What do you think about this? You know I only have a day left to spend with you. Would you be willing to skip school and spend the afternoon with me?"

"What would I tell Sharon?"

"You don't have to tell her at all. Just walk to school with her and then once she's in class, you leave and meet me at the park. You know the one, its two streets north of the school?"

"Yes, I know where it is."

"NU? So will you?"

She looked into his eyes. They sparkled like deep blue crystals in the starlight. "Yes. You'll be there waiting for me?"

"Of course."

Chapter 31

Gilde walked as fast as she could to the park. It was another frigid day and a blanket of snow had fallen the night before. But the sun was shining and her heart was light. In fact she was filled with joy and she couldn't wait to see William.

He was rubbing his hands together to keep them warm when he looked up and saw Gilde. A smile that rivaled the brightness of the sun came over his face.

"You look beautiful"

"My face is all red from the cold."

"Rosy cheeks become you, my dear." He said and smiled. Then he looked into her eyes bent down and kissed her softly

"Let's go into town or we'll freeze to death." She said

They walked four blocks into town. Gilde's legs hurt from the cold, but she had never felt as content as she did walking beside William. He looked so handsome and strong that she wanted him to put his arm around her. She looked up at him.

"I'm so cold…" She said fetchingly.

He smiled and put his arm around her. "You're my girl now. I guess it's alright for me to pull you close."

When they got to town they wandered through the shops trying to stay warm. Finally they found a used book store. It had a musty old smell and two floors of shelves filled with dusty books. Although it wasn't very warm, it was a lot warmer than being outside. Gilde and William spent several hours looking through books and discussing books they'd read. His eyes sparkled with such passion when he talked about the biographies he'd read of doctors who'd made huge strides in medicine.

"Someday, when this is all over, I am going to be a great doctor. I 've always wanted to do that."

"I know you will be a wonderful doctor." She hesitated. "William?"

"Yes, love."

He'd called her love. That threw her off and she blushed and looked away. He took her chin in his hand and with a tenderness that almost made her cry; he turned her face towards his. "What did you want to say?"

"I don't want you to go back to the navy. I am afraid for you." Her voice was so soft it was almost a whisper.

"I don't want to go. But I have to. If everyone backed out and no one went to fight the Nazi's, Hitler would take over the world. I can't expect other men to go and fight if I am not willing to. Isn't that right?"

She bit her lip. "I wish you were a doctor already. Then maybe you would be stationed at a local hospital"

"I have plenty of training to help as medic. But as much as I care for you, I can't stay here. I want to help the men at the front who need me. I'll be a medic and help the doctor on board the ship."

"But you could be there when they go in to battle."

He nodded and took her hand in both of his "Your hands are so small. And …cold."

"It's cold in here. And…I am nervous."

"I know. But now I have a special reason to return safely. And because of you I'll be extra careful."

William took Gilde to a restaurant for lunch. She couldn't remember the last time she'd been out for a meal. And she'd never been to such a fancy place. He opened the door for her and pulled out her chair. It made her feel pretty and special. He was tall, and heart wrenchingly handsome, his light brown hair cut short. His most attractive features were those eyes, azure blue eyes full of depth and compassion, and that smile. His smile felt like a secret embrace between them.

A waiter handed Gilde a menu. When she opened it, the entrees were listed but there were no prices.

Gilde read the menu over several times having no idea what to order. She had never been on a real date before but she did know that the man always paid the check. She was uncomfortable with the whole process, what if she ordered something that was very expensive. Without prices listed on the menu, she had no idea of what everything cost. If she were so bold as to ask William what to do, she might embarrass him. So, maybe she would just wait and order whatever William ordered. William was watching her and smiling. He could see that she was struggling. He reached across the table and put his hand on hers," Gilde "when he said her name it sent fireworks through her body. "Order whatever you want. This is a special day."

Gilde lifted her eyelids from the menu and their eyes linked.

"Can I chart this as our first official date?" William asked

"Yes." Gilde said. "Our first date." Gilde was blushing again.

"Or was our first date the other night at the old house that you are sure is haunted?"

"That was a lovely night. After we were inside the house it no longer felt haunted to me."

"I know. I knew it wouldn't. I want every date, every minute, every hour that we spend together to be special."

"You're really nice to me, William. "

"How old are you Gilde?"

"I don't want to tell you."

"Why?" he looked at her concerned.

"Because you'll think you'll think that I'm too young for you."

"Are you too young for me?"

"I hope not. I'm young but I've been through a lot and I feel a lot older than I am. But, the truth is, I'm only fifteen."

"You're right, fifteen is young, but you're not too young for me. Lots of Jewish couples marry young. And my intentions with you are respectful and proper. Like I said before, I wasn't raised exactly orthodox, but I was raised to respect women, so, I'm not looking for a good time girl. I want to get married and start a family, and it's important to me that my wife is Jewish and once the war is over I sure would like to try to keep a kosher home."

"Is that all you want from a girl? A wife to give you children and keep your house?"

"Not at all. I have to have feelings for her. Very special feelings. Like the feelings I have for you."

"Well, I'll tell you the truth; before I came to live with your family I didn't know anything about keeping kosher. Sharon and your mother have told me a little, but because of the rations they've had to make exceptions in the dietary laws just to survive."

"It's a lot of work. But I'd like to try to raise my children in a Kosher home. There is really no reason why, only because when I was a young boy that's the way it was in my house. It's a nostalgic thing I suppose. But, I wouldn't want to be so frum like the Weiss'."

"Frum?"

"I thought you knew a little Yiddish?"

"I do, a little, but not that word."

"It means pious, very religious."

"Oh I am glad that's not what you want. Because, quite frankly, I wouldn't know how to keep up with that."

"Boy oh boy, we're starting to sound pretty serious." He said

"Oh, I..." She stammered and looked away.

"Gilde, I am serious about you. That' why I am saying I would like my children to know the Jewish traditions. I'd like my son to have a bar-mitzvah at thirteen. I'd just like to keep up some of the stuff I was raised with. How do you feel about all of this?"

"I do have to admit that I wasn't raised this way. We had Shabbat dinner, my mother lit the candles. We celebrated Hanukkah, and Passover. But my father never fasted for Yom Kippur. I guess my family made their own rules. I don't know how you feel about that, but for the right person I could learn the traditions, and more about the religious practices."

"Am I that person, Gilde?" He said. "I guess what I am trying to say is that I have to leave here tomorrow afternoon. I don't have time to woo you the way I would like to. The way a decent fellow should woo a girl he would want to marry. And believe me if I had the time I would show you the way a beautiful and special girl like you should be treated. But, I like you Gilde. I like you a lot. I guess you could say, I more than like you. I think I might be falling in love with you."

"Oh..." she said and the menu slipped out of her hand and on to the ground. The waiter appeared immediately, picked it up and handed it back to Gilde. "I don't know what to say."

"Do you like me? Even a little?"

"A lot."

He smiled. I'm glad. I'm very glad. I know this is very soon, but I don't have time to waste. I ship out tomorrow. I want to ask you...if maybe you could think about us getting engaged. I mean I don't know if your feelings for me are as strong as mine are becoming for you. But just knowing you were here waiting for me to get home would give me the courage to go forward"

"Marriage?"

"Yes, marriage."

She was stunned.

"Just say you'll think about it."

"I will. I'll think about it." She said

"Would you like me to order for you?" William asked

"Yes, would you please, Wil?"

"Of course, anything for you, Gilde."

He ordered a beautiful meal. It seemed to be far more than the rations allowed. But Gilde didn't say anything. The food was wonderful and she was enthralled with William's company.

She watched him eat. His mother was right, he was slender and could use a few extra pounds.

They ate slowly wanting to stay in the warmth of the moment as long as they could, but finally it was time for Gilde to meet Sharon at school. "I want to be there when Sharon gets out of class so she doesn't suspect that I wasn't in school today." Gilde said

"I hate to part, but I think it's a wise choice." William said "It's probably best if we keep all of this quiet until you decide whether to accept my proposal."

Gilde nodded. So, in order to prevent any suspicion, Gilde would meet Sharon as she did every other day. William took Gilde's hand as they walked quickly towards the school. She liked him, she really liked him. But she hardly knew him.

"Now your little hand is even colder." He said taking her hand in his up to his lips and blowing warm air on her hand and then kissing it. Then he touched her face.

"I do like you William." She said

He pulled her head towards him and kissed her. The kiss was soft and sweet and it made her feel secure in a way she had never felt before. She did not have blood relatives in Britain. She didn't know what she would find when she returned to Germany. If she was engaged, she would have a future. God willing when the war ended she would have a husband and maybe in a few years a child. Then no matter what she found when she returned to Germany to look for her family, she wouldn't feel so lost and so alone. Yes, Gilde thought I could see a life with William.

"Well, Gilde, I am falling for you hard and fast."

"William, I really care for you too." She said

"Enough to marry me?"

"Yes… Yes. "

He lifted her up like she was weightless and spun her around then he kissed her lips again. She was giggling. "I am so happy Gilde. Can we tell my parents and sister tonight?"

"Yes." She said

"Then I guess it's alright to say it."

"To say what?"

"To say I love you." He said and kissed her. A tear dripped down her cheek. She was not alone any more. The Lawrence's were her family. William would be her husband.

"I love you too." She said and she meant it.

The tear had frozen on her chin. He tenderly wiped it away with his thumb. Then he kissed her again.

Sharon was just turning the corner as Gilde and William arrived. William left quickly.

"Was that Wil?" Sharon said

"Yes." Gilde answered.

"What was he doing here?"

"Oh nothing. I was just leaving school and he was here."

"What, that doesn't make sense, Gilde? Are our parents all right."

"Yes, everything is fine." Gilde smiled "Perfect in fact. So, Sharon, how was your day?"

Sharon just looked at Gilde skeptically. Gilde said nothing. Everything would be explained tonight.

Chapter 32

"Mazel Tov" Sam Lawrence stood up and clapped his hands. Lenore put her arms around Gilde and kissed her on the forehead

"Welcome to our family. You'll be our second daughter." Lenore said "I'm Kvelling, I'm so happy."

"And you'll be my sister." Sharon smiled then as soon as Lenore let go of Gilde, Sharon hugged her.

"So…let's go downstairs to the store and pick out a diamond so I can I make a ring for Gilde."

"Oh that's not necessary." Gilde said "You've done so much for me already."

"Of course it is necessary. You're marrying our son. Right William? Don't you want Gilde to have the most beautiful engagement ring?"

"I want my Gilde to have everything in the world. No chazeray for my future wife. And when I get out of the service, I am going to work hard and provide a good life for you, Gilde and God willing, our children." William said. His eyes were shinning with pride. Gilde could see how happy he was, and happiness overflowed from her too.

Gilde choose a small ¼ carat diamond that had been cut and polished in to an emerald shape.

"Are you sure you don't want something bigger?' William asked

"I'm sure. My hands are so small. This is perfect."

"And you just want a simple band?" Sam Lawrence asked "you know you can have whatever you choose."

"I know, and I am very grateful. But this is all I want. It's so much more than I ever expected."

"Well, I am going to stay up all night so that I can have it finished before William leaves in the morning. I want he should see it before he goes"

"That's not necessary Papa. I know you'll make my Gilde a beautiful ring." Then turning to Gilde William said "As long as my Papa has the diamonds, you should chose something bigger."

Gilde shook her head. "I'm happy with this ring. It's more than I would ever have hoped for." She said

"OY, she's such a mensch." Sam said "a treasure." He reached over and pinched Gilde's cheek. "Now it's your responsibility to bring me plenty of beautiful grandchildren. Such naches that will be for this old man. With pride I'll show all of my old friends my precious grandbabies."

Gilde blushed and looked away.

"Maybe we can take a photograph of the ring when it's finished and send it to Willie." Lenore said. "That way you won't be so rushed."

"Good idea." Sam answered.

The hours before William had to leave passed quickly. No one in the family wanted to go to sleep. They wanted to savor the time they had left with William. Everyone sat in the living room and talked, telling stories of William's years growing up, until five in the morning when they were all so tired they could no longer keep their eyes open. William's train was to leave at eleven in the morning. And although the family only had four hours of sleep they were all awake at nine. Mrs.

Lawrence used up all of the egg rations and made a breakfast of scrambled eggs. Everyone, even Sam, took just a little and said they were full leaving the largest portion for William.

Gilde sat beside her new fiancé. She was quiet. If only she could find the words that would convince him to stay. But there was nothing she could do or say and she knew as much. William's convictions were too strong. So, she just sat beside him praying that he would return.

Chapter 33

1941

It was late afternoon when Gilde and Sharon took the ration books for the family and went shopping for their rations. The jewelry business had fallen off even more since the beginning of the war. So because the family needed the money Lenore found a job driving a bus. Since she was working most of the time and Sam was trying to drum up business in the store, the household chores fell to Sharon and Gilde.

They were waiting in the butcher shop when they ran into a friend of Sharon's from school.

"Have you met my future sister in law, Gilde Margolis?" Sharon asked Wilma

"No, we've never met. But I didn't know William was engaged."

"Yes, he got engaged when he was on leave a couple of days ago."

"Your family must be very excited?"

"Yes. We are"

"But it must be difficult for you, Gilde to have your fiancé so far away. I can imagine how hard that must be. By the way, Gilde is a lovely but certainly an unusual name."

"Oh, thank you. Yes, everyone says that it's an odd name, and yes it is hard for me to be away from William when we just got engaged. Very hard. I wish he would come home."

"I know what you mean. I'm only in town for a few days. My brother was killed in action. She crossed herself. My parents got the death notice and I came home right away."

"Oh, I am so sorry." Sharon said.

Gilde felt sick. The words Sharon had just spoken poked at Gilde's greatest fear. "I'm sorry too." She stammered

"Yeah, me and my folks are brokenhearted. My mother is inconsolable. I'm afraid she's going to get sick. Worse yet, I still have another brother in the service and after this happened I'm sick with worry about him."

"Of course you are." Sharon said "I haven't seen you around town for a long time. Have you been gone?"

"I've been working in Birmingham in a factory building parts for planes for the war effort. I'm doing what I can to help."

"That's admirable. Very." Sharon said.

Gilde just nodded and tried to smile. All she could think about was William.

"Write to me sometime, let me know how you're doing." Wilma said to Sharon. "I'll give you my address."

"I will. I'll do that."

Wilma wrote her address and gave it to Sharon." We all have to do what we can to keep Hitler out of Britain. Because if the Nazi's ever come on our shores, it will be a dark day in hell for us."

Gilde felt like she was in a trance, her mind unable to function as she and Sharon stood waiting for their turn with the butcher.

"Are you all right?" Sharon asked.

"Not really. Are you?"

"Not really. She scared me. Of course we all know what can happen, but, when it gets this close to home it becomes more terrifying." Sharon said

"I know. I feel it too."

They finally finished making their purchases and walked home quietly for several minutes. A block from the apartment Sharon said "Wilma is a nice girl. But I don't think she knows that I am Jewish."

"You don't?"

"No, I don't think she'd be as friendly if she knew."

"Do you think that's why she was questioning my name, Gilde?"

"Maybe, who knows." Sharon said "There is far too much hate in this world."

Chapter 34

December 7th 1941

On the morning of December 7th, 1941 The Empire of Japan waged a sneak attack on the United States of America. Without warning Japanese planes plummeted bombs down upon the American Naval base at Pearl Harbor. America shook with rage, like a giant volcano about to erupt. The world stood breathless as President Roosevelt of the United States of America responded over the airwaves : **President Franklin D. Roosevelt**: Yesterday, December 7, 1941—a date which will live in infamy—the United States of America was suddenly and deliberately attacked by naval and air forces of the Empire of Japan.

The United States had now joined the allies as they entered the war. American service men enlisted by the thousands. As America came forth with a vengeance fighting on two fronts, in the Pacific against Japan and alongside her allies Great Brittan and Russia on the European stage. Isoroku Yamamoto, a Japanese general couldn't have been more correct when in reference to Japan bombing the US he said "I am afraid we have awakened a sleeping giant."

Chapter 35

1941

Gilde and William wrote to other fervently, like young lovers who are forced to be apart will do. Sometimes the mail was slow because of the war. But Gilde usually received a letter at least once a month. She would read the words over several times and then hold the letter to her breast. I have someone who loves me. She would think to herself. I am not alone in the world.

On a Tuesday morning late in February Sam Lawrence woke up with a terrible headache. He got out of bed to splash his face with cold water. When he turned on the light, he found that he was disoriented, dizzy and his vision was blurred.

"Lenore." He called out, but his speech was slurred. "Come quick. I don't feel right."

Lenore got up and ran into the bathroom where she saw that Sam was on the floor.. When she saw him, she screamed. In order to sooth her fear, he tried to get up but he couldn't. Both girls got up quickly and came running to the bathroom. When Gilde saw Sam on the ground, she ran to call for help.

An ambulance arrived and took Sam to the hospital. For Gilde the blaring lights of the ambulance and the alarming sound brought back terrible memories of the Nazi's. Gilde loved Sam like her own father and seeing him unable to move was horrifying. She dressed quickly. Then Sharon, Lenore and Gilde walked to the bus stop and waited. It took a half hour for the big red bus to turn the corner. They entered through the back paid their fare and sat down. No one spoke, because they dared not give voice to their fears that Sam might be dead.

Lenore was shivering. Gilde took her hand. Sharon took her mother's other hand. And thus they rode for a half hour until they reached a stop that was two streets from the hospital.

The corridor to Sam's room was stark blinding white and smelled of paint and alcohol. Gilde felt her hands trembling as the three women walked up to the reception desk.

"I'm looking for my husband, Sam Lawrence. He was brought in by ambulance" Lenore's voice was small and weak

"Have a seat in the waiting room. I'll let the doctor know that you're here." The receptionist said.

They did as they were told. The sat and they waited. Lenore was so nervous that she bit her lip and it was bleeding. Gilde had a handkerchief in her handbag. She gave it to Lenore to wipe the blood. And still they waited. It was taking too long. Gilde feared that Sam was already dead. If that was the case she would have to be strong for Sharon and Lenore. And worst of all she would have to tell William in her next letter.

Gilde gently rubbed Lenore's shoulder.

The hospital was busy, nurses in uniform raced from room to room. Doctor's wearing white coats dashed through the halls, sometimes in pairs. Still no one came to talk to the Lawrence's. Lenore had begun weeping softly. And the sound of it broke Gilde's heart, but even more than heart break it made her angry. She got up and went back to the receptionist.

"We need to speak to someone now. My father in law is in the hospital, he was taken by ambulance. We don't know if he is alive or not and we have been waiting for a long time. Please, find someone for us now." Gilde said. Her voice was stern. The receptionist was fairly young and Gilde's stern reproach affected her.

"I'll find someone. Give me five minutes."

"Five minutes. Please. We can't wait any longer. We're going out of our mind with worry."

"I promise. Just five minutes"

"Thank you." Gilde said but her voice was still stern

But the receptionist was true to her word and a doctor came to speak to them a few minutes later.

"Mrs. Lawrence?"

Lenore stumbled as she got up. Gilde reached for her. Sharon was shaking.

"Yes,"

"The good news is your husband is alive. The bad news is that he had a mild stroke. I can't say that he will be perfect, there may be some nerve damage but if all goes well, he'll be functional. However, it won't be an overnight recovery, it will take some time."

"Oh Dear God, thank you." Lenore said falling back down into the chair. She put her hands over her face and wept.

"Can we see him?" Gilde asked.

"Yes, how soon can we go in?" Sharon took Gilde's hand

"In a little while." The doctor said "I'll send someone out to get you when he is fully awake."

Chapter 36

Sam was in the hospital for three grueling weeks. Gilde and Sharon kept the business open which concerned Sam very much and he mentioned it constantly. But Gilde reassured him that because she had been helping him for so long, she knew enough about the work to take good care of things. Sam had liked Gilde from the start, but once she and William became engaged, Sam showed Gilde where the keys to the safe were. "You're part of our family now, Gilde" He'd explained that everything the family had of value was inside that safe. Gilde felt honored that he trusted her as much as he did and she was very careful to protect everything that Sam had shown her.

Every couple of days Gilde and Sharon made sure to stop by hospital for at least an hour. They usually went when Sharon got home from school. Gilde would close the shop and the two girls would take the big red bus over to see Sam.

Because Sam had always been so full of life, until he got sick, Gilde had lost sight of his age. But since the stroke, he looked older every day. Although he denied that he was in pain, Gilde could see the agony on his face. The area around his eyes was now deeply lined and he had little control over the left side of his body. For the first two weeks following the stroke he was unable to form words and so he didn't speak at all. His mouth hung limp and with a trembling hand and difficulty holding a pen he tried desperately to communicate by writing. Most times the writing was illegible. Finally, after a couple of difficult weeks Sam slowly found he was able to move his lips and make sounds. He tried to speak but his voice had changed. It seemed as if his tongue had gotten too big for his mouth and it was hard to understand what he was trying to say.

"Vision blurred. Sometimes, see double." Sam said

Gilde and Sharon nodded.

"Thank God you're alive, Papa." Sharon said "We have to be thankful for that. You'll get better."

Sam nodded his head and tried to smile, but only one side of his lips moved the other stayed stationary. "

"Gilde has been doing a wonderful job of watching the shop. So you don't have to worry about the business." Sharon said trying to give Sam words of comfort and encouragement.

"Gilde… a blessing." He tried to say.

One afternoon when Lenore was not at work, she joined Gilde and Sharon on their visit to see Sam.

Sam was sitting up in bed. Up until now, his pallor had been gray but his color was a little brighter and less gray today.

When they entered the hospital room, Gilde and Sharon kissed Sam's forehead. Then Lenore stood beside his bed and took his hand in hers.

"Something important … ask you." Sam stammered. Trying to make his speech as clear as possible. "Lives depend on me watch for fires. Someone does my job?"

"Don't worry Papa. Sharon and I take turns doing your job at the factory and we will keep doing it until you get home and are back to your old self." Gilde said patting Sam's arm.

When Sam was finally released from the hospital he was very weak. It was hard for him to walk or to see and he was out of breath with the slightest exertion. However, his speech had improved to the point where he could be understood when he talked. Sam told Gilde again and again that he was grateful for her help. But he was eager to get back to work, he felt old and unproductive.

"Stay in bed and rest for few more days, Papa" Gilde said. After she and William had become engaged Lenore and Sam told Gilde to call them Mama and Papa. They insisted on it and she loved it. She finally felt like she belonged somewhere. "I'll take care of everything."

"But what about school?" Sam asked.

"I've stopped going. I stopped when you were in the hospital. I've decided that I want to learn the business. Yes, that's what I want to do." Gilde said

"The business isn't what it was before the war. We aren't busy, we don't earn much money. You'd be better off in school" Sam said. When he spoke he still sounded like he had a mouth full of marbles, but Gilde had gotten used to it and she understood him perfectly now.

"Let Sharon go to school. She's much more studious than I am. I'll stay at home and work with you until you are all better. Then we'll see. I might decide to go back to school."

"If you take all this time off you'll probably fail a grade. That wouldn't be good for you."

"I'll be just fine. I am going to marry William and be a wife and mother anyway. School doesn't really fit into my plans anyway."

"Maybe Sharon could pick up your school work and you could study at home?" Sam said

"If that's what you want, Papa. I'll do it."

"It would make me happy."

"Then, I'll do it. Will you explain the situation to my teacher and bring my work home, Sharon." Gilde asked

"Of course. You know I will."

"I know." Gilde said "you're a good sister."

And so Gilde worked the business for a month until Sam was finally well enough to come back. At night she did her school work as she promised. When Sam returned, he was semi- functional. He limped very slowly and the left side of his face drooped.

While Sam had been out, Gilde remembered what she'd learned and began to repair watches and jewelry. She ran the business with the efficiency she inherited from her father, organizing everything. And when Sam returned he was surprised to find everything in better order than he'd left it.

Chapter 37

1942 May

It was a brisk spring morning. It had rained the night before and buds had begun to form on the trees in the yard. Sam had returned to work but he was not able to stay all day. After a few hours he was exhausted and returned to his bed. He was concerned with his oblation to watch for fires. But Gilde and Sharon assured him that they would not shirk the responsibility. It was a lot for Gilde. Between the shop, the school work Sharon brought home, and fire watching one night a week, she was constantly busy.

She was in the store. Her hair was pulled back with a black velvet headband and she was double checking a repair on a watch as the customer was waiting to make a payment.

"It's running perfectly now. Here have a look. Gilde said. When she looked up from the watch to the customer she saw William standing at the back of the store. Gilde dropped the customer's ticket on the display case and ran into William's arms and he lifted her in the air.

"Oh God, it's good to see you." She said. She was laughing and crying at the same time.

He kissed her. "I missed you, love. I really missed you…" William said.

"I'm going to leave the money I owe you on the counter." The embarrassed customer said

Gilde nodded. Her eyes never left William's face. "I missed you too, so much."

"What are you doing here in the shop? Shouldn't you be in school? Where's Papa?"

"I'm working. Your father was sick. He's better now. But, I've decided to help in the shop. How long can you stay?" She said squeezing the arm of his uniform. Wanting to hold on to him forever.

"Two days, then I ship out. This time for real."

"What do you mean for real? Where are they sending you?"

"I don't know. They won't tell us. But I'm pretty sure I'm leaving the country."

"What? Why won't they tell you where?" She squeezed his arm.

"It's top secret. But let's not worry about that now. I am here with you and it feels so good to see you and hold you. Let's enjoy these two days. What do you say?"

She squeezed him tighter.

"Damn you look beautiful." He said "Even more beautiful than I remembered. And every night since I've been gone, I would lay on my bunk and retrace every detail of your face." He kissed her again.

"I cherished your letters. I read them over and over. The paper you wrote them on is falling apart. That's how often I read them." She laughed a little

"Was it difficult to get paper to write to me?"

"Yes, but your father's connections helped."

He smiled "Gilde…"

"Yes?"

"Let's get married today. I love you. We have these two days…"

She interrupted him. "Yes let's."

"You'll marry me today?"

"Yes. I will."

"Yes!" He lifted her in the air and she laughed. "Yes."

Chapter 38

Gilde put a sign outside on the door of the shop that said "Back in an hour" then she locked up and she and William went upstairs to the apartment to see the rest of the family.

"Wil, you're home!" His mother screamed in excitement when she saw him. Then, she put her arms around him and squeezed. William hadn't realized how short his mother was. She'd always seemed so tall to him. He'd grown and she'd gotten shorter with age.

"How's Pa? Gilde said he was sick" William said.

"He's doing better. Come in and see him. When he sees you he'll be so happy." Then she called out "Sam, Willie's here."

Sam came limping out of the bedroom, he was smiling. "Willie. How'd you get home?"

"I have two days leave, Pa. What's the matter with you?" William saw his father limp and he saw that the side of Sam's face sagged.

"I'm fine. I had a little problem. But I'm much better now."

"Why didn't anybody tell me? Gilde, you never wrote anything about my father being sick. What happened?"

"You're father had a mild stroke. I knew you wouldn't be able to leave and come home. I didn't want to worry you when you were so far away."

"Gilde." He shook his head "You can't do this to me. I have to be able to trust that you'll tell me if anything is wrong. I need to be sure that you'll tell me, you're my lifeline, my connection to home…"

"If that's what you want William. I will. I was just trying to protect you."

"Yes it's what I want." His voice was harsh and louder than usual.

Gilde almost cried. She was hurt. He'd never been mean to her before, never had he spoken to her in that tone of voice. Tears threatened to fall from her eyes. William took a deep breath. "I'm sorry Gilde. I shouldn't have spoken so harshly to you. It was just the shock of seeing my father this way. Forgive me?"

She nodded. "Yes."

William walked over to Gilde and put his arms around her. This was the first time he'd shown her affection in front of his family and she could see that they were embarrassed. They all looked away. "I'm really sorry, Gilde. I would never do anything to hurt you. You have to believe that. I was just upset is all."

"I do believe it and I know you are upset."

"Gilde and I are going to get married today." William said "Right Gilde?"

"Yes, right." She smiled.

"Today?" His mother said.

"In the Rabbi's study." William said "Go and put on your prettiest dress, Gilde. You too, Ma, and when Sharon gets home from school we'll go to the Shul and see old Rabbi Silverman. Then I'll make Gilde my wife."

Chapter 39

"Rabbi Silverman," William greeted the Rabbi who had performed his bar-mitzvah when he was thirteen.

"William, boychick, how are you? It's good to see you...and, I see you brought the whole mishpocheh, the entire Lawrence family. It's always a pleasure to have you in my Shul. "

"We've come here today with a purpose." William said looking tall and handsome in his uniform "This is Gilde, she is my fiancée. I have two days leave and we want to get married."

The Rabbi nodded. "First let me say, Mazel Tov! She's a beautiful young lady."

"And she's a good girl a haimish girl, she'll make a good wife and mother." Lenore said

"We like her very much, she's already like a daughter to us." Sam said

"I'm glad to hear it." Rabbi Silverman smiled. Then he said to William "And because we are in war time your situation is not so unusual. Sometimes things have to be rushed in war time. So we will do things a little bit different than we usually do. I am sure God will understand" He smiled. "It just so happens that we have a four post canopy here. It's nothing fancy, just a cloth draped over four posts, but it will work. My Secretary and the caretaker who is one of our congregants can help hold up the canopy. Do you think you can manage to hold a post, Sharon?"

"Of course I can."

"Sam, are you strong enough?"

"I'll manage. My son will be married under a chupa."

The Rabbi took a bottle of wine down from one of the bookshelves in his study. "I keep this for very special occasions." He said and smiled "For the Kiddush."

"The blessing over the wine." William smiled.

"Yes that's right" Said the Rabbi. But first let's fill out the Ketubah, the wedding contract. Will your parents be coming, Gilde? I'd like your father to sign the Ketubah"

"No. I wish they were." Gilde said "My father is stuck in Germany. My mother too. I came here to Britain with the Kindertransport."

"You're Jewish I assume?"

"Yes, I am."

"It's funny but you sound British, you have no German accent."

"Sharon and I have been working on it for a long time and I've gotten rid of it."

"From what I am hearing it's not good for our people in Germany." Rabbi Silverman said

"No, it was bad when I left."

"Yes I know and we will say a prayer for our Jewish brothers and sisters in Germany. So, if your father's not here you'll have to sign the Ketubah, the marriage contract, for yourself, Gilde."

"I'll sign." She smiled.

The Rabbi wrote up the Ketubah and both William and Gilde signed the paper.

Before the wedding service began the Rabbi said a few words asking God to watch over the Jews all over the world.

Then the four people chosen to hold the posts held them up and created a chupa or canopy. The couple got beneath the canopy. Then Rabbi took a wine glass from the drawer of his desk and filled it half way with wine. Next he took his handkerchief out of his breast pocket.

And…the ceremony began.

Baruch, Attah, Adonai, Eloheinu…

When the Rabbi finished the prayers Gilde said her vows then William pledged his. They each placed simple gold bands that Sam had given them on each other's hands. Once the rings were in place the Rabbi handed the wine glass to Gilde. She took a sip and handed it back to the Rabbi who then handed it to William who emptied the glass.

Now, Rabbi Silverman wrapped the goblet in the handkerchief that he'd taken from his pocket and placed it on the floor at William's feet. William stomped on the handkerchief wrapped package. The sound of the chalice bursting into a million tiny shards brought a chorus of 'Mazel Tov" from everyone in the room.

"May you have as many healthy and happy years together as there are tiny bits of glass in that Kerchief." Sam said

William kissed Gilde and even though the world was in flames with war, Gilde was so happy she felt like she could fly.

Chapter 40

The Rabbi said Mazel Tov and shook William's hand. He said a special blessing for William because he was leaving to fight and wished him a safe return.

Then each member of the family embraced Gilde and welcomed her.

"You are already like a daughter to us." Sam said "Only now it's official."

"Mazel Tov." Sharon said hugging Gilde. "Sister."

Gilde hugged Sharon tightly

"And you're my precious second daughter." Lenore said

"Today is a very special day for our little family. Let's all go out and have a meal." Sam said. "I know a restaurant where there are no rations.

They gathered around a round table. Real white bread was served, not the grainy brown bread that had become a staple since the war.

"Gilde was such a help to us when I was sick." Sam explained to William. "She took over the business. She took care of everything. It's a good thing too. Because neither you nor Sharon ever wanted to learn anything about the Jewelry business."

"Sharon, you're still going to the university in the fall aren't you?" William asked

"Yes, I'm hoping to go. Although a lot depends on the war."

"Of course she is going. I am feeling much better. Gilde and I are partners we'll run the business together…" Sam said

"Is this what you want Gilde?"

"Yes, it is."

"Are you sure?"

"I'm sure."

"You're not obligated you know."

"I know." She smiled "I asked your father if I could help him in the store before he got sick. Then when he needed me, I knew enough to be able to work the business."

William took Gilde's hand. "My beautiful wife." He said and smiled. She blushed and Sam said "This calls for a bottle of wine. We have to make some toasts."

Chapter 41

Gilde couldn't look at the rest of the family as they said goodnight when she and William went to his bedroom. She kept her face cast down to the floor until the door closed. Of course it was expected that the Newlyweds would sleep together. After all they only had two nights as a married couple before William shipped out again. But Gilde's face was scarlet with embarrassment because the family knew what was going to happen behind William's closed bedroom door. Gilde was a virgin and this sort of thing was very private to her.

For months, William had written Gilde beautiful romantic letters but now that they were, alone and the time had come to make love, she was nervous and shy.

"I brought you a present." William said

"Oh? You didn't have to."

"I wanted to." He smiled. "Give me a minute. Sit down on the bed and close your eyes."

She raised her eyes and looked at him. "What did you do William Lawrence?"

"Come on, close your eyes so I can surprise you."

She did as he asked.

"You can open them."

He handed her a pair of real silk stockings and a bar of sweet smelling soap. "This stuff was hard to get. But I wanted you to have it. I wish I could have brought you more."

"Oh William, I've never had silk stockings before. I'll save them for special occasions."

"If you like them, I'll try to get another pair and send them to you."

"I love them. But this is plenty. I have no place to wear silk stockings. My cotton ones are just fine for working at the store and going shopping for food." She smiled "I'll save these for us. For when you come home" She said then she put her arms around him and was overcome with emotion. "Just come home to me, safely. That's all I ask."

"I will Gilde. Don't be afraid."

"I'll count the days." She said

"I have a single Yahrzeit candle. It's the only candle I have. I've been saving it for a long time. I am going to light it…" William got up and took it down from a shelf and then lit the candle. He turned off the light. A golden glow came over the room.

William sat down beside Gilde. "You're trembling," he whispered. She nodded her head. After reaching up to caress her face he leaned over and brushed his lips against hers. She touched his face. "I love you." She said

"I love you too, Mrs. Lawrence. And when this war is over, I am going to come home to you and be the best husband any woman ever had."

He kissed her again. "Let me take your shoes off." He said getting down on his knees and removing her shoes. Then he gently raised and massaged each foot. No one had ever massaged her feet before. It was calming. Then he kissed her calf. She looked down into his eyes, they were even deeper blue by the light of the candle.

William stood up and raised Gilde from the bed and into his arms. Then he kissed her gently at first, then more passionately. He took his time, didn't rush. Slowly he undressed her until she had nothing on but panties and a bra Gilde had never been naked in front of a man before and she wondered what he thought of her body.

It was as if he had read her mind "In case you're wondering what I'm thinking , I'm thinking that you're the most beautiful woman I have ever seen. Even now as I am looking at you, I can't believe that you're my wife. How did an average fellow like me ever end up with a magnificent wife like you? I am blessed. God has truly smiled on me."

His compliments reassured her, but she blushed.

"Come lay down beside me. Let me hold you in my arms. Let me remember the smell of your skin and the silk of your hair."

She got into bed and he quickly undressed himself. Then he lay beside her and stroked her hair, his fingers cherished her neck. He kissed her lips, her eyes. She sighed. Something inside of her stirred and the fear she'd felt earlier turned to desire. All of her nerve endings were responding to his adoring touch and he knew how to gently coax her body until she was aching to feel him inside of her.

With loving hands he undid her bra and removed her panties.

He took something from the night table, tore open the paper and smoothed it over his erect penis. Then he straddled her and looked down in to her eyes.

"What is that?" she asked

"It's something I learned about in medical training. I don't want to bring a child into the world until this war is over."

That was all he said. Then not to spoil the mood he leaned

down and kissed her lips then gently kissed her breasts "My beautiful Gilde…my one true love, my beshert. I will always be good to you all my days on earth."

He moved slowly, very slowly. She felt a single stab of pain as their bodies joined to become one and then the pleasure was more glorious than any she had ever felt before.

They lay wrapped in each other for several minutes. Gilde felt William's heart beat against hers. "I should put the candle out, so we will have a little left to use again." He whispered softly in her ear.

She nodded. "You're right."

Chapter 42

Gilde relished the warm strength of William's arms as he held her close to him through the night. They made love again in the morning. Then fell back asleep for two more hours. When they woke up they were both so hungry that the need to eat forced them to leave the bed.

The family was in the living room. Gilde still couldn't look anyone in the eyes.

William had two slices of toast with margarine and marmalade, Gilde had one.

"What would you like to do today?" he asked. "Would you like to go and see a film?"

"No, I don't want to spend our time together in a dark theater. I want to look at you."

"Then let's take a long walk…"

"Yes, let's do that."

"We can talk about the future. I want you to tell me all of your dreams so I can write them down and make them come true one at a time…."

They walked arm in arm down several streets, passing the park, and then the Shul where they had just gotten married. William took Gilde's hand in his. She looked up at him and smiled.

"William, I was so worried the whole time you were gone. When I wrote to you and asked where you were stationed you never answered. Why?"

"Top secret. We aren't supposed to send information like that through the mail."

"Can you tell me now? Were you in battle?"

"No, I wasn't. I've been training at a training facility. But I wasn't allowed to divulge the location. Just in case, the letter somehow got into the wrong hands. Then the Nazi's could bomb our training base"

"Can you tell me now?"

"I'll tell you that it was in Britain."

"Is there a chance that you might be in Britain for the rest of the war? Maybe you won't see any battles at all?" She held her breath saying a silent prayer that this might be true.

"No, love, I got this two day leave because when it's over I ship out. I don't know where they're sending me."

"Oh William." She turned and hugged him. He kissed her hair. "I'm so scared. Are you afraid?"

"Of course I am. Only an idiot wouldn't be afraid. But I have you to live for, so I'll be extra careful."

"Please…" She said, her hands were trembling "be extra careful."

That night as William slept Gilde nuzzled her face into his neck and listened as he took each slow easy breath. Where were they sending him? She didn't push him for an answer, because even if he knew, she didn't want to know. Her lips brushed his neck and in his sleep he pulled her closer to him. It was hard to believe that she was a married woman. It was even harder to believe that she had no idea when she would see her beloved husband again.

The precious seconds passed so quickly that Gilde couldn't believe that the magical hours with William were coming to an end. She sat on the edge of the bed watching as William was packing his duffel bag preparing to leave again. He took down his uniform shirt that had been hanging on a hanger in the closet. Gilde had taken extra time to make sure it was pressed perfectly for him. He laid it on the bed. She reached over and ran her fingers over the fabric, but what she really wanted was to bury her head in his shirt and cry. As he was carefully folding the rest of his things Gilde noticed the long lean muscles in his arms flex with the movement. My husband is so good-looking. She thought. He doesn't even realize how handsome he is. Not that it mattered to her right now, right now all that mattered was his life. She had to practice control or she would have started crying and begged him to stay. She might even have fallen down on her knees and held on to his legs so he couldn't walk, so he couldn't leave. If only somehow it were in her power, she would do anything to keep him safe. But she knew he couldn't stay and even if he could, he wouldn't. Integrity, that's what William called it. He loved her, she saw it in his face every time he looked at her, and she knew that he wished he didn't have to leave her. But, Gilde knew even before she'd signed the marriage license that she was wedding a man with convictions. A man who would do what was right rather than what was comfortable, or easy. That was why he'd enlisted and why he was going now. She loved him for his strong character, and at the same time, she hated it. Right at this very moment in time, she wished he were a coward, a coward who would shirk his responsibilities so that he could stay safely at home in her arms.

But finally, the time to go had come, the farewell kisses had to end. William held her tightly "You be a good girl, and you stay safe. I'll be back. And, take care of mom and dad. Alright?"

She nodded tears had stained her cheeks.

"Listen Gilde. I'll be just fine. Don't you worry about me. " William said, he smiled at her and touched her face "I love you with all my heart." He said and then he left.

From the window, Gilde watched as William swung his duffel bag over his shoulder. Her eyes were glued to his form until he turned the corner and she could no longer see him.

Reaching down she turned the wedding band on her finger and whispered, "Come home to me…"

Chapter 43

June 1942

The cloudless blue sky and bright sunlight of the June morning made it hard to believe that there was a war going on. Tender baby blades of grass were poking through the ground. Tiny flowering buds had formed on some of the trees, and Mother Nature seemed totally unaware of the pain and suffering of mankind. Gilde and Sharon sat outside on the stoop in the front of the building sipping weak tea. Gilde had wrapped her hair into a twist so it wasn't hanging on her neck.

"Do you ever wake up at night in a panic? I mean in total fear?" Sharon asked

"For William."

"Yes, of course for William, but for us too. I mean what if we lose the war? What if the Nazi's come here and take over Britain, what then?"

"I've thought about that. If I let myself think about it too much, I'll be paralyzed with fear. So, I try to put it out of my mind and I try to believe that we'll win. Believe me, I was a child in Germany, I know how brutal the Nazi's are. I will never forget the night that my father was arrested. He was arrested for nothing. Nothing except being a Jew."

"If they get to our shores, "Sharon sighed "It won't only be the Jews here who will suffer, it will be all of the people here in Britain."

Gilde nodded. "Let's hope our brave soldiers can keep them away from our shores. And let's pray that William comes back safely."

Sharon nodded. They sat quietly looking at the winter turning to spring

Then Gilde spoke "What's left of the inventory of jewelry from before the war is running low. I don't know what we will use to trade on the black market once it's gone. The rations that they give us are very small. I suppose we'll have to adjust the best we can."

"Mama hardly earns enough to keep a roof over our head. And Papa is far too sick to go to work anywhere. He can't even go back to the fire watching. And as you know, the rent for the store is more money than the store brings in every month"

"I know. Believe me I know all of it. And poor Papa, he's lucky to stay awake for two hours at time. He comes down here to the store when he can, but he gets tired so quickly." Gilde said "We are always a few weeks behind on the rent. So far, we're paying it, but just barely. I don't know how long we can hang on. Do you think that the landlord will put us out on the street?"

"I don't think they will, they've known my family for years, but you know how Papa hates to be indebted to people. He is always saying that he is not a schnorrer, he says that he always paid his own way and never expected charity from anyone." Sharon said. "Before the war I was planning to go to the University, but I am thinking about going to work instead. I could probably get a full time job as an overnight firewatcher. Or I might even get them to train me to drive an ambulance. I think I'd like to be a part of a rescue team it would make me feel like I was doing something worthwhile."

"Going to school has always been your dream. You'd have to give it all up."

"Yes, but what difference does it make. With the war going on I am not going to be able to go to the University. I was hoping it would be over by now. But, in a few months I'll be eighteen and then I'll have to register for a job working for the war effort anyway. Why not start now?"

"I can see what you mean. Every day I wish it would end, but only if we win. If God forbid we don't, things will be much worse than they are now.

Chapter 44

September 1942

A month earlier, in early August, Sharon got a job as an ambulance driver in Stoke Newington, London. After a month had passed in order to save the daily bus fare she moved in with Frances, a friend who lived walking distance from the ambulance station. Frances was part of the same rescue team as Sharon and working together in emergencies they'd become close friends as they learned to depend upon each other. They worked well together, and often joked that they knew instinctively what the other was thinking. Most weekends Sharon tried to come home. Sometimes she brought Frances with her. Sharon and Frances had a bond that was deeper than the bond Sharon and Gilde had shared. They cast knowing glances back and forth. Sharon sometimes whispered in Frances' ear. Gilde felt left out, and watching them, she realized how much she missed having a surrogate sister in the house.

The business was failing miserably. They had not been able to make the rent the previous month and now it was time to pay again and they were a month behind. Lenore had talked to Gilde about closing the shop. But they both knew that Sam would be hopeless if they closed the business and it might have an effect on his health. He'd worked at that little shop for his entire life. It was all he knew. Every day he forced himself to come downstairs for at least a couple of hours. It was the only reason Sam had to get out of bed and without it, Gilde and Lenore were afraid he would slowly fade away. The results of that could be fatal.

Since Sharon left, Gilde spent a lot of her time alone. Sam was asleep, the store was empty and Lenore was at work. Most of her spare time she spent thinking of William or writing to him. It was hard to get her hands on any paper. Money was tight and spending it for paper seemed frivolous, but she'd made friends with Sam's black market connection and occasionally they would bring her a few sheets as a gift. Gilde had also taken up knitting. An old lady who attended the same shul came to the shop one day to have an old watch fixed. It didn't need much work and the old woman didn't have much money. "No charge today." Gilde had said feeling sorry for her. "You're a good girl. How about if I teach you to knit as a payment? I'm very good at it?"

And so that was how Gilde learned to knit. It proved to be a useful past time. If an old sweater, hat or mittens became worn or unbearable, she took it apart and then used the yarn to make something new. With the clothing rations, it helped to be able to reuse everything.

Although she hadn't shared her fears with anyone because she didn't want to alarm them, Gilde was riddled with worry. She hadn't received a letter from William in over a month. In fact, the last correspondence she'd received was in July. She checked the mail every day, and she knew that his family had not heard from him either because she always got the mail and there had been no letter. It is just the mail. She told herself. The mail is slow. But her fear filled her belly and in her heart she knew something wasn't right.

Then it came…the telegram from the British War Office. She'd tried to fight the nagging dread but in truth she'd been expecting it. And even though she'd known it was coming when she saw who had sent it her heart dropped even before she opened it. The boy who had delivered the telegram stood at the door waiting for a tip. Gilde was too stunned to get him any money. In fact she didn't even thank him for making the delivery. She just took the paper and closed the door. Her heart was beating wildly. The paper cut her finger as she forced the letter open. Blood dripped on the white sheet as she read the words that had haunted her every nightmare since William had left turning the corner of the street and disappearing to where she could no longer see him. "We deeply regret to inform you..." the letter began….

She read on. He had been somewhere off the coast of France. His ship was destroyed; a memorial would be erected at a later date.

This couldn't be true. It wasn't supposed to happen his way. All they had together as a married couple were two days? William would never hold her in his arms again. "Why God? Why? Haven't you taken enough from me? Why William too?"

Sam was asleep, Lenore was at work. Sharon was not at home. Gilde had to cope with this sad and horrifying moment all alone.

She read the telegram again hoping that she'd somehow made a mistake. But, she hadn't. What happened, how did he die? Did he suffer? Oh God she hoped he hadn't suffered. Her dear sweet lover, husband, and best friend. Gone forever...no more hope, no more letters.

Gilde slumped down on the sofa and put her face in to her hands. "Oh William…all of our dreams….all of our hopes…the home and children we'll never share…." The cut in her heart was so deep that she wept a loud.

Chapter 45

Gilde told Lenore about William. Lenore stood unable to speak, trembling when she heard the news. Then she began to cry. She reached out to take Gilde in her arms. But Gilde wanted to be alone. Her pain and loss was too great to share. She wanted to bury her face in William's pillow. She hadn't washed the pillowcase since he left. Now she never would. If there was even a trace of his essence, still there she wanted to inhale it, to take it deep inside of her and hold it there forever. Gilde walked slowly up the stairs to the room she and William had shared for those two nights. Two nights she would remember for the rest of her life. Her body felt heavy and burdensome. Once she was alone she threw herself on the bed where she and William had made love and buried her tears in his pillow. Let Lenore call Sharon, or even worse tell Sam. She couldn't hold anyone else up. Her grief was too much and she just couldn't bear it.

Chapter 46

When Lenore told Sam about William, he turned over in his bed and stared at the wall.

Sam died that night. He had a heart attack in his sleep. Gilde didn't find out until the morning when the ambulance was making a lot of noise taking his body away. She was alerted by the roaring of the siren and all of the movement in the hallway, and then the strange voices in the house. Gilde would have liked to stay locked in her dark room forever, until she too died. But there was far too much commotion in the house for her to remain hidden in her bedroom.

She wore her housecoat over her nightgown with an old pair of slippers that were broken and flapping as she walked. She'd meant to fix them, but she kept forgetting. Right now, she no longer cared.

Lenore was sitting curled up in the corner of the lumpy sofa and weeping. Gilde sat down beside her and ran her fingers over the floral fabric.

"What happened?" Gilde asked gently

"I told Sam about Will last night. He died in his sleep. I found him this morning."

"Oh my God." Gilde put her arms around Lenore and held her. Lenore laid her head on Gilde's shoulder and watched as two medic's carried Sam's body covered with a sheet, out on a stretcher. Gilde rubbed Lenore's back. They sat that way for almost an hour then Gilde asked "Did you call and tell Sharon?"

"Yes, I called. She should be on her way home." Lenore's shoulders slumped. She'd lost so much weight since the food rations began, and now the tragedies of the past two nights were carved in deep wrinkles on her face. Her eyes were sunken and red. Gilde looked at her and felt guilty for not having embraced her the previous evening when Lenore had tried to hug her. Yes, it was true, Gilde was hurting, and Gilde had lost her husband. Last night the emptiness and the ache inside of Gilde was eating her from the inside out and all she wanted was to bear the weight of the pain alone in her dark room, but she was being selfish, should have thought about Lenore. After all, Gilde wasn't the only one who'd been shattered, her mother in law had lost her son. Gilde should have been with Lenore to give her strength when she told Sam. But Gilde had thought only of her own pain and now she was overcome with grief and regret about how she'd behaved. And, to add to the weight of the tragedy that had become her life, her father in law who was such a good friend was gone now too.

"I'll make us some tea." Gilde said to Lenore, her heart was heavy, but she filled the pot with water and put it over the gas flame then she sat back down beside Lenore and waited for the water to boil.

Lenore rambled incessantly, going on in fits of nostalgia about William when he was a child and Sam when they were first married. Gilde listened because she knew Lenore needed to talk, but she wished she could get away and be alone.

Chapter 47

Sept 1942

Sharon and Frances arrived and Gilde was glad to see them. She was weak and overwhelmed. And Lenore needed comforting, perhaps they could take over with Lenore for a while. Gilde could use the break. Frances was a blessing, she made all of the funeral preparations for the family. She telephoned Rabbi Silverman who arrived at the house within the hour. He arranged for the funeral home to take care of Sam's body. Then Frances contacted all of the people on a list of close friends that Lenore dictated to her. As Gilde watched Frances comfort Sharon, she realized what she had overlooked before. Sharon and Frances were lovers. It was apparent to Gilde in the way they communicated with each other with their eyes. Gilde had been jealous of Sharon's closeness to Frances, but now she understood. It was the same closeness she'd shared with William. Gilde had not lost her surrogate sister, Sharon had not replaced her. Sharon had found her true love. It was good that Lenore didn't see the relationship for what it was. She would have been upset. And right now, Lenore couldn't cope with much more. Gilde would never mention it to her or to Sharon. But as she watched Sharon and Frances together a lot of things became clear to her. Like why Sharon had never shown an interest in any of the boys they met. Gilde smiled to herself. Although she was facing agonizing grief, she was glad that at least her dear sister Sharon had found happiness.

The burial for Sam was to be the following day. There would be a service at the chapel for both William and Sam. But because there was no body the service at the gravesite would be only for Sam. Rabbi Silverman called one of the congregants who had been a friend of Sam and Lenore's to act as the Shomer and stay with Sam until the burial. Later that night Frances put together a small meal and tried to insist that the family eat something. But no one was able to eat.

The following day they walked to the chapel for the memorial service. Rabbi Silverman told wonderful stories about Sam's kindness and generosity. Then since the Rabbi had known William all of his life. He told a funny story about William preparing for his bar-mitzvah. Tears came to Gilde's eyes as the Rabbi talked about the wedding between William and Gilde. He mentioned a private conversation he'd had with William years before he'd ever met Gilde. William had asked the Rabbi questions about looking for his beshert. "How will I know when I find her, how will I be sure that she is the right one? William asked me one Friday night after services." Rabbi Silverman said "I told him your heart will tell you William." The Rabbi looked directly at Gilde. "The day William and Gilde came to me to ask me to marry them William turned to me and whispered. You were right, Rabbi, my heart has spoken. Gilde is the one"

Gilde wept openly. She imagined William as a younger man asking the Rabbi about his bershert. She thought about how kind William was to her, about how he'd surprised her at the old abandoned house, about the North Star. She couldn't remember what life was like before she loved William, she couldn't recall how she felt before she knew him. Now, she had no idea how she was going to go on with her life without him."

The entire group walked to the cemetery which was just a street away from the Synagogue. Gilde stood beside Lenore on one side, Sharon stood on Lenore's other side. The heat of summer still lingered. A thin line of sweat trickled down the back of Gilde's neck and found its way in to the black dress she'd borrowed from Sharon. The sun beat down on Gilde's head and shoulders. This was all too much. Her eyes burned from crying and her throat was raw and dry. The Rabbi was speaking, but she couldn't hear him. Her heart was screaming in pain. It was saying that after today her life would never be the same. How many times would she have to change course, she had been uprooted so many times? How many people who she loved would she have to lose before she could finally go to her own rest?

Most of the people who were at the cemetery had been at the chapel, they'd come up and said their condolences to Gilde, Lenore and Sharon. They were neighbors, friends from the Shul, customers from the store. They were gathered in a circle. Some of them patted Lenore's arm trying to give her strength. A customer came up behind Gilde forcing her to turn around. "I'm so sorry for your loss." She said. Gilde nodded.

The woman had made Gilde look behind her. What she saw was all of their dear friends, standing in the hot sun at the cemetery, so devoted, and proud in their worn clothes and wholly shoes. There was no doubt that she'd suffered from some anti-Semitism in the UK. The British were not perfect. But she couldn't help but admire them, the English were fighters, no matter what was thrown at them, they refused to surrender they would not be broken. All of the people she knew had endured so much since the beginning of the war, the death of friends or family, fear of invasion, and terrible shortages of everything, with the bravery of lions. William was born and raised in London, and she could say without a doubt that he had been a fighter. Tears filled her eyes. She was broken without him, but so proud of his courage, his character, and the wonderful integrity that was her dear William.

Sharon wept softly. Frances patted her arm and whispered something softly in her ear.

Lenore was dry eyed, but grief worn and disheveled. Her eyes were bloodshot and her hair which had turned gray over the past year had not been combed.

In a deep haunting voice that broke the silence of the afternoon, the Rabbi began the Hebrew prayers. Gilde had never learned Hebrew, but the musical rhythm of the soulful words expressed the depth of sadness and loss in her soul.

When he finished the prayers the Rabbi said in English "This war has brought tragedy to many families. Today we must trust in God's plan as we say our goodbye's to Samuel Michal Lawrence and his son William Jacob Lawrence….."

There was no breeze that day, only relentless heat. Gilde watched the Rabbi and remembered how happy she was the day she'd married William. It was the best day of her young life. Her heart had never been so joyful. And in equal measure her heart had never been as sad as it was today.

The casket was lowered into the ground. The family each took turns shoveling a small bit of earth upon the grave. This was the Jewish way of saying goodbye.

Gilde walked silently beside Lenore, Sharon and Frances, all the way back to the apartment. Mrs. Weiss the neighbor who lived next door had set up the Shiva. She'd left a towel and a little bit of water in small glass on the steps. It was a good thing it was only a bit of water because recently a water shortage had been declared. Now bathing was to be done once a week. People living together were expected to use the same bathing water and most importantly, bathtubs were only to be filled to four inches deep. For Gilde this was the most difficult of all the rations. Sharon knew how fastidious Gilde was so she always insisted that Gilde bathe first. Gilde was generous about sharing her rations, but this was one thing she relished and never offered to give up.

Lenore arrived at the door first. She carefully poured a couple of drops of the precious water on to their hands then dried them with the towel before entering the Shiva house, the house of mourning. Next was Gilde and then Sharon. This was a symbolic a cleaning of the hands which was the Jewish tradition for those returning from a cemetery following a funeral. Then each of the visitors who'd come to pay their respects followed suit

Gilde didn't know where Mrs. Weiss had gotten the food, but a small spread was laid out on the table. There were a few slices of brown bread cut into quarters then toasted and smeared with a thin coat of margarine, a few slices toasted and thinly covered with canned beans, and a few more with a light spread of marmalade. And two eggs sliced very thin. The mourners removed their shoes. They would spend the entire seven days of the Shiva in their stocking feet, sitting on hard surfaces. Out of respect the visitors waited until the mourners, the immediate family, had taken their food. Gilde had no appetite. She put a half slice of bread with margarine on a plate and went to sit down. Mrs. Weiss had done a good job of preparing the house. All of the mirrors were covered with sheets, so that the mourners would not see their own grief. This would normally continue for the next seven days, but Sharon had an important job to do, and it was necessary for her to return to work the following morning.

Sharon and Frances sat close to each other in the corner. While Gilde sat beside Lenore. Neither of them was able to eat.

The Rabbi had gathered ten old men who were friends of the family and members of the congregation to do a minion, prayers for the dead. Gilde had never attended a traditional Jewish funeral before. The customs were strange to her. She wasn't sure what they all meant, but her grief was far too great for her to bother asking. She sat quietly beside Lenore. Friends of the family came over to say they were sorry and share pleasant memories of the deceased. Some of the visitors brought a few cookies, or a few small pastries. It was a custom to bring something sweet and leave it for the mourners and guests. Then each visitor was to have a bite of something sweet before walking out of a Shiva house. But during wartime it was very difficult to come by any baked goods. The reason for a Shiva is to help to divert the family from their grief and the visitors seemed to distract Lenore, to help her escape the pain even for a few hours. But it didn't help Gilde at all. If it weren't for Lenore, Gilde would have retreated to her room and stayed there. Every night after the visitors left, Gilde went into her room and reread all of William's letters.

By the seventh day most people had already come to pay their respects. Very few were coming any more. Sharon had returned to work several days earlier and so only Gilde and Lenore were left in the flat.

"You know, just between us, Willie was Sam's favorite. He was so proud of that boy. From the time Willie was born, he saw great things in him. I guess maybe every man wants a son."

Gilde nodded. "I know Sam loved him."

"I am not surprised that losing Willie was what put Sam over the edge. He was so sick and weak already."

"Yes…" Gilde said

"I have something that I want to talk to you about." Lenore cleared her throat.

"Go on." Gilde said

"First off, you should be filing for a widow's pension. You're entitled to it. Do, you know that?"

"Yes, I know." Gilde said "I will."

"I'm telling you this for two reasons. One, we are going to have to close the business. Now, with Sam gone, there is no point in keeping it open and paying rent on it. And second of all…I think I'd like to move to a smaller flat. Something more affordable. You're welcome to come with me if you want to."

"I've been thinking a lot about what I am going to do now. I've decided that I am going to sign up for nurses training. I want to do something that would continue what William started. Something that would make William proud. Do you understand what I mean? I want to work for the war effort. If it's possible I'd like to be sent to the battle front and work with wounded soldiers."

"That's terribly dangerous, Gilde. When you turn eighteen you' can get a local job and help with the war effort that way"

"Yes, I know. But I think I want to go to nursing school. I want to save lives the way William did. I guess I want to carry on where he left off…"

"Do you know where you are going to go to school yet?"

"Yes, I am going to try to get in at the hospital in Birmingham. I've heard good things about Queen Elizabeth Hospital. From what people are saying they have a good nursing program. It costs twenty pounds to get in. But the training is supposed to be superior. So, that's my plan for the future I suppose. One thing I've learned, is that my future is always changing." Gilde smiled a sad half smile.

"Do you need some money? I have a little that I can give you"

"I'm all right, William gave me some money before he left. He said it was in case of an emergency."

"Will you stay in contact with me?"

"Of course. I don't suppose you have an address where I can write to you yet?"

"Not yet. But if I am accepted in to the nursing program I will write to you through the Queen Elizabeth Hospital and forward my address." Gilde said

"Write to Sharon, because I am moving to a smaller flat. So, I'll stay in touch with Sharon and she can tell you where I am. I will miss you Gilde."

"I will miss you too; you've been like a mother to me…"

Chapter 48

1942

The night before she left London to go to apply for the nurses program, Gilde packed the few things that she owned. She called Sharon to let her know about her plans to study nursing. Lenore, had already moved in with an old friend three days prior. But she was looking for a place of her own. The family had only two days rent left paid on the apartment. So, Gilde was leaving just in time. She and Sharon reminisced for a little while about the past and about William. Then heartsick and frightened of the future Gilde went back to the bed she had shared with her husband for just a few precious days and tried to sleep. When the sun rose she got up in order to get ready. It was a three-hour bus ride from London to Birmingham. She planned to take an early bus. Then just in case of travel delays she'd arranged her appointment at the hospital for late afternoon.

Gilde wore the nicest dress she owned for the appointment with the admissions office at the Queen Elizabeth hospital. Her dress was old and she'd repaired it more times than she could count. But it was clean and ironed and for the first time, she wore the silk stockings that William had given her. She had styled her long hair in a neat twist with a curl at the top which was the latest fashion. Gilde wanted to make a good impression, she wanted to get accepted into the program. "God forgive me" she whispered as she removed Alina's Star of David necklace. Being Jewish might prevent them from choosing her. Then she whispered "I'm sorry my love, my dear husband, I know you would understand" as she removed her wedding ring. Being a married woman could be prohibitive, why give them any reason to turn her away?

When the bus let Gilde off, she saw that Birmingham looked as bad as London. The same bombed out buildings surrounded her and dust and smoke filled the air. This came as no surprise, after all, Gilde knew that Birmingham was where a lot of the factories were that supported the war effort. This was where they built army vehicles, planes, arms, and more. For a moment, she thought that perhaps she should have gone to a hospital in a safer area. But then she squared her shoulders and remembered William's bravery. I will carry on his work. She thought.

The Queen Elizabeth Hospital was a large, modern, and imposing building. Not at all like the infirmaries she had seen pop up all over London. As she went inside to report to the nurses training admissions office, she was intimidated. After all, she had no medical training or background. How was she ever going to convince them to accept her?

"Gilde Lawrence?"

"Yes…"

"Miss Brown will see you now. Go through the double doors to the office on the right." The receptionist a young attractive girl with her long hair in a bouncy pony tail said.

"Thank you."

Gilde knocked on the door of the office. A large sturdy woman who looked like a man in the face, but had heavy breasts and wore her salt and pepper hair very short looked up from a pile of papers. She tapped the pencil she was holding a few times stared at Gilde, then put the pencil down on the desk.

"Well? Come in…"

Gilde walked in.

"Sit." The woman said critically scrutinizing Gilde, looking her up and down. "So, you want to be a nurse?'

"Yes. I want to save lives, to help in the war effort."

"Do you know the rules here?"

Gilde shook her head "No, I'm sorry I don't."

"Well, before you decide that this is where you want to be, let me make the rules clear to you right now. Training takes four years. During this time, you may not get married. If you are dumb enough to defy this rule and we find out that you have secretly eloped you will be expelled. It is required that you pay twenty pounds for your books and uniform. It's expensive, I know but it's worth every penny. You'll get the best nurses training here and you will earn eighteen pounds as salary each year you are in training. Don't be mistaken you'll work hard. But you will learn a great deal and you'll be given room and board. So, how does that sound to you?"

"It sounds good to me."

"And how can I know you will not be getting married. You're a young pretty girl. I'll bet you have a fellow in the service."

"My husband was in the service. He died. He wanted to be doctor, to save lives. I want to carry on his legacy. I believe I will be an asset to this hospital. I'm not looking for anyone else." Gilde said. Then she hesitated. "I want this very much. I am asking you to please accept me."

Chapter 49

Elias 1943

Elias found himself working in a nightclub under the name of Earl Schmidt, with forged papers. The British intelligence had set him up in a modest one bedroom apartment on the border of Belgium and France. His good looks and fearless manner made him popular with the Wehrmacht and SS officers who frequented the bar. He told them jokes and laughed at theirs. When one of them who was sitting at the bar saw a girl who he found attractive he asked Elias to intervene. Elias winked at the SS Officer and said watch this. He poured the girl another beer and brought it over to her. "You see that man over there?" Elias pointed to the SS officer "That's Obersturmfurher Shulman. He's a very important man."

Shulman heard Elias and stuck his chest out.

"He wants to buy you a drink." Elias put the beer on the bar in front of the girl. She looked over at Shulman and smiled. Shulman got up and walked over to sit beside the girl, and as he did he nodded his approval to Elias.

That night Shulman left with the girl he'd met at the bar and as he walked out he looked over her shoulder and nodded to Elias who smiled back at him.

All the Nazi's who frequented his nightclub came to love the way Elias praised them and made them feel important. He knew just when to talk and just went to keep his mouth shut. And, because he always appeared to be distracted by telling a joke or busy wiping down the bar when they were discussing covert operations, they began to trust him and converse easily and loosely in his presence. The Nazi's affectionately called him a cad, a ladies' man looking for nothing more than a good time. And he played the part well. He bought them drinks. They gave him generous tips. And if he hadn't hated the Nazi's as much as he did, he probably would have made some friends among his customers. But, Elias was always listening to the conversations around him, even when he appeared to talking to another customer. He never, not for a single second, forgot who they were and who he was. And because his ears were always open he learned before most of the world even knew, what was really going on in the concentration camps.

If he hated Nazi's before he despised them now.

Everyone had heard bits and pieces about work camps in Germany. Elias still remembered that after Kristallnacht many of the Jews had been taken to these prisons. But now, he'd heard real life horror stories from the Nazi's themselves, not only of the concentration camps but of mass shootings of Jews, and Gypsies, and other sub-human's as the Nazi's called them. He learned that the mentally and physically handicapped were being euthanized. And that Hitler planned to take over all the surrounding countries in the east and eventually maybe the world. Once a country came under Nazi rule, Hitler planned to eliminate all of the people he considered to be undesirables then turn the rest of the population into slaves for the Aryan race. Aryan breeding farms had also been established where children of racial purity were being breed. Yes, Elias was learning a lot.

Every week Elias met with several other men, they too

were spies who posed as ordinary citizens of Belgium. They were his British intelligence contacts. Once a week they went to a restaurant where they shared drinks and dinner. They laughed, told jokes, flirted with girls in case they were being watched. And they were careful never to speak openly of anything of any importance. At the end of the meal, Elias would walk towards his flat with one of them, both of them acting drunk and disorderly. Then Elias would discretely hand the other British spy a piece of paper that contained all of the information Elias had gathered from overhearing the Nazi's at his bar that week.

If he were caught by the German's he would be killed. Worse, if they found out that not only was he a spy, but he was a Jew, things would be even tougher on him He might end up being tortured in one of those camps he'd heard about. And, sadly, he also knew that the British didn't trust him entirely either because he was born in Germany and also because he was a criminal who had killed a man. Elias was alone in a strange country and friendless, walking a daily tightrope, and playing a dangerous game of cat and mouse. But he enjoyed the secret game he was playing. He loved that the Nazi's thought he was their friend, all the while he was secretly working towards their demise.

Chapter 50

Elias Late 1943

One of Elias' British contacts came to his bar one night. This was highly unusual. But Elias acted happy to see his old friend.

"Jan, what brings you here?" He asked

"I was in the neighborhood. I did some handy work for an old woman who lives a few minutes from here so I thought I'd come in for a beer. She needed to have some pictures hung, it took me a few minutes, but I made a little extra money."

Elias poured him a beer. Something was going on. Jan sat at the bar talking about his job at a factory. I've been seeing this girl." Jan smiled "She is an actress, in Paris. Very sexy. I am going to see her at the end of this week. If you can get the time off, she has a girlfriend staying with her another actress. We could have a good time. You know how women who are in the entertainment field can be? Huh? Easy?"

Elias smiled. "I'll see if I can get the time off work. We're busy on the weekend."

"It will be worth your while, my friend. Besides, you can help me pay for half of the hotel room."

"I knew there was a catch." Elias laughed. But he was

concerned. There was more to this than just a date with two women in Paris. Earlier in the year, in March, he'd reported hearing about two planned attempts on Hitler's life. Both of them had failed. He'd just recently sent information that another attempt was being planned. Could this have anything to do with this trip to Paris?

"So, if you can make it, I'll write down the name of the theater, and I'll meet you there on Friday night. The performance is at eight o'clock. I'll have her leave a complimentary ticket for you at the box. Just pick it up. I'll be inside waiting."

Elias had no trouble taking the time off. His boss was part of the operation.

On Friday he purchased a train ticket into Paris. Once he arrived, he took a taxi to a theater called the Grand Guignol. It was a small bizarre theater; he'd heard that it was known for offbeat productions. Apparently, the show was a series of short plays. The man behind the counter at the box office handed him his ticket, and under the ticket was a note folded very small. He whispered, "Go to the bathroom right after the first short play ends and just as the second is beginning when you get there read this." Then louder he said "Enjoy the show."

Elias took his seat. Jan was not there. No one joined him.

He glanced at the program. The show was to be a series of macabre short productions with frightening costumes and images. The curtain opened to a dark and dreary set. Elias felt a cold chill run up his spine as he watched what appeared to be an actual suicide taking place on the stage. A young man shot himself in the chest, the gun shot sounded very real and the blood that flowed from the wound looked authentic. When Elias had lived in London he'd been to the theater a couple of times, but he'd never seen anything quite like this. Where was Jan? Had something gone wrong? From living on the border of France and Belgium and working in the bar, he'd picked up enough French to understand the play. It was called "The Kiss", it was the story of a young man who had fallen in love with a prostitute. She grew tired of him and he'd attempted suicide. As he lay dying a beautiful nun sat at his side, the boy became delirious and imagined that the nun was his girlfriend the prostitute that he loved. In his delirium the boy kissed the nun, and even though she was a sister and had sworn a vow of celibacy, it was obvious that she kissed him back like a lover. The premise, the set, and the costumes were disturbing, especially since they hit Elias so close to home in his own life. After Glenda, a prostitute, had turned on him, he no longer cared if he lived or died. In fact, because his life meant so little to him, Elias had killed for Glenda and now he walked a treacherous path every day. The actor on the stage, who'd shot himself in the chest and the beautiful nun somehow woke him up as if he'd been asleep and had been living in the illusion of an unrealistic sense of safety. And, it suddenly all became very real to him. Until this moment, he'd never actually believed that he could die. Really die. He'd been willing to take chances because somehow he'd always felt invincible. But this play had struck a nerve, and now for some unexplainable reason, for the first time Elias was afraid. He felt the small folded paper in his pocket and his fingers twitched.

When the first play ended everyone clapped. He was trembling as he waited until the first actor in the second play came on stage. Then, he had to contain himself so he didn't sprint to the bathroom. Walk, he thought, But Elias was unnerved, unsettled. After he checked all of the stalls and was sure he was alone, he went into the last stall in the row and opened the paper

"Go behind the stage door and wait. The password is Bumbleberry."

He quickly tore the paper with the information written on it into small pieces and then flushed them down the toilet.

Before he left the bathroom, Elias looked in both directions. His fingers were trembling but poised on the gun under his jacket. The British Intelligence had trained him to use the weapon before he left Britain, but as of yet, he'd never been in the position to use it. He was on edge, like a zebra being pursued in the jungle. Every nerve ending in his body a live electric wire. Did he remember how to shoot the gun properly? How could he have been so lax up until now? Remember the steps, Elias, remember everything they taught you, your life could depend upon it. He thought. They'd given him several weeks of target practice, with a profession trainer, but he was still by no means a perfect shot. In fact he hadn't paid as much attention as he should have when he had the opportunity to learn. All he could think about was getting through it, because he hated the sound a shot being fired and the smell of gun powder.

As Elias slipped out the side door of the theater he jumped because heard the audience scream in terror. He was beginning to hate this weird theater. All he could hear was his heart beat in his temple as he waited for his contact. For a quarter of an hour, Elias hid in the darkness and the shadows behind the building. Then a small sprite of a girl emerged from the stage door. Her blond hair had been cut in a short boyish style.

"Bumbleberry." She whispered in to the darkness. Elias immediately took note that she spoke English with a British accent.

"I've been waiting for you." Elias stepped out in to the light.

"Elias right?" She said

He didn't answer. He just watched her

"Listen" she said "You have to get back to Britain quickly. One of your connections has been arrested by the Nazi's. We think he probably ratted you out. So, if you go back to Belgium they'll be waiting for you and were pretty sure you'll probably be next. I have to get out of here too. So, the plans are that you and I will to travel together as husband and wife. I can't tell you much more right now. But, wait here stay out of the light, and, as soon as the show let's out, I'll meet you in the alley.'"

"What happened to Jan?"

"Just wait here." She said "No time for questions right now."

Elias watched her disappear back into the building. Then he went behind the stage door exit into the dark alleyway and huddled in a curve in the building structure. His senses were on high alert.

The girl returned with a wig, a hat and glasses. Could she be trusted?

"I took these out of the costume pile. It will be a while before any one misses them and by then we'll be safe in Britain."

She helped him put on the disguise.

"I can't see without a mirror. How does it look?"

"Good. You'll pass. By the way, in case we are caught, remember all of this information, it might save your life, my name is Anne. We are French and you're my husband Claude. Our sir name is Bellamy. We are from Paris. You are a shoemaker. I am a bit part actress. Can you remember all of this?" She said handing him the papers that had been made for him even as she rushed him out of the alley. She was talking fast.

They walked north two streets then got into black automobile that was awaiting their arrival.

The car started to speed away

Once they were traveling at a good clip, the man who was driving began speaking to the girl who called herself Anne. He was speaking in German and he sounded like a native. Suddenly Elias felt a pang of fear shoot through him. Have I been tricked? He thought.

Chapter 51

1943

Gilde straightened her starched apron and carefully pulled her golden curls away from her face pinning them neatly on each side with barrettes. The white collar and cuffs looked crisp and professional and the soft pink color of the junior nurse's uniform dress flattered her blond hair and gave her skin a rosy glow.

Nursing wasn't easy. When she first arrived, she learned quickly that she hadn't realized how weak her stomach was. The senior nurses laughed when she vomited at the site of large amounts of blood the first few times. But she was getting better every day. Some of the more seasoned nurses or even the sisters were cruel when she was weak stomached and unable to cope with the gore of an injury, or when she gagged and choked at the smell of a GI bleed. They made it apparent that no one was to be handled with kid gloves. She was expected to be a professional and cope with whatever was thrown at her.

Gilde passed out at her first training session in the operating theater. The presiding doctor, Alden Thornbury, had cut into the patient. When the blood ran on to the floor and pooled, Gilde fainted. It was the first summer that she'd been in training and between the heat and the smells in the operating room she got dizzy and passed out. When she awakened she was in a hospital bed, embarrassed, and sure she'd made a mistake trying to become a nurse. Two senior nurses came to check on her. They were both kind. They assured her that she would get stronger as time went on, but she wasn't sure that would be the case.

"Stay in bed for a bit, then come on back to work. It happens to all of us in the beginning." One of the senior nurses a young girl who'd come to check on Gilde said as she was taking the hair out of Gilde's eyes.

Gilde lay there feeling like giving up. She was missing William and the rest of the Lawrence family. Perhaps she should have taken a desk job somewhere. That was when Dr. Thornbury came in to the room.

"You must be Gilde Margolis?" He said with a smile.

Gilde nodded. Alden Thornbury wasn't a particularly handsome man. He was tall and gawky, his light brown hair was full of cowlicks, but he had kind eyes and a genuine smile. "How are you feeling?' He asked

"Foolish for trying to become a nurse." Gilde said "I don't have the stomach for it."

"Would you believe me if I told you that the same thing happened to me when I first started studying medicine? And, now look at me, I'm a surgeon." He smiled "I won't lie to you, it takes getting used to. But you'll make it."

That was a little over a year ago and now she and Alden were the best of friends. She was about to graduate from a beginner to a Senior nurse, and she found that she was now able to cope with most of the gory aspects of the job, but her heart still broke a little every time someone died. She and Alden often discussed how difficult it was to detach from the patients.

"Don't get me wrong. Every time we lose somebody I feel terrible. But, you have to try to separate yourself or you'll go nuts." Alden said. "It's hard to accept but death is a part of life. We, as doctors and nurses, do what we can, then all we can do is leave the rest up to God."

They tried to have lunch together at least twice a week when their schedules coordinated, and dinner at least once a month outside of work. Gilde told Alden about William. He listened as she poured her heart out about how William had wanted to be a doctor.

"He was so strong and kind." Gilde said "I miss him every day."

"I bet you do." Alden said.

"Do you have a girl?"

"Never had time to get serious with anyone. I was always too busy studying. Then war broke out and then…well… I really had no time for anything."

"So, you never had a girlfriend?"

"I've dated, but nothing serious. I guess when the time is right I'll meet someone. Right now I'm too busy for a wife and a family. With the war going on I'd be worried about them constantly. It's bad enough that I am worried about my parents."

They were sitting in the hospital lunchroom.

"Want some baked beans? I have a half of a can." He offered.

"No thanks." She said

"How about you Gilde? Where are your parents?"

"That's a long story." She said. Gilde had not shared her past with anyone at the hospital. No one knew that she was Jewish, or born in Germany. No one knew anything about the Kindertransport. Her accent was British, she could thank her dear friend Sharon for that. So, there was no need to share the details of her life.

Alden tilted his head to a side. Working in medicine, he'd learned a lot about people. He was like a bloodhound and he detected that there was a secret in Gilde's past, something that made her uncomfortable. But he also knew she wasn't ready to talk about it with him. At least not yet, and he wasn't going to force it. "Listen, I'm not going to push you to tell me anything. I just want you to know that if you ever want to talk, I'll be here for you."

She smiled "Thank you Alden. Thank you for your friendship, your kindness and your understanding.

Damn, she is pretty. He thought.

Chapter 52

Elias

The black automobile sped through the city of Paris. As Elias watched out the window, he saw the world flying by him, a pair of lovers face to face on a bench under a tree, several Nazi officers in uniform sauntered arrogantly in to a night club, two women with a small dog disappeared in to an apartment building. Then, as they left the city behind, the surroundings became more rural. Until the auto came to a stop in a dark remote area where a private plane awaited. It was as if the runway had been carved out of a forest because the large open field was surrounded by trees. Elias had never flown an aircraft but he wondered if there was enough room for a safe take off. The blond girl took Elia's hand and pulled him along. There were no words spoken, but Elias could see a bulge in the man's coat and he assumed it was a gun. Elias figured he could take the man if it weren't for the weapon, but a firearm made even a small man powerful. And this man was a spy, he was probably well trained in the use of the gun, not a fool like Elias. If these were German spies and he was on his way back to Germany he was in serious trouble. "It's all right, come on, we have no time to lose." The girl said to Elias. He followed her because he didn't know what else to do. If he tried to take the man, she might shoot him.

The man who had been driving the car sat in the pilot's seat in the cockpit.

"Hier gehen wir, wir sind auf unserem Weg zurück nach Großbritannien" the pilot said. Elias stared at the back of the pilot's head. He'd just said they were on their way to Britain but he'd said it in German. Elias was confused.

"No need to speak in German, Ralph, he speaks perfect English." The blond girl said to the pilot of the plane as she smiled at Elias "No need to worry. We're on the right side, we're Brits. Ralph just wasn't sure if you spoke English or not. We all speak at least a couple of languages. So…From what I understand you spent many years in Britain. Isn't that right, Elias?"

"Yes, it is. I was born in Germany, but I consider myself British." Elias said

"Well, you must have done something right. From what I understand you're going to be decorated for your service." Ralph said.

The plane rumbled and shuttered. For a minute Elias thought it was going to explode, but then the plane sped down the runway and just in time, before they were going to go straight into the forest, the plane lifted into the sky. They missed the top of the trees by a few feet and then, the sky opened up for them and they were airborne.

"By the way, Elias, my real name is Babette Desmaris."

"You're French?"

"Yes, but I speak English like a Brit and German like a Kraut. That's why I'm an actress." The girl smiled. "I hate the Nazi's so having this talent made me perfect for the position of a spy."

Elias wouldn't have called her beautiful or glamorous. She was cute, small in stature, all of her features were small except for her eyes. Her large eyes were bright green and slanted like a cats. Her light blond hair was short and stylish. She was missing a tooth in the back of her mouth on the right side, but it only showed when she smiled. And her smile was so engaging that he forgot to care about the missing tooth. Elias was nineteen and from looking at Babette he took her for somewhere close to his age. In the past he'd always liked older women. But this girl was different. It took spirit to be a spy. And he had to admit this young girl who was so petite in stature had guts.

Chapter 53

Gilde August 1944

On a Monday morning Gilde came to report for work. The head nurse on the floor had assigned her four patients. That wasn't unusual, sometimes she had more. Three of them were men she'd been caring for, for the past few weeks. But there was a new name on her list. Archibald Notman. The notes in Notman's chart said: RAF pilot. Shot down in a training accident. Surgical repair went well on his lower right leg. Everything looks good. But, change bandages often and keep an eye out for any signs of infection.

Archibald was sitting up in his bed with his arms crossed over his chest when Gilde went in to his room to introduce herself.

"Good morning, Mr. Notman. My name is Gilde Margolis. I am going to be taking care of you. How are you feeling today?"

"How should I be feeling? I'm stuck here in this bed like an invalid and there's a war going on. I feel lousy."

"I'm sorry to hear that. Do you have any pain?"

"Of course. My leg is a bloody mess and ask if I have any pain. Now that's a stupid question."

"There's no need to be disrespectful, Mr. Notman. I am trying to help you."

He softened "I'm sorry. I'm just frustrated."

"Let me go and get you some breakfast. How does that sound?"

"I'm not hungry. The food here stinks."

"Well you're going to have to eat if you want to get well. So, I'm not going to stand here and argue with you. I'll get you something and then you can eat it or not. Your choice." Gilde said

He nodded and turned away from her to look at the wall.

Ornery bastard. She thought as she went back to the nurses' station.

"Notman's a difficult one, isn't he?" Sally, the nurse at the desk said. "I've tried reasoning with him. He is just a miserable difficult bastard of a man."

"Yes, I can see that. I was just wondering how I got stuck with him."

"Truth is, all the girls have tried to handle him but he is such a pain in the bum that we thought you might give it a go."

"Thanks a lot." Gilde said

"He is handsome though." Sally said almost apologetically.

"Is he? I didn't notice."

Chapter 54

Elias

When they returned to Britain, Elias was treated with respect for the first time in his life. His work at the border of France and Belgium had been helpful to the British, it had saved lives and been instrumental in making important arrests. It seemed that the nasty business with Bart was forgotten and the intelligence agency was glad to have him as a part of their team. Elias and Babette were put on various small jobs as interpreters for the British intelligence. And, Elias was decorated. He received a metal and honors.

Within the first month of their return to Britain, Elias and Babette began dating. This girl was different than any of the others Elias had dated in the past. She was not a foolish child who followed him around because he was handsome, but neither was she an older woman looking for a relationship with a younger man to make herself feel as if she were still attractive. Babs as Elias affectionately called her, had her own mind. Although she was an actress and a free spirit she wasn't glamorous and over dressed like Glenda. And there was no denying that she was smart. In fact he'd learned that she was very educated, like Mary, but unlike Mary, she didn't need anyone else's approval to feel her own self-worth.

"Why should we pay rent on two flats" Bab's said one day as she drank a beer right from the bottle just like a man. "We spend all of our time together anyway. Let's move in together."

They were together as often as possible and Elias had to agree, it wasn't a bad idea to cut back on expenses. So, they found a small apartment in a quiet area and moved in.

They were still working with the British intelligence but neither of them had been asked to leave London for a while.

Since she was a child Babette had wanted to be an actress. She auditioned and was cast in a few bit parts on the London stage. But she wasn't successful. Her career was failing. Elias knew it. The few productions in which she worked got terrible reviews from the critics. The lack of success in her dream career was sending Babs in to a state of depression.

"Go ahead and audition. Quit your job. I can afford to pay the rent. "Elias said.

But Babs just shook her head. "I'll keep working until I get I get the big break I've been waiting for."

Chapter 55

Gilde

Gilde was the first nurse who was not willing to put up with Archie's temper tantrums. He made it very apparent to the staff at the hospital that he was angry that he was weak and stuck in a hospital bed. His family was very wealthy, when Archie contacted his father, his father sent money to have Archie transferred to a private room. 'Spoiled brat' Gilde thought when she saw that Archie was no longer in one of the beds in the long line of beds where the other patients were lined up. The week after Archie's surgery one of the doctors examined him and informed him that it would be at least three weeks before he could even try to walk and even then there was no guarantee that his leg would be able to sustain his weight.

"You're lucky that you still have your leg." The doctor said "Be thankful for that."

"Go to hell." Archie said to the doctor and turned over to face the wall. Gilde had been in the room while Archie was being examined. She had removed the bandage and cleaned the area, and now that the doctor had left she was covering his wound with fresh bandages. Everyone else in the hospital, all of the doctors and nurses had come to hate dealing with Archie, but Gilde couldn't help but feel sorry for him. After she'd finished covering his leg, Gilde stood there at Archie's bedside trying to think of something to say.

"What do you want?" He asked her

"I don't know." Gilde said "I suppose I just want to say that I'm sorry you have to go through this. But there are a lot of others who are in much worse shape."

"And that's supposed to make me feel better?"

"Actually, yes…it is."

"Well, it doesn't.

That night before Gilde was getting ready to sign off, she brought all of her patients their evening dose of medicine. When she handed Archie his pain pill he refused to take his medicine.

"Listen, you can suffer all you want. If you don't want the pain killers there are plenty of people who are suffering and who would be happy to have them."

"Then give them to somebody else. I don't care what you do." Archie said

Gilde took the pills back to the nurse's desk. Archie made her angry. She was disgusted by his entitled attitude and the fact that he had a private room while the other men suffered in large open areas lined with beds. Who the hell did he think he was? Just because his family had money, he thought that he was special. Everything about him infuriated her, it irritated her so much that she thought about him constantly, and even discussed him with Alden the following afternoon when they had lunch in the hospital cafeteria.

The following morning one of the orderlies brought Archie his food for breakfast. The orderly set the tray on the table beside the bed. When Archie saw what was on the tray he threw it against the wall.

Gilde came in to work later that afternoon. She was scheduled for the evening shift. When she went to the nurses' station to check in for the day, the head nurse on duty told her about Archie's episode with the food earlier that morning.

"He's impossible. The day nurse couldn't get him to let her examine his wound." The head nurse said shaking her head. "If he doesn't let us keep it clean it's sure to get infected. To tell you the truth…I don't really care what happens to him. Whatever he gets he deserves." The head nurse said

"I'll check on him tonight."

"Do you really think you can talk him into letting you change his bandages? I sure doubt it. "

"I don't know. But I am going to try." Gilde said. "If we can't keep that wound clean he's going to lose that leg."

"We all realize that."

"Have you told him?"

"I haven't. I can't stand him, and like I said, I don't' care what happens to him anymore. "

"I'll talk to him." Gilde said.

Archie's room was in an area right off the main community room where all the other patients lay in rows of beds. The size of Archie's room was so small it looked like it had once been a broom closet.

Gilde stood in the doorway leaning against the wall with her arms crossed over her chest and watched as Archie lay on the bed with his head turned towards the wall. She took a deep breath and steeled herself for the confrontation. Then she went in.

"Good evening. It's Gilde Margolis, I'm going to be your nurse tonight."

He didn't answer.

"Archibald? "

When he still didn't answer, she walked around the bed to face him. He quickly wiped the tears from his cheeks.

"This room would be a lot better with a window." He said

"Yes, it would." She said "But it was difficult enough for the hospital staff to find you a private space. You could be in main room with sick and dying men all around you."

"I know." He said and something in his tone of voice let her know he wasn't fighting. He sounded broken.

"Can I get you anything?"

"No, thanks."

"Archibald? May I call you Archie?"

"Yes, sure, why not?"

"Archie. I'd like to examine your leg. Would that be alright?"

"No. It wouldn't"

"Archie. Please. I am afraid that if we don't keep that wound clean…"

"It's already happened."

"What's happened?" She asked.

"The doctor was here a few minutes ago. I guess they didn't tell you. Or maybe they don't yet."

"Who doesn't know, what?"

"The other nurses at the station probably don't know yet. The doctor probably hasn't had a chance to tell them. He just left right before you got here. He examined my leg, it's full of infection. He says it has to be amputated."

"Oh" Gilde slumped. That was why he was crying. Poor fellow. She thought and she felt her heart break for this stubborn difficult man. "I'm sorry."

"No need to be sorry. It's not your fault. You didn't do it."

Gilde closed the door so that they could speak privately. Then came back and sat down on the edge of Archie's bed. That's why he was no longer so ornery. He had lost his fight. Now it all made sense.

"When do they plan to do the surgery?"

"Tomorrow. I figure the doc will let the nurses know tonight"

"Listen, let me go and see to my other patients and as soon as I get them settled in, I'll come back and sit with you."

"You don't have to, I'm fine."

"But I want to…Would that be alright with you?"

He shrugged. But then he looked into her eyes and nodded. She smiled at him.

"Gilde?"

"Yes?"

"Thank you." He said

Chapter 56

By the time Gilde finished with her other patients the doctor had come to the main nurses' desk and told them about the plans for Archie's surgery the following day. Since Archie was Gilde's patient that night, one of the nurses told her about the amputation to take place the following day.

"I'm going to spend some time talking to him tonight. I don't want to leave him in there alone. Can you cover for me and keep an eye on my other patients? If you need me, just come in and get me." Gilde asked one of the senior nurses.

"Yes, I agree with you, he shouldn't be alone tonight. I know he's a real jerk, but I sort of feel sorry for him." The nurse said

"Me too." Gilde said

Gilde spent the evening sitting on the edge of his bed and talking with Archie. He told her about his family. They talked about Christmas at his house when he was just a boy.

"Christmas at the Notman house was something to see alright. My mother loves to entertain. Before the war she spent a fortune on holiday parties. All of my relatives would come from wherever they were living at the time. We had plenty of bedrooms so some of them would stay with us. It was always a lot of fun. I looked forward to it all year. There was so much confusion with so many people in the house that when I was little my sister and I would wait until everyone was asleep and then sneak out at night and go sledding down the hill in the snow. If we would have gotten caught my parents would have killed us. But of course we never did." He reminisced. "Those were good times."

"Yes, it sounds like it."

"My good times are over in this life, Gilde. I'm going to be a cripple. What kind of a life is that?"

"You're a strong handsome man. I mean, heck, look at the President of the United States, Roosevelt. He's in a wheelchair for goodness sake. And he's a very powerful man. Everyone respects him."

Archie's eyes were glassy but he didn't shed the tears that threatened to spill down his cheeks. He just shrugged. "Gilde." He said his voice barely a whisper. "Will you be here tomorrow when I get out of surgery?"

It was her day off. She and Alden had arranged their time off to coordinate as often as possible. They had plans of going to a film the following day. But how could she tell Archie, who was such a pathetic man, a hard man who had finally let her break through his tough exterior that she wouldn't be there for him when he needed her most?

"I'll be here." She said.

Chapter 57

Gilde and Alden had become the best of friends. He helped her with all of her work as she struggled to get through her nurses training. There was nothing they couldn't discuss. In fact finally when she'd come to trust him more than she trusted anyone else in the world, She told him that she was Jewish. He listened patiently as she told the whole story of the Kindertransport and how she'd been torn away from her family. Alden knew all about how Gilde had been shuffled around until she met William. Gilde explained how being married to William had given her a sense of security, how she'd become a part of a family. And she wept when she told Alden how much she loved and missed William. "I've kept in touch with his family. At first they wrote often, but over the last six months I haven't received a letter. I don't have any idea what's become of them." Gilde said.

"You've written?"

"Yes, several times. Neither Sharon, William's sister or his mother have answered."
"It could be the mail." Alden said gently patting Gilde's shoulder.

Alden told Gilde about Judith, the girl who he'd been attracted to in medical school. "She never paid much attention to me." He said. "I didn't know what to do, so I put all of my focus on becoming the best doctor I could be". And, he was. Everyone at the hospital said he was a miracle worker. But when Gilde complimented him on his work he just smiled and said. "It's not me who is the miracle worker, I'm just a vessel. You know before I go in to surgery I always ask Jesus to use my hands to heal." Alden said.

He was a religious Christian, but he loved and respected her Jewish roots.

"Christ was Jew." He said one day as they were discussing the fact that Gilde kept her Judaism a secret from everyone else. "Most people never think about that. Or they don't even realize it."

"Let's face it, Alden, if the other staff members knew I was Jewish they would not accept me as easily as they do now. Look at how they treat the other Jewish staff."

"Yes, you're right. Well, as long as you want me to, I will keep your secret. After all, you're my best friend. And best friends have to be able to trust each other."

"I am so glad to have you in my life, Alden. You are a wonderful friend, confident and....medical trainer. I don't know how I would ever have gotten this far working as a nurse without you. You helped me so much."

'You had it in you all along. I just tried to help you bring it all out."

The following morning before Archie's surgery, Gilde called Alden to tell him that she would have to cancel their plans to go to the movies that afternoon.

"Alden?"

"Hello Gilde."

"I have some rather bad news. I can't make the film today. One of my patients is having an amputation and he asked me to be there for him when he comes out of surgery. I feel sorry for him, Alden. He is a difficult man, but I think deep down he's a sad boy. He's losing a leg, and it's hitting him hard. He doesn't feel comfortable with the other nurses."

"Archibald Notman, right?"

"You know him?"

"Everyone knows about him. His family is loaded. They own Notman Candy Company. Old wealth. Very old wealth. I hear he's very hard on the staff."

"It's true."

"If you're going in to the hospital and we can't spend the day together. I don't' mind if you want me to come in and assist in the surgery."

"Would you Alden? I'd feel better if you were there. He has an infection and after all, this is a big operation."

'I'll be there. While he is in recovery, we can have lunch. Then you can go up and see him when he wakes up."

"Sounds perfect. Thank you."

"You don't have to thank me, Gilde. I'm here to serve."

Chapter 58

Archie was in bad shape but he made it in to recovery. He lost a lot of blood during the surgery and his life hung in the balance for a week. Gilde came to see him every day, even on her days off. In the beginning, he drifted in and out of morphine induced sleep. She wasn't even sure he knew she was there.

"He's in a lot of pain, Gilde" Alden said when he and Gilde left the room after he came to examine Archie one afternoon.

"Do you think he'll make it?"

"So far it looks good. Keep an eye on his temperature. Infection is our biggest concern right now."

By the second week, Archie was still on morphine, but they'd reduced the dosage and he was awake more often. His incision was healing and so far he was not showing any signs of infection. Gilde cleaned and redressed his wound every day even on her days off.

"You realize that you saved my life." Archie said to Gilde "I'm not sure my life is worth much anymore. But I owe you a great deal."

"Archie, you're young, you'll do great things with your life."

"Of course I'll never fly a plane again."

"I know. But there are so many wonderful things you can do."

"Like take over my father's business? I never wanted that."

"Don't be so hard on yourself, Archie. You'll figure it all out. For now, rest, and heal. That's what's most important."

And he did. By the end of the month Archie was able to stay awake for hours at a time. Gilde would come in and prop up his pillows, then she read to him.

"You're voice sooths me. Do you know that you have the most beautiful speaking voice? Do you sing too?"

Gilde laughed. "I guess I can sing. It's kind of funny, but I haven't done it in forever. I mean not in front of anyone."

"Will you sing for me?"

"Oh Archie, really? Here in the hospital?"

"The door is closed. Sing softly. I want to hear you."

She shook her head "I feel foolish."

"Please?" He sounded so sweet when he asked that she agreed and sang a short song for him.

"Just as I suspected. You do have a beautiful voice, Gilde. With your looks you should be a film star." Archie said. There was something about him when he was sweet that touched her very deeply. Maybe it was because he was always so mean, that when she saw his soft underbelly she melted.

"It's funny that you think that. When I was a child I wanted to be on the stage. Even now, I love to go to the movies. I always wonder what it would feel like to be up there on the big screen and have a whole audience watching you."

"Gilde…" Archie took her hand. "You've come to mean more to me than I can say. I look forward to your visit every day. In fact I wait for you. I find myself glancing at the doorway constantly and hoping you'll be there."

He needed her. Her heart ached with yearning to care for someone who needed her so desperately.

"I think I am falling in love with you." Archie said taking her hand. "I doubt you could ever love me. I'm damaged. But, I think I love you."

This was the first time since she'd lost William that a man had touched her heart this way. She wanted to make things better for him. She wanted to save him. And perhaps she was confusing the need to rescue a shattered creature with falling in love.

She squeezed his hand. He brought her hands to his lips and kissed her fingers.

"Kiss me, "he said.

She leaned down and her lips brushed his. It had been a long time since she'd felt the desire to lay with a man. But Archie was attractive and adoring and he needed her. God, how he needed her.

Gilde got up and locked the door. Then she took off her uniform, and lay down in bed beside him.

It wasn't easy to make love with all of the bandages and wires. But they managed. And, from that day on, Archie started to recover quickly.

Chapter 59

Elias

In the beginning of their relationship, Elias thought that Babs was different from the other women in his past. But as their relationship grew, he began to see similarities. Bab's was working for the intelligence agency less and less. But, Elias had become even more involved, he was now doing translations for a sector of the British intelligence agency that was tapping into the German communications system.

After more auditions than Elias could count, Babs finally landed a bit part in a show. Elias suspected that Babs had slept with the director to get the part. When he asked her about it, she shook her head and accused him of being suspicious. Maybe he was, after all he hadn't had much success with women. They'd all treated him like a joke, and as he'd grown up he found he wasn't able to love anyone completely. Because he had developed a mistrust of women, he didn't feel bad about being unfaithful to Bab's. If she asked him, Elias would say that he loved her. But he told himself that he would never be a fool for another woman the way he'd been for Mary or even worse for Glenda. No woman would ever have the power to hurt him like that again.

The years had taken his boyish charm and replaced it with an older more suave attractiveness. Working with intelligence had taught him to put himself and his own needs first. He liked having Babs around. He wanted to have a couple of kids, he thought that children might fill the emptiness in his heart. So, he'd been thrilled when Babs accepted his proposal of marriage. They had wonderful sex and she was a sweet caring girl. She'd make a good wife. He was on her side, he wanted to see her succeed in her career. In fact, he was willing to help her in any way he could. But no matter what, no woman, not Babs or any other, would ever own his heart entirely again.

Chapter 60

October 1944

Gilde helped Archie to learn to walk on crutches. It was frustrating for him and sometimes he became angry and threw the crutches down. When he did he fall. Embarrassed and aggravated he cursed as Gilde helped him up from the ground.

"I wish I was back to normal. I hate the way this whole bloody thing turned out. Why me? Why did I have to end up like this?" He said the week before he was to leave the hospital.

She gently took his hair out of his eyes and as she did she could see him warm to her.

"I'm sorry." He would said. "I was out of line talking that way to you."

"You're doing fine." She said "You'll be going home next week."

"I know. But I'm going home half of a man. My father will think I'm a failure."

"How could he? You're a war hero." Gilde kissed Archie's cheek.

"My sweet Gilde." He said

It seemed like the perfect time to tell him. But she was trembling.

"Archie?"

"Yes, sweetheart."

"Archie. I missed my period."

"Oh?'

"I think I might be pregnant."

He was quiet for several minutes. She looked up at the clock then back at his face.

"When will you know for sure?" He asked

"I'd say another month."

"I'll be home in Yorkshire by then."

"I know."

"We'll stay in touch. I'll write and call all the time. I love you Gilde. I'm going to be here for you."

She took his hand in both of hers.

Chapter 61

Elias

Bab's knew Elias was unfaithful. Several people had come to her and told her that they saw him with other women. One of her close female friends said she saw him coming out of the doors of a hotel with his arm around a girl. Bab's always stood up for Elias against their accusations of his infidelity. But secretly she knew they were all true. She also knew that he'd begun drinking to excess. Many times, she would find him passed out drunk. But Bab's wasn't one to give up easily. Slowly with the patience of a woman in love, she'd pulled painful stories of his past from the deepest hidden regions of his heart. There was no doubt in her mind that he loved her. But he didn't trust her. He didn't trust anyone. And she wasn't sure how to convince him that she wouldn't betray him the way every woman in his past had done.

Against her better judgement, Babs married Elias on November 1, 1944 in a public ceremony. A few of their mutual friends attended. They left the courthouse and walked to a local pub to have a drink to celebrate. A wicked chill was in the air foreshadowing a cold winter.

After a few drinks Elias was flirting with the waitress. Babs watched him. Maybe part of the attraction, she thought, is that he is so elusive. Just like this damn career I've chosen.

But as she watched him, she began to feel a bitterness burning like bile inside of her.

Chapter 62

Gilde

Archie was released from the hospital and went home to Yorkshire. He called every Sunday morning and Gilde received letters twice a week. In his correspondence, he told her that he had settled in with his family, and was doing better with his crutches. But he never mentioned her pregnancy.

She was hoping he would tell her that he'd told his parents about her and that he would propose marriage. But he said nothing.

Gilde's breasts were swollen. She was sick to her stomach most of the day and she hadn't had her period for over six weeks. She was pretty sure that she was going to have a baby. She hated to do it, but she had to talk to Archie about it again. That Sunday Archie called.

"I'm sure you remember what we talked about before you left the hospital. "

"What are you talking about?"

"Archie" the receiver was shaking in her hand "I'm pregnant."

"Are you sure now?"

"Yes, I have all of the symptoms."

"Don't worry. I'll be there next weekend. We'll work this thing out."

"I'm scared Archie."

"I told you not to worry. I'll see you next Sunday."

Work it out? What did that mean? He hadn't mentioned marriage. Work it out?

The entire week, Gilde was on edge. She avoided Alden not wanting to tell him anything about the pregnancy and afraid he would see that something was wrong in her eyes.

No letters arrived from Archie that week, and Sunday came and went without any trace of Archie. Gilde waited another week, but when she didn't hear from Archie, she looked up his home phone number in the hospital records. Part of her wanted to believe that he was ill or something had happened that kept him from coming to Birmingham. But deep inside she knew that he was running away and she prayed that she was wrong.

Gilde dialed the phone number. It rang, it rang again.

"This is the Notman residence." A woman's voice said with a cockney accent.

"May I speak to Archie, please?" Gilde's voice was shaking.

"I'm sorry he's not here."

"Is this his mother?"

"No love, this is the housekeeper. His mother isn't here either. They went to stay at Archibald's fiancé's house to plan the wedding."

"Wedding?'

"Oh yes, love. Archibald is getting married. He and his fiancé went to boarding school together. Did you go to school with them?"

Gilde was tongue tied. She lied because she didn't know what else to say "yes."

"Then you'll probably remember Corrine Hildabard? They are going to get married, Archibald and Corrine. The families have been friends for as long as I can remember and that's a long time." The housekeeper laughed.

"Who can I tell him called?"

"Oh…" Gilde stammered. Think quickly. She made up a name "Mary Smyth. Tell him that…" Gilde said and hung up the phone.

Gilde leaned against the wall trying to catch her breath. What was she going to do? The only thing she could do. Ask, no, beg, Alden to put his license at risk and perform an illegal abortion for her.

Chapter 63

"How's your schedule look this week?" Gilde asked Alden when she telephoned him that night.

"I'm off on Thursday if all goes according to plan. But of course, as you know that's always subject to change."

He was colder than he'd ever been to her and she knew it was because she'd been avoiding him.

"I'm working Thursday. Let me see if I can switch and get the day off. If I can get off work would you let me buy you lunch?"

"To what do I owe such an enticing invitation?" He said. There was the old Alden. She could hear the smile in his voice.

"I just haven't seen you in a while and I missed you."

"Well then of course. I wouldn't miss a lunch date with you for the world. But hey…it's my treat." He said

She couldn't help but adore him. He was so kind and even though she'd been unavailable and not answered his calls for a while he'd already forgiven her.

"You are too sweet, Alden."

They hung up and Gilde called Ruth.

"Ruth can we switch days off? I'm off on Saturday. Can you work my Thursday and I'll work your Saturday?"

"Yeah sure. A Thursday for a Saturday? Sounds good to me." Ruth said.

"Thanks so much. I'll call the Nursing Supervisor and have the schedule changed.

Chapter 64

Gilde met Alden at a café down the street from the hospital. Alden was waiting when Gilde arrived. He got up and gave her a hug.

"It's really good to see you. Gilde. I felt like you had abandoned me." He said

"No, I've just been so busy."

"I'm glad you're here now." He said smiling

They ordered.

"How have you been?" She asked

"Good, busy too." He said and she saw that he was studying her. "Gilde? What's wrong?"

"Nothing. " She stammered "why do you ask."

"Because I can see that something isn't right. I see it in your eyes. Talk to me, come on Gil."

She could hardly swallow her tea. Her throat closed and she felt the tears well up in her eyes. Gilde was so ashamed. How could she tell Alden what she'd done? It was so shameful to admit that Archie had made a fool of her, had used her. And beside that how could she ask Alden, the kindest most wonderful friend in the world, not to mention the best doctor, to put his medical license in jeopardy? If the abortion somehow went wrong as they often did and she died, well, everyone knew she and Alden were good friends. So, Alden would be suspected as the doctor who performed the surgery.

"Gilde?" He said again.

Her hand was trembling as she lifted the teacup. But she couldn't speak. She sat staring down at the table for several minutes. Then in a very soft voice she said "I'm pregnant. It's Archie's and he wants nothing to do with me…or the baby."

Alden leaned back in his chair. Just then, the waitress brought the food and put it down on the table.

Alden waited until the waitress had gone and then in a very quiet voice he said "Let's take a walk. We'll pack this food up and go somewhere we can talk privately."

"Let me pay. I asked you to meet me. You shouldn't have to pay for lunch too."

"You silly girl. Meeting you is the highlight of my week. Now don't insult me. I'm the man here and a man always picks up the tab when he takes a lady out for a meal." He smiled at her and touched her hand.

"It's too cold outside to sit in the park. Let's go to my flat." Alden said.

"Don't you have a roommate?"

"I did. He got married and moved out two months ago. I would have told you but we haven't talked. See, it's been that long since you and I had a nice long chat."

Everything in Alden's apartment was warm and welcoming like Alden. The sofa was overstuffed and comfortable with an old teddy bear holding a book propped up on a sofa pillow."

"What's this?" Gilde said when she saw the stuffed animal

"Oh, that's my teddy from when I was kid. I've taken it all over the place with me. We're old buddies."

"That's so sweet. I can't' believe you still have your old teddy bear."

"His name is Goliath"

Gilde laughed "like David and Goliath?"

"Yes, I guess so. When I got him as a very young child, my father said his name was Goliath and he was a giant who could defend me from any monsters who might come and get me while I was sleeping."

"I had a teddy bear when I was young."

"Do you still have it?"

"No, I didn't have room to bring it with me when I left Germany."

"You can have mine if you want him. He's very powerful against monsters and bad dreams."

She smiled. "I think I might have out grown teddy bears."

He sat down beside her and took her hand in his.

One entire wall was a bookcase filled with books that Alden had accumulated over the years, many of them medical journals. Then off the main room was a small kitchen with just enough space to fit a wooden table and two chairs.

"Do you like the place" he asked

"It's nice and homey.

"Right down the hallway is the bathroom. And then a little further down are the two bedrooms".

"It must cost you a fortune to rent this place without a roommate."

"Yes, it's expensive. I'm looking for something smaller."

He said. "Let's have our lunch." Alden said

Gilde sat on the sofa while Alden put the sandwiches on plates. Then he put a pot of water on the gas burner to make tea. Once it was ready he poured two cups and sat back down beside Gilde on the sofa.

"Thank you." She said as he handed her the cup of hot tea. The weather was chilly and she wasn't feeling well so sipping the hot liquid was comforting. Gilde drank the tea but couldn't bring herself to eat. Her stomach was in knots.

"Now that we're alone we can talk freely about your problem." Alden finally said. "What do you want to do, and how can I help?"

She could tell that he already knew what she wanted him to say. "I don't know how to ask you this. I mean, of course I'll pay you. I guess I could probably go to another doctor. That would probably be the best thing for you. I would have to ask around and see who was doing this. But, it's so damn dangerous."

"Gilde, you're rambling. I am assuming you want me to perform an abortion for you."

"Yes." She looked away "You're the only doctor I really trust."

"I don't want your money. And I wouldn't let you go to anyone else. Your life means too much to me. If this is what you want I'll do it."

She bit her lower lip and the tears began flowing down her cheeks. "I'm so scared, Alden. I am sick with guilt about what I did with Archie. I should never have slept with him without being married. There was just something about him, I don't know what it was. I don't know what made me do it. I have no excuse I only know that I am really terrified and I can't believe he abandoned me. I feel so alone…"

"Don't be afraid. I'm here. Nothing will happen to you. You'll be fine. You're not alone, Gilde you have me. You've never been alone. At least not since the first day I met you."

He gently put his hand under her chin and lifted her face so he could see her eyes.

"Why did Archie do this to me, Alden? He said he loved me. I don't understand. When I called his house the housekeeper said he and his mother were away visiting his fiancé. She told me her name…Corrine Hildabard. It keeps going through my mind like a freight train. Apparently they have known each other for years. I don't know why he did this to me. I was so kind to him."

"Well," he took both of her hands in both of his "The Hildabard family is an old wealthy family they are well known in Britain they own a lot of real estate. Corrine and Archie were born in to the same circle. I'd bet that they probably met when they were kids, and I wouldn't doubt it if they were betrothed at a young age."

"You mean, you think he knew he was going to marry her even while he was seeing me?"

"I'm sorry to say it, but yes. Most of the people in that class, the upper class, stick together. They might have a romance with someone outside of their little world. But, they're expected to marry one of their own."

"So you really think Archie knew? He was just playing with me?"

"I don't want to put it that way, but I'd say yes. Can I ask you something?"

"Of course. I mean, it's none of my business, but did he know you are Jewish?"

"I can't remember if I ever told him. I've kept it a secret for so long."

"That's a big problem with the upper, upper class. There is a lot of anti semitisim. Now, Archie probably cared for you, but I am sure he knew that his family would never have allowed him to marry you."

"Because I am Jewish?"

"That's part of it, but you don't have their kind of money. You're not one of them. They don't let outsiders in. If Archie wanted you, he would have had to fight them and it would have been a tough fight. Believe me, I know. This was just the easy way out. For all of his ranting and raving old Archie is nothing but a coward."

"I'm so ashamed. I feel like a fallen woman for what I did with Archie. And now this..."

"Shhh. Gilde, we all make mistakes. I've made plenty in my lifetime and I'm sure I'll make more. But I'll tell you something that I know is not a mistake."

She cocked her head. "What?"

"I'm in love with you, Gilde. I've been in love with you for a long time now. And even when I thought Archie might be a man and stand up to his family and marry you, I still never felt like my love for you was a mistake."

She gasped. "And now, now that I've made a mess of my life. What do you think of me now Alden?"

"Now? Now, I know that loving you is what I was meant to do. And I am going to be here to help you through this. You don't have to love me too. Just being here for you is enough for me."

She had never kissed Alden. But at that moment, she wanted to kiss him to feel even closer to him. His kindness lit the darkness of her uncertainty. She looked into his eyes and leaned forward. But before she had the opportunity to kiss him, he had already gotten up to pour her another cup of tea.

"Gilde, I don't want your love out of guilt or need. If you are ever to really love me, it has to be without conditions. It has to be the way you loved Archie, or William. "

He smiled as he handed her the cup.

Chapter 65

Alden arranged to do the abortion at his flat on the following Friday. That was the next day that they were both off of work together.

Every minute of every day, Gilde thought about the baby she was carrying. Was it a boy or girl? She even began to think of names. All of her life, she'd wanted to be a mother. Now she was pregnant. If she went through with the abortion, she would be free of the pregnancy by the end of next week. And after all, wouldn't that be for the best? It would she thought, and yet, she couldn't stop thinking about her unborn child. If she didn't have the abortion, she would be thrown out of nursing school as soon as she began to show any visible signs of pregnancy. Then, she would be in the worst position of all, an unwed mother, without a job or a home to raise her child. The only place to go then would be a home for unwed mothers, and they had a terrible reputation of being brutal. She was so angry with Archie that she could have killed him, and yet at the same time she missed him terribly.

As she walked back to her dormitory one night after work she saw two young women with babies in carriages. Then the following day on the way to the bakery, she saw a pregnant woman walking arm in arm with a man. Had she seen so many things having to do with babies before this? Perhaps they were always there; she just didn't notice them until now.

On the Thursday night before the day that Gilde and Alden had planned to terminate her pregnancy, Gilde had a nightmare. A frightening dream that was so real that she couldn't catch her breath. The following day the day she was to terminate her pregnancy was a Friday, the day of the Sabbath. In the nightmare she had visions of demons shouting curses at her and telling her that she was committing the sin of murder. She sat up in bed covered in sweat and shivering. Her stomach turned and she ran down the hall to the bathroom and vomited. When she got back to her room, one of her roommates was awake.

"Gilde are you all right?"

"Oh yes, I'm fine. Just sick to my stomach. It must have been something I ate." She said. But she began to wonder if the other nursing students on her floor might be noticing that she was vomiting often.

She lay in bed trying to catch her breath and looked at the wall not wanting to fall back to sleep in case the nightmare returned. Was she making a mistake having this abortion? An irreparable mistake? If she went to the home for unwed mothers she could give the baby up for adoption. Gilde had to talk to someone. There was only one public phone in the dorm and it was downstairs in the main living area. She had never telephoned Alden in the middle of the night before but he was her closest friend and right now the only person she felt she could trust. She listened until her roommates breathing slowed and she was sure the other girl was asleep. Then as quietly as she could she slipped down stairs and went to the phone.

"Alden, it's Gilde."

"Are you all right?" He asked his voice full of sleep and concern.

"I don't know if I can do it. I had a nightmare and I'm so

afraid. Alden I don't know what to do." She was whispering but hysterical.

"Listen to me. Try to relax. I have an idea. We'll talk tomorrow."

"I can't believe I am such a nervous wreck."

"It's understandable, your hormones are changing with the pregnancy and you're frightened and confused. Just put your trust in me. You know I've never let you down. We'll talk tomorrow. Everything will be fine. You'll see. Do you believe me?"

"Yes, Alden, and thank you."

"What are friends for?"

Chapter 66

Gilde went to Alden's flat as soon as the sun rose. She rang the downstairs buzzer.

"Who is it?"

"Gilde."

"I wasn't expecting you until nine."

"Do you want me to come back?"

"Of course not. I'll buzz you up." He said

Her eyes were red and swollen with crying, her hair was uncombed.

Alden looked like he had just tumbled out of bed, and Gilde was pretty sure that he had. His hair was standing up in every direction, and he had a flannel robe over his pajamas.

"I'm sorry to be such a pest."

"You're not a pest. Sit down, please. Here, hold Teddy, he'll help." Alden said putting the teddy bear in Gilde's arms. "Come on, Gilde, smile. It will be all right. I'll put up a pot of tea."

She sat on the edge of the sofa with the bear on her lap.

"Here you go" He put the tea cup in her hands. "Now, a good hot cup of tea, the strength you get from teddy and the support of a good friend, that's me and you'll be just fine. I'm the doc and that's what the doctor orders." He smiled

As soon as he sat down beside her and gave her the tea cup, she began to relax. It was the first time she'd felt at peace since she'd made the decision to terminate her pregnancy.

"All right. Now, let's talk." He said taking one of her hand in his.

She sipped the tea and then put the cup on the coffee table "I don't think I can go through with this. I had a night mare and I am afraid I am doing something terrible. Oh, Alden, I am really afraid. Do you think I am doing something terrible?"

"I would never judge you or anyone else Gilde."

"I'm so confused. All of a sudden everywhere I look I see children. I've always wanted a child. I am afraid that if I have an abortion God will punish me and I'll never be able to have another child."

"I don't believe in a hateful God like that, Gilde."

"I'm lost, Alden. I'm thinking about going to a home for unwed mothers and giving the baby up for adoption once it's born."

"Well, I think I might have a better suggestion." He said and cleared his throat "Why don't we get married. You and I? As I told you before, you don't have to love me the way I love you. I wouldn't want you to tell me that you did unless it's the way you really feel. But if you want to have the baby I love you enough to marry you and we can raise the child together."

"I'd feel like I was taking advantage of you."

"Would you be? I don't think so. We're best friends. We'd have a great life together. I mean, if you don't think you would be happy being married to me, just say so and you can live here until the baby's born and then if you don't want the child you can give it up for adoption."

Either way, if she had the baby she would have to drop out of nursing school. They would not allow her to attend pregnant. And, she did like Alden. He made her feel safe, and he made her laugh. They would probably do well as a couple. Her feelings for him weren't the sweet emotions of young love she'd had experienced with William, or the wild physical need she'd shared with Archie. The feelings she had for Alden were calmer, more relaxed. But she had to admit, she cared for him and appreciated him. He made her feel like nothing bad could ever happen to her as long as he was with her. And, he made it clear that he would always be there for her. She'd never had that kind of safety in her life.

"I'll marry you." Gilde said

"You will?" His eyes brightened, and he looked very happy but surprised

"I will." She said smiling. He looked so excited. And suddenly everything in the world seemed all right.

Chapter 67

No married or pregnant women were allowed in the nurses training at Queen Elizabeth hospital. Gilde reread the rule book that she'd received when she first started the program at the hospital.

"I'm going to have to go to the office and drop out of nursing school." Gilde sighed as she talked to Alden an hour after they were married in a civil ceremony.

They'd gone out for dinner to celebrate and were sitting at a corner table in a restaurant.

"Do you want me to go with you?" he asked. "I will if you want me to."

"No, I should do this alone."

"I guess it's a good thing that we have that second bedroom. I don't think we should move now. We'll use it as a nursery."

"Can we afford such a big apartment without me working?"

"We'll manage. You don't have to worry about anything, Gilde. Just leave it to me." Alden smiled.

Chapter 68

Elias

Babs caught Elias in their bed with another woman and threw him out of the house swearing she never wanted to see him again. He was dead drunk and fell asleep on the lawn in front of the building. The next day when he awoke he returned to the apartment. They fought, yelling at each other so loud that the upstairs neighbor called the police. But when the police came, Babs told them that everything was fine and that she and Elias would be quiet. Then she allowed Elias to come back home. They had angry passionate sex that night. Then to secretly punish him she had a casual affair with an actor she met at an audition. It was a quick and meaningless tryst that only happened a hand full of times. But Babs made sure to leave evidence of her infidelity all over the apartment. She wanted to hurt him. But when Elias realized Babs was cheating, he accused her of having been unfaithful all along.

They fought again. This time Elias hit her and they separated. He found a small apartment on the other side of town. But he missed her terribly and began taking the bus to the old neighborhood where they'd lived. He watched outside her apartment to see if he could catch a glimpse of her, but he couldn't. Elias needed something to keep him going. He was drinking and obsessing about Babs. So, he decided to put in a request to the British intelligence agency for a more challenging job.

Elias, along with another male agent, was sent on a mission to rescue two important fellow agents who had been taken prisoner in Germany. During the mission, things went badly and Elias was shot and wounded. If it hadn't been for the other agent he was working with he would have bled to death. The bullet struck his upper arm and he had never felt such pain. With the help of his coworker he was able to get to the location of a private plane and return to a hospital in Britain.

"Is there anyone you would like us to notify?" The nurse who came in to Elias' room asked. "Yes, my wife. Babs. Let me give you her number. Call her right away." He said.

He gave the nurse the phone number. When she left he looked at his wound. If it would have been just a little to the right he would have been hit directly in the heart and he would be dead right now. The near death experience made him long to see Babs. They had a volatile relationship, but he loved her. He knew he did. All of the other women he was unfaithful with meant nothing to him. They were shields against the true depth of his emotions. If only he could explain this to Babs. If only he could be sure she was really in love with him, maybe he could stop it and allow her to be his one true love. But, hadn't she just had an affair with another man, some actor, unsuccessful too? And wasn't that proof enough that she was just like the others? Women were ruthless. They could break your heart and leave you without a thought.

Damn he wished he could get a drink. But of course that was impossible in the hospital.

Babs would be here soon. He knew her. She would be a wreck when she heard he'd almost died. But that still didn't keep her faithful. Well, maybe if he was real nice and asked her sweetly, she'd smuggle in a pint for him. That would help, at least for now.

Chapter 69

February 1945

Doctor Alden Thornbury had never been happier. He and Gilde were enjoying every step of her pregnancy. As soon as he signed the marriage license, Alden decided to put Archie out of his mind and out of their lives. From that day forward in his mind the child that Gilde carried was his. The little one would bear his name and he would be a good father for the rest of his life. If it had taken a disastrous affair with Archie to make Gilde see that she would be happy with him, then all he could do was thank Archie. Because Alden was in love and all of his dreams seemed to be coming true.

For the first trimester of her pregnancy, Gilde couldn't keep any food down. Alden tried everything, even pulling favors with patients who had friends on the black market to get food he thought Gilde might find more appealing. However, no matter what she ate it had a strange metallic aftertaste and she vomited within a half hour. However, now that she was well into her second trimester she was hungry all the time. Not only was she able to eat, but she was able to eat more than she had ever eaten at one sitting than she'd ever eaten in her life. Her belly grew big and hard, and Alden loved to rub it or put his ear up against it and listen to the baby. Sometimes he talked or sang to the baby. Gilde often did the same. Again, Alden went to friends who were able to get him extra and appealing food through the black market.

He loved delighting Gilde. And there was no question that he would do anything in his power to make her enjoy being his wife. He brought home small gifts of hair ribbons and occasional soap or perfume. Gilde knew that these things were available on the black market, but the price was high and she wondered how Alden afforded all of it. But when she asked him all he ever said was "Anything for you my darling."

Alden adored his young beautiful wife, and he was beginning to believe that she might be falling for him too. She laughed a lot and always seemed so happy. Sometimes, he wondered if he were just dreaming, but other times he was sure he saw something twinkle in her eyes when she looked at him. It was a special light and dare he say, loving look. But most of all Alden was sure that he had not seen it there before they were married.

The first time they made love, on the night they were wed, he was nervous like a virgin girl. This was not because he hadn't been with women before. He had, but they were only casual dates, and he had never wanted to please anyone as much as he'd wanted to please his wife. After they'd finished she'd breathed a sigh of contentment. Even now, when he thought of that sigh, he could still hear her in the darkness and the sweet, tender sound of knowing that he'd satisfied her made him smile.

Until Alden and Gilde were wed, he'd willingly taken extra hours at the hospital without a thought. He loved his work, but he found that he loved his new wife more. And since his marriage, he'd changed. Now, from the time he left no matter where he was going until his key turned in the lock and he opened the door to their apartment and saw her lovely face, he longed to go home.

Chapter 70

1945

In her final trimester of pregnancy, Gilde was miserably uncomfortable. Her belly was so large she couldn't find a comfortable position at night when she tried to sleep her breasts ached all the time. The baby lay on her bladder all night and if she finally did fall asleep she'd wake up several times a night to urinate. On a rainy afternoon when the sky was the color of burnt charcoal in the last week in April, Alden got off work early. It was a chilly day and he thought Gilde might enjoy something warm so he brought home a pot of hot soup from the hospital cafeteria.

Gilde was surprised to see him.

"I missed you, so much today that I took the afternoon off."

"Just like that?"

"Sort of. I told them I wasn't feeling well, and the head Doc on duty let me go home. It's been ten days since I had any time off."

"Are you sick?" She was genuinely concerned.

"No, I'm fine, just wanted some time with you." He said

She was sitting on the sofa wrapped in a blanket reading one of his books.

"I brought soup. Let me get you a cup."

He brought two cups of the steaming broth. "I raced all the way home so it wouldn't get cold."

She laughed. "We could have warmed it up."

"I didn't want you to feel like you had to do anything. I know how exhausted you are."

"I can't believe it's almost over. A couple of months and the baby will be here."

"Yes." He smiled.

"You know, I have been meaning to ask you. Your family? Do they know that you and I are married? You've never mentioned them." Gilde asked "have you told them anything?"

"You're right. I haven't mentioned my family." Alden said "And for a good reason. Do you remember when I told you that Archie was in for a hell of a fight with his folks if he married you? Well, my family and Archie's family run in the same circles. He didn't recognize me when I came to examine him because although we went to the same boarding school, he was the big popular athlete on campus. I was in the science lab, constantly studying. I knew, even then that I wanted to be a doctor. The same way, I knew from the first day I saw you that I wanted to marry you. I'm not an indecisive kind of man. I am not like Archie. I don't care what my family thinks…"

"Do they know that were married?"

"Yes, I called and told them before we tied the knot."

"And what did they say?"

"They disapproved. They had someone in mind who they thought would be the perfect wife for me. She's a nice girl, rich, from a rich family, all the criteria they expect. But she wasn't you. And I don't love her. So, I told them, I was going to marry you. They could accept it or not, but either way, no matter what they did or said, it wasn't going to change my mind."

"They didn't accept it." She said as she took his hand and held it to her cheek. "You're so cold."

"Yes, it was freezing out there. But, no they didn't accept it. And, quite frankly I don't care. I love you and I'm the happiest I've ever been."

She curled into him and he held her close taking in the fragrance of her freshly washed hair.

"I love it when you use the special soap I got you to wash your hair."

"It smells like lavender. I love it too, but I try to save it."

"Well you don't have to. Things are looking very good for us as far as the war goes. Russia is advancing towards Berlin. Soon it'll be all over. The allies will be victorious and I'll be able to get you plenty of soap."

His arms encircled her while she rested in the embrace.

He felt the fire stirring in his loins. "I'd love to carry you into the bedroom and make love to you for the rest of the day. But, I don't think it's safe for the baby."

"Hmmm." She said disappointed, she would have loved to spend a relaxing and sensuous afternoon with him, but she knew he was right. "I know. We'll have to wait."

"That will only make our love making sweeter when we can be together. I love you so much, Gilde. I don't care about anything else. I used to think that my job would be my whole life. I'd be a doctor. Probably never, marry. But even if I did, I never dreamed that life could be this blissful."

"Alden." She took his hand from around her waist and put

it to her lips. Kissing it gently. "I realized something..."

"What."

"I love you."

"Really?"

"Yes, I really love you."

He turned her around and kissed her. Then he cuddled her in his arms and gave silent thanks to God.

Chapter 71

At the end of April two days after Gilde declared her love for Alden making him the happiest man alive, the U.S forces liberated Dachau concentration camp. The atrocities they found behind the barbed wire fence stunned the world. Piles of dead skeletal bodies, thousands of starving tortured people. Many of them were Jewish. When Gilde read about it in the paper all she could think of was her family. Were any of those she loved among the dead?

Chapter 72

Then on April 30th, Adolf Hitler and his wife of a few hours, Eva Braun committed suicide in his underground bunker, the Wolf's Lair, in Poland. Before Hitler died, he saddled Admiral Donitz with the responsibility of handling the mess he'd made of Germany. Hitler insisted that Donitz continue to fight to the end. However, the Nazi surrender had begun.

On May 7, 1945 in a city in France, Germany signed the document of surrender. Then late on the evening of May 8th, the fighting stopped. The following day at Stalin's insistence, another signing of surrender took place in Berlin.

The allies rejoiced. After six bitter years of sacrifice, war, and death, they had finally destroyed Hitler and his terrible Third Reich.

Chapter 73

June 1945

Gilde awakened early at around four o'clock on the morning of June 16th, 1945 with slight cramping. Alden lay deep in sleep beside her. The baby is coming. She thought. My baby is going to be born in to a peaceful world. A world without Nazi rule. The pains were a half hour apart and not very strong. She'd let Alden sleep for a little while. How wonderful it would be to go home to Germany and see her parents, her sister, Lotti and Lev again. Or would it? Once she found out the truth, who was alive, who was dead, who was injured, she could no longer delude herself that everything would be okay, she would have to face and accept whatever awaited her. In a way, she was relieved that they couldn't get in to Germany yet, however, she'd already decided that as soon as the boarders opened, even though she was afraid of what she might find, she was going. It had been so long since she'd allowed herself to even dream of the day when she could be reunited with her family. She'd stifled that wish long ago because it seemed like the war might never end. Very soon now, she would be able to go back to Germany, to her childhood home. But sadly, she could never really recapture the lost years…

The pains were coming more frequently.

"Alden" Gilde whispered "I think I am in labor."

At four-thirty that afternoon, Victoria Lynn Thornbury was born. Alden and Gilde named her Victoria in honor of the victory of the allies. In reality she was a wrinkled red little bundle. But Victoria was healthy and had a set of lungs like her mother's. And to Alden and Gilde she was the most beautiful baby that had ever been born the entire history of the world. They counted her fingers and toes. Marveled at her tiny earlobes. And because they were so happy and in love, they both seemed to have forgotten, that Alden wasn't her birthfather.

The next three months were chaotic. Victoria or Vicky as they called her had colic and almost never slept through the night. Alden and Gilde took turns walking with her and rocking her. Alden bought Gilde a second hand wooden rocking chair. The motion seemed to soothe Vicky's stomach. Gilde couldn't help but notice that the chair had been hand carved. One night as she rocked Vicky to sleep, her eyes examined the arm of the chair. It had small intricate rabbits and butterflies carved into the wood. Suddenly she was flooded with memories of her father. He made furniture like that, with beautiful carvings. She remembered watching him work when she was just a child. He would be so intent, such a perfectionist that every piece he turned out was a work of art. Gilde didn't realize it but she was weeping softly. Alden was asleep in the other bedroom and even though he was exhausted, he heard Gilde and got out of bed. When he saw her sitting in the chair with Vicky asleep in her arms and tears rolling down her cheeks, he went to her and knelt beside her.

"Sweetheart....you're tired. Let me take the baby for a while."

She shook her head "I'm all right."

"What is it? What's wrong?"

"You see this? These tiny little rabbits and butterflies? My father used to make furniture like this. My Papa is a real artesian."

"You miss him?"

"Very much."

"Well as soon as we can get in to Germany, we'll go and find him."

"He was arrested before I left. I never saw him again after that night. Do you think he is all right? Do you think he's alive? I mean do you remember that article about the concentration camp and how terrible it was." Her voice was ragged with emotion.

"I don't know what we are going to find, when we get to Germany, Gilde. But I am going to do everything to help you look for your family and no matter what we discover I'll be there with you. I wish I could promise you that all of your loved ones are all right. But, I won't lie to you. I can't make that promise."

He stroked her knee.

"I love you Alden, and it is such a comfort to know you'll be with me"

"Of course I will. I'll always be with you no matter what we have to face. I'll spend the rest of my life taking care of you and showing you how grateful I am that you do love me."

Chapter 74

By early September Vicky's colic had settled down. She was sleeping through the night. Now Gilde was able to get some rest, but raising a baby was still more work than Gilde had ever anticipated. Finally, Alden decided that Gilde needed to get away. They'd been invited to a friend's wedding in the east end of London. He thought the trip would be good for her, so he arranged for one of their mutual friends, Ruth, a senior nurse, to stay with Vicky. At first Gilde resisted. She didn't want to leave the baby. But, Alden reminded her that they both knew Ruth was a very capable nurse.

"Come on, Sweetheart. You need the break." He said "We'll only be gone a few days."

Gilde reluctantly agreed. Ruth arrived at eight o'clock the following morning but it took Gilde over two hours to explain all of Vicky's needs.

"I raised my two sisters. My mum was sick. I am sure I can handle this." Ruth said winking at Gilde "Go and have a good time. You both need it."

Chapter 75

It had been quite a while since Gilde had been in London. And being there brought up memories. So much had happened to her in London. She thought of Jane, William, Sam, Sharon and Lenore. So many people had come and gone in her life. Gilde said a silent prayer begging God to take her before he took Alden. Please God, she prayed silently, I don't want to ever have to face losing him. But she never mentioned it to Alden.

Alden had arranged for them to stay in a nice hotel. The room was decorated beautifully.

"This is like our belated honeymoon." He said. They made love a half hour after they arrived. But Gilde couldn't get Vicky off her mind. She called Ruth twice that first day to make sure everything was all right.

Ruth assured her that everything was fine. The wedding was scheduled for the following evening. The first night Gilde and Alden were on their own to enjoy a nice evening out in London.

They went to dinner at a fancy pub right in Piccadilly Square. Gilde hadn't worn her high heels or the silk stockings that William had given her in over a year. She got dressed and although in the back of her mind she was constantly thinking of her baby, she felt pretty for the first time since she'd gotten pregnant.

Alden ordered wine. As they sat close together at a corner table sipping the wine slowly, a crowd of people entered the pub. It was a group of both men and women and they were loud and laughing. Gilde glanced over at them and recognized a very familiar face. The man with the familiar face saw her too.

"Gilde Margolis? Is that you?"

"Elias? Elias Green?"

"Yeah, it' me..." Elias said walking over. "How have you been?"

"Fine. And you?"

"I've been doing well."

"Were you in the war?

"Yeah, actually, I was decorated by the British intelligence office for my service."

"Very impressive." She smiled. "We'll you look terrific. By the way, have you seen Shaul?"

"Never saw him again after we all separated at the train depot that morning."

"This is my husband, Alden. Alden, this is Elias Green. We were on the kindertransport together when we came to Britain from Germany."

A woman with short blond hair came walking up "Elias, the party is in the other room," She said. Gilde thought she was rude.

"Babs, I want you to meet an old friend of mine. This is Gilde Margolis. I've known her since we were children. We came over from Germany with a group together." He said then he made sure to add "This is Alden her husband."

"Nice to meet you." Gilde said "It's not Gilde Margolis

anymore," She smiled at Alden "It's Gilde Thornbury."

"Say, why don't you two join us? My wife, Bab's is an actress and that group in the other room, well, they are all part of her cast party. What do you say Babs?"

"Sure, come as my guests." She said without enthusiasm, looking Gilde up and down and scrutinizing whether to worry about Elias trying to sleep with her or not.

Alden shrugged. "We don't want to intrude."

"Don't be silly, come on, it'll be fun." Elias said

Gilde and Alden entered the private room. A piano player was playing show tunes. Everyone was dressed in formal attire.

"Sit with me, come on let's catch up." Elias said to Gilde. "So, it's been years the last time I saw you, you were just a twelve year old standing outside the train station. Do you remember?"

"Yes, I remember every minute of that trip. I was so afraid."

"I think we all were. I always wonder how Shaul is doing."

Just then a man in his early forties, tall, and well-groomed took a microphone and stood by the piano.

"Welcome everyone. Mr. Jacobson and I would like to thank all of you for your hard work on "The Song of the Blackbird. Every one of you did a wonderful job…."

"That's the director." Elias whispered "Jacobson is the producer. Babs was lucky to land this part. Even though it wasn't a lead, it was a big step in her career." It was easy to see that Elias had been drinking. His speech was a little slurred his eyes were red and his voice was too loud.

"I'll bet you're really proud of her." Gilde said

"Yes, I am." Elias said "Hey, didn't you want to be an actress when you were young?"

"Yeah, that was a long time ago." Gilde said

"She still has the most beautiful voice." Alden said taking Gilde's hand "She sings to our daughter all the time."

"I remember that you had a good singing voice. You used to sing sometimes when we were at school at the orphanage. "

"Now I sing my little girl to sleep and hope the singing works." She laughed

"I can't believe you have a child!"

"Yes, she's wonderful. She's three months old."

"That's really something."

"Do you have any children?"

"No, not yet. Not with our careers. It just hasn't been the right time." He said. Then changing the subject, his eyes brightened up and he said "I have an idea. This should be a lot of fun. I'll be right back."

"Where's he going?" Alden asked leary of Elias.

"I don't know."

"He's a heavy drinker. I can see that." Alden said

"I would have to agree with you from what I can see. But, I hardly know him. I haven't seen him for years."

"Ladies and Gentleman, Babs' husband has asked us for a special favor. He'd like to invite an old friend up to sing a song for all of us. We've agreed to indulge him. So, Gilde Margolis, please come on up to the stage."

Alden and Gilde looked at each other. "I couldn't." She said "But thank you for asking me."

"You can and you will." The director said "Come on, nobody here will bite you."

Gilde shrugged. Elias came back to the table and grabbed Gilde's hand. Alden said lamely "her name is Gilde Thornbury, not Margolis." Then as soon as the words left his lips, he felt foolish.

"Do you know any American music?" The piano player asked.

"Some." Gilde said.

"Do you know Chattanooga Choo Choo?"

"Actually I do know that song."

"Okay then, let's go." The piano player's fingers danced over the keys as the lively tune sprung to life.

Gilde hadn't sung in front of a crowd in years, and she'd never sung in front of a group of professional entertainers before. Her knees wobbled. But as soon as she opened her mouth and began to sing, she forgot that anyone was watching. Her natural rhythm kicked in and she began singing and moving with the beat. When the song was finished, the entire audience stood up clapping. Her face flushed and she whispered "Thank you." Then handed the microphone to the director of the play and turned to leave.

"Hey, wait a minute." The director said taking the mike away from his mouth "You're name is Gilda right?"

"Gilde."

"Gilde that was sensational. I have a part for you in my next production. Are you interested?"

She had to hold on to the piano or she might have fallen over. "A part? In a play?"

"Yes, a professional show. On the London stage. Here's my card. Call me tomorrow."

Gilde took the card and went back to her table

"You were wonderful, sweetheart." Alden said

That night back at the hotel room. Alden and Gilde made love. She lay in his arms knowing she had to talk to him about the offer from the director but not wanting to disrupt the bliss of the mood.

"Alden. I don't know how you're going to feel about this, but the director offered me a part in a real professional production. It's been my dream to do something like this since I was a little girl. But if you don't want me to do it, I'll understand. If I take it, I'll need to move to London. At least until the show closes. I could take Vicky with me. I'd have to hire a nurse to watch her during rehearsals and when I was on stage…."

Alden cleared his throat. "You want this?"

"Yes, I really do." She said

"Well…it won't be easy on us. But, I love you too much to ever stand in your way. I've always told you that I would stand behind you no matter what."

"Oh Alden, really?"

"Of course. It makes you happy, so we'll find a way to make it work. I'll find a job in a hospital in London. We'll hire a nurse to help with Vicky." He kissed the top of her head "If this is your dream, sweetheart, then I am going to do everything I can to help you make it come true."

Chapter 76

When Bab's heard that Gilde had landed a part in the next production she was furious with Elias for interfering.

"Don't be jealous, Babs it doesn't become you." Elias said

"I might have gotten that part if you hadn't put your nose where it didn't belong."

"You and Gilde are different types. I doubt you would be competing."

"We'll don't doubt it. You might be my husband, but you aren't my friend. I am sick and tired of you, of your drinking, of your risk taking, of your cheating. I have had it, Elias. I'm done. I'm leaving. Don't come looking for me. This time it's really over."

"You're making more of this than it is" He said

"I don't care what you say. I'm done. You have all kinds of problems that you can't let go of from your past. It's not my fault that you were orphaned or that you had bad relationships with women before me. All I know is I can't fix you Elias. I've tried. God knows I've tried. You hurt me, I forgive you and take you back and then you hurt me again. I won't do it anymore. This is it. I'm done with you for good."

Elias poured himself a drink and gulped it down while he listened to Babs slamming her suitcase in the bedroom. He knew she was packing. What could he do or say? It didn't matter anyway. Women would come and go, and in the end they would all prove to be the same. He poured another drink.

Chapter 77

The first meeting of the cast was at the playhouse the following week.

"You have one week to be off book. We have another week of rehearsals, and then the show goes on." The director said as Gilde sat listening.

She couldn't believe that she was going to perform in a professional show. Would she be able to memorize her lines in time? She had to, she had no choice.

As soon as Gilde received her script she went home and began working on memorizing her lines. Even while she was feeding and bathing Vicky, she had a copy of the script beside her and she was rereading the lines over. Her part was small, but it did include a singing solo and she wanted to get it right. If she wasn't ready in a week, she was sure they could easily replace her.

With his medical experience during the war Alden had easily landed a position at a prestigious hospital in the West End of London. The salary was better than he'd been earning at Queen Elizabeth hospital, and they found a spacious second floor flat a few streets from his job. The hours were long, but even though he came home exhausted, he insisted on staying awake and helping Gilde by running lines. They hired a young capable nurse, Brenda, who Alden knew from the hospital to help with Vicky. She came to their house on a part time basis. During the two weeks before the show opened, Gilde wanted Brenda to come as often as possible so that Vicky could get used to her.

The first night that the show was to open Gilde sat backstage in the community dressing room contemplating running out of the theater before her cue was spoken by her fellow actor. But, she didn't. At first when she walked out on stage she was dazed by the large crowd in the audience, but once she started singing she forgot that anyone was watching at all, and her voice rang through the auditorium like a silver bell. The audience loved her. By the end of the first month, she was offered and accepted a bigger and better part at another theater not far away where she even had a small private dressing room. Although she was not quite famous her name was becoming known amongst the regular theater crowd. And the directors were beginning to take notice of the bright young vivacious Gilde. She had all the makings of a star, a strong voice, a pretty face, a voluptuous body, and a brilliant sense of humor.

Alden never wavered in his support of his wife and because of he was always her best friend, besides being her husband and lover, her admiration for him grew and she loved him even more for his quiet stability and reassurance.

Every night of the show, as was expected of the cast, following the performance Gilde came outside the back door in her gold lame gown to autograph programs for the fans. It was on one such night that she walked out the back door, pen in hand to the music of loud applause, when she glanced over the crowd and saw Archie. He stood there on crutches, still handsome, with a dark haired woman on his arm, a pale, slender woman. Archie's eyes caught Gilde's. His face broke into a smile. "Sign my program, please, Mrs. Thornbury" someone said "Mrs. Thornbury will you please autograph this for my son?"

She was surrounded by fans. They were all calling out to her at once. For a moment she felt as if the wind had been knocked out of her. Then all the memories of her and Archie and what she had done and the shame she'd brought upon herself, came rushing at her in a surge like a tidal wave.

Gilde felt herself flush. Her knees seemed to be giving way beneath her. Keep calm. She told herself all these people are watching you. Then she raised both hands in the air. "I'm sorry to disappoint all of you, but I am not feeling well tonight, so there will be no autographs. However, I want to thank you coming to see the show. Please know that your support means a lot to me" She said trying to force a smile. Then she turned around and with her head high she quickly went back inside the theater.

Her heart was beating wildly as she disappeared behind the door in her dressing room. She dropped into the chair and put her face in her hands. It was hard to breathe. But only a moment later there was a knock at her dressing room door.

Oh no. She thought. Could Archie have paid someone to let him come back stage?

"Who is it?" She said in a curt voice

"Miss Thornbury? There's a telegram for you." It sounded like an adolescent boy. How had he gotten back stage? Archie must have paid someone to allow this child to deliver a telegram to her. That didn't surprise her. Archie, that coward, it was easier to send a message than to face her.

She opened the door and signed for the telegram. Then she grabbed a few coins from her purse and tipped the boy.

Damn you Archie. She thought. Why was she still so damn attracted to him?

"I have to see you. There are so many things that you don't know. Things I have to tell you. Things that influenced me to break up with you when I did. But, I shouldn't have left you. I made a mistake Gilde. I love you. Meet me tomorrow at eleven am in front of Big Ben. I'll be waiting and praying for your forgiveness. Please show up, Gilde. All I ask is that you give me a chance to explain, Archie."

Part of her wanted to see him, to punish him, to make him sorry for what he did to her. Part of her wanted to tell him about his child, to tell him about Alden, and how he'd abandoned her at the hardest time in her life. But the biggest part of her was afraid to see him, afraid that somehow all of the anger, the attraction, and the mixture of emotions she felt towards him would draw her right back into loving him. The whole thing made no sense but it made all the sense in the world. Could she walk away, she'd waited so long dreaming that the day would come when she could hurt him the way he hurt her, but if she did would she get caught in her own web? And besides that, what the hell was he talking about? What had caused him to leave her? What were the secrets that she didn't know?

Big Ben at eleven tomorrow morning. She read the letter again. He wanted to meet her at Big Ben the following morning. She would have to be out of her mind to show up....but would she be able to resist?

Chapter 78

1945 December, France

William Lawrence was finally going home. He'd spent two and a half years in a Marlag, a POW camp for Naval prisoners. It was a hell hole surrounded by barbed wire with bunk beds and a charcoal burning stove in the center of the room where the prisoners huddled through the winter trying to stay warm. He'd lived on thin watery soup and one piece of black bread twice daily, always hungry. When they were captured his fellow Naval men warned him to get rid of his tags because they had a Star of David on them indicating that William was Jewish. William refused. According to the Geneva Convention the prisoners were to be treated humanely. But this did not include William. By wearing his Star of David, he set himself up for constant persecution. When the war ended, he was taken to the hospital undernourished, blind in one eye and too sick to make it all the way to Britain. He spent the next six months in the French hospital trying to recover from the nightmare he'd lived through all the while enduring constant questioning about his treatment by the Nazi's.

"How were you treated?" The Red Cross asked

How could he ever explain? They had so many questions. And he was far too tired from the ordeal. He didn't want to talk about it anymore, and didn't want to think about it anymore. However, even though he refused to discuss his captors, their memories were always present waiting for him to try to sleep and then making their appearances in his nightmares. Many times during his imprisonment, he'd longed for death to free him from his misery, but his memories of his lovely young wife, his sweet and beautiful Gilde at home awaiting his return had kept him alive. When he got to the hospital he'd asked one of the nurses to send a letter to his family. He had been too weak to write it so he dictated it to her. She promised to send it. But months passed and he received no answer. He tried again as soon as he had the strength to write it himself, but the letter was returned unopened.

Finally it was time. He was well enough to be discharged from the hospital. William would never be in good health again, his body was twisted from torture. His bones were weak from lack of nourishment, but he had a train ticket, and soon, very soon…he would be back in London, home. He would hold his precious Gilde in his arms, see his parents and his sister again, and give thanks to God that he had survived.

Coming soon….the final book in the Michal's Destiny series **"1945, 11 million murdered."**

MORE BOOKS BY THE AUTHOR AVAILABLE ON AMAZON

All My Love, Detrick

Book One in the All My Love, Detrick Series

Detrick, a German boy, was born with every quality that the Nazi's considered superior, this would ensure his future as a leader of Adolph Hitler's coveted Aryan race. But on his 7th birthday, an unexpected event changed the course of his destiny forever. As the Nazis rose to power, Detrick was swept into a life filled with secrets, enemies, betrayals, alliances and danger at every turn. However, in spite of the horrors and the terror surrounding him, Detrick would find a single flicker of light. He would discover the greatest gift of all, the gift of everlasting love.

You Are My Sunshine

Book two of the "All My Love, Detrick" series

Munich, Germany 1941

A golden child is genetically engineered in the Nazi's home for the Lebensborn. She is the daughter of a pure German mother and a member of Hitler's SS elite. With those bloodlines, she is expected to become a perfect specimen of Hitler's master race. But, as Germany begins to lose the war and the Third Reich begins to crumble, the plans for the children of the Lebensborn must drastically change.. Alliances will be broken. Love and trust will be destroyed in an instant, secrets will rise to the surface and people will prove that they are not as they seem. In a time when the dark evil forces of the third Reich hung like a black umbrella of doom over

Europe a little girl will be forced into a world spiraling out of control, a world where the very people sworn to protect her cannot be trusted.

The Promised Land:

From Nazi Germany to Israel

Book Three in the All My Love, Detrick Series

The Holocaust robbed Zofia Weiss of all she holds dear. The Secret State Police have confiscated her home, killed her friends, and imprisoned the man she loves. After searching through displaced persons camps and finding nothing, Zofia is sure that her lover is dead. With only her life, a dream, and a terrifying secret, Zofia illegally boards The Exodus, bound for Eretz Israel.

Along with a group of emaciated Jewish survivors, Zofia sets out to find the Promised Land. Despite the renewed sense of hope, Zofia lives in constant fear since the one person who knows her dark secret is a sadistic SS officer with the power to ruin her life and the life of an innocent, Lebensborn child.

When the Nuremberg trials convict the SS Officer of crimes against humanity, Zofia believes she is finally safe and does her best to raise the beautiful girl entrusted to her care. As the child becomes a woman in her own right, can she find true love and belonging in a post-war society, or will the secrets of her heritage tear apart the only family she's ever known?

To Be an Israeli

Book Four in the All My Love, Detrick Series

Elan Amsel understands what it means to be an Israeli. He's sacrificed the woman he loved, his marriage, and his life for Israel. When Israel went to war and Elan was summoned in the middle of the night he did not hesitate to defend his country. Even though he knew, he would pay a terrible price for his decision. Elan is not a perfect man by any means. He can be cruel. He can be stubborn and self-righteous. But he is brave, and he loves more deeply than he will ever admit. This is his story.

However, it is not only his story; it is also an account of the lives of the women who loved him. Katja, the girl who he cherished but could never marry, who would haunt him forever. Janice, the spoiled American that he wed to fill a void, who would keep a secret from him that would one day shatter him. And…Nina, the beautiful Mossad agent who Elan longed to protect, but knew that he could not.

"To Be An Israeli" spans from the beginning of the Six-Day War in 1967 through 1986 when a group of American tourists are on their way to visit their Jewish homeland.

This book is a saga of a people who to this day live under the constant threat of war and terrorism. It is the story of a nation built on the blood of her people, a people who understand that if Israel is to survive they must put Israel first. These are the Israelis.

Forever My Homeland

The Final Book in the All My Love, Detrick Series

A group of Americans go on a tour of Israel with their Synagogue. One of them has a secret.

Meanwhile, a group of radical Islamist's plan to use the visitors to bend Israel's policy of never negotiating with terrorists in order to free members of their group who are being held in Israeli prisons..

However, the terrorists must contend with Elan Amsel a Mossad agent who's devoted his life to the preservation of his beloved Israel. Elan believes that nothing can break him, that is, until the fate of two innocent girls is thrust into his hands.

Forever, my Homeland, is the story of a country built on blood and determination. It is the tale of a strong and courageous people who don't have the luxury of backing down, They live with the constant memory of the Shoah, and a soft voice that whispers in the desert winds... "Never Again'.

THE VOYAGE:

A Historical Novel Set during the Holocaust

Inspired by true events. On May 13th 1939, five strangers boarded the MS St. Louis, Promised a future of safety away from Nazi Germany and Hitler's third Reich unbeknownst to them they were about to embark upon a voyage built on secrets, lies, and treachery. Sacrifice, love, life, and death hung in the balance as each fought against fate but the voyage was just the beginning.

A FLICKER OF LIGHT

Hitler's Master Plan

The year is 1943...

The forests of Munich are crawling with danger under the rule of "The Third Reich," but in order to save the life of her unborn child Petra Jorgenson must escape from the Lebensborn Institute. Alone, seven months pregnant, and penniless avoiding the watchful eyes of the armed guards in the overhead tower, she waits until the dead of night. Then Petra climbs under the flesh shredding barbed wire surrounding the institute and at the risk of being captured and murdered, she runs headlong into the terrifying desolate woods. Even during one of the darkest periods in the history of mankind, when horrific acts of cruelty became commonplace and Germany seemed to have gone crazy following the direction of a madman, unexpected heroes came to light. And although there were those who would try to destroy it, true love would prevail. Here, in this lost land ruled by human monsters, Petra will learn that even when one faces what appears to be the end of the world if one looks hard enough one will find that there is always "A Flicker Of Light."

THE HEART OF A GYPSY

If you liked "Inglourious Basterds," Pulp Fiction," "Django Unchained," You'll love "The Heart of a Gypsy!"

During the Nazi occupation, bands of freedom fighters roamed the forests of Eastern Europe. They hid, while waging their own private war against Hitler's tyrannical and murderous reign. Among these Resistance Fighters, there were several groups of Romany people (gypsies).

The Heart of a Gypsy is a spellbinding love story. It is a tale of a man with remarkable courage and the woman who loved him more than life itself. This historical novel is filled with romance, and spiced with the beauty of the Gypsy culture.

Within these pages lies a tale of a people who would rather die, than surrender their freedom. Come, enter into a little known world, where only a few have traveled before... The world of the Romany.

If you enjoy romance, secret magical traditions, and riveting action....you will love "The Heart of a Gypsy."

Please be forewarned that this book contains explicit scenes of a sexual nature.

A NAZI ON TRIAL IN GOD'S COURT

This is a very short story. It is 1,235 words Himmler; Hitler's right hand man has committed suicide to escape persecution after the fall of the Third Reich. What he doesn't realize is he must now face a higher court. God's court. In this story he will meet Jesus and be tried in heaven for crimes against humanity and the final judgment may surprise you.

MICHAL'S DESTINY

Book one of the Michal's Destiny Series

Siberia 1919.

In a Jewish settlement a young woman is about to embark upon her destiny. Her father has arranged a marriage for her and she must comply with his wishes. She has never seen her future husband and she knows nothing about him. Michal's destiny lies in the hands of fate. On the night of her wedding she is terrified but her mother assures her that she will be alright. Her mother explains that it is her duty to be a good wife, to give her husband children and always to obey him. However, although her mother and her mother's mother before her had lived this way, this was not to be Michal's destiny. Terrible circumstances would force Michal to leave her home and travel to the city of Berlin during the Weimar period where she would see and experience things she could never have imagined. Having been a sheltered religious girl she found herself lost and afraid trying to survive in a world filled with contrasts. Weimar Berlin was a time in history when art and culture were exploding, but it was also a period of depravity and perversions. Fourteen tumultuous years passed before the tides began to turn for the young girl who had stood under the canopy and said "I do" to a perfect stranger. Michal was finally beginning to establish her life However, the year was 1933, and Michal was still living in Berlin. Little did she know that Adolf Hitler was about to be appointed Chancellor of Germany and that would change everything forever.

86724798R00183

Made in the USA
Columbia, SC
05 January 2018